MELANIE LEAVEY

Skelly

Book One of the Sea Glass Trilogy

THREE RAVENS
P R E S S

Second edition

ISBN: 9781777143107

This book was professionally typeset on Reedsy.
Find out more at reedsy.com

for the magic-keepers

Contents

Acknowledgement

I feel like if I thanked 100 people, I'd be leaving out 100 more; I just don't really know where to begin.

So instead, let me just thank all of you - whether you're reading a free/ARC version of this book, or have had enough faith in the possibility of it by putting down some hard-earned cash.

Thank you for taking a chance on this story, and on me. For those of you who've been with me since the beginning - since those hastily-scribbled *ink-blot stories* that found their way into your actual mailbox - and those who have crossed my path only recently…thank you for waiting, with far more patience than could be expected.

The world is on fire - at the time of this writing, COVID-19 is turning life upside down. When I decided to re-write these stories, I did so because I wanted to give something back to the world of books for all of the years and in all of the ways, that books have saved me. I believe with all my heart and soul, that we need all the magic and wonder we can get our mitts on.

And, sometimes, we just need to escape for a while.

extra special thanks to Seumas Ferguson for Scots Gaelic translation, all errors are mine alone….

…and to Helen Redfern, for talking me off more ledges than I can begin to count; Indigo Carlton, for taking Skelly's words and turning them into art; Antoinette Martin, for knowing just the right thing to say to keep me going, even when she wasn't trying to and to Liz Galgavolgyi for her big, beautiful, generous heart.

I shall endeavour to be worthy.

~m. xo *March 18, 2020*

Chapter 1

"You can't be serious!"

Frances held the phone away from her ear as Sophie shrilled down the line. A pile of boxes teetered precariously as she tried to shuffle between it and the tower of rubbish she'd cleared from the back part of the studio.

"I most certainly am," she replied, trying very hard to sound calm and sensible. "It's a studio space and it's affordable. What more is there to say about it?"

"But it's a cow-shed!" exclaimed her friend, genuine horror palpable in her tone. "It must be stinking. Honestly, Frances, I've no idea where your head is. Jack is perfectly willing to let you have the new spot in their shared space. Lois has already moved her stuff out. Wouldn't you rather…"

"No," said Frances, more firmly this time. "I may not be sure of much right now, but I absolutely *do* know that I don't want to be anywhere near Scaffold Street Gallery and everything associated with it. Including Jack and Lois."

"But they're our friends," said Sophie, her voice tinged with reproach. "They had nothing whatsoever to do with what happened at the gallery. They've always been very supportive of you."

1

Frances stifled a sigh. Sophie couldn't possibly understand. Any minute now she'd age into her substantial trust fund and was already living the life she'd always envisioned for herself by having opened up a boutique bookstore cafe in the village. Frances, on the other hand, was having to make other plans.

"Look, Sophie. I appreciate their offer; you know I do. I'm just not interested in a shared studio. Besides, it's a bit out of my price range at this point and it was *you* who suggested I move to Thistlecrag in the first place. Also, this isn't a cow-shed, it's a converted outbuilding. There's a difference."

Frances glanced around at her new space, letting her gaze slide over the dubious stains which seemed to be seeping in from under the whitewash. She gave a surreptitious sniff. The faint whiff of damp covered up any possible remnant of the building's former inhabitants.

"Anyway, is that all you called for?" she said, cradling the phone between her shoulder and ear. "I really need to get on with my unpacking. The light's going and…"

"Fine, fine," interrupted Sophie, with a good-natured chuckle. "I can see you're going to be pig-headed about this. I think you're mad but then again, that's probably not news to you."

Frances laughed, shooting a glance at the faery that was rummaging through the box marked 'tea supplies'.

"Right you are there," she said. "Give my love to Stuart and take some for yourself."

Sophie sent a smacking kiss noise down the line and rang off.

"Get your grubby mitts off that, Moss," she said, marching over to flap good-naturedly at the little house-brownie. "There'll be no tea until we've got this rubbish cleared out. If I know Sophie, she'll be around for a nosy and I don't want her to see this place in such a state."

Moss crossed his arms in an exaggerated flounce.

"I don't know why you're bothering with this charade," he said, his voice piping like wind through reeds. "Moving us out to this hovel when we could be staying with Sophie and Stuart in that glorious flat above the shop. It's just too selfish. I could have the run of that cafe…all those beautiful books and a thoroughly modern Aga in the cafe kitchen. So warm, so toasty…"

He broke off and looked at the damp walls and grimy kitchenette that hid behind a drooping partition. The Aga in residence was of a vintage that didn't inspire confidence.

"Instead I'm to be consigned to chilblains and toxic mold. Tell me again why we're here?"

Frances opened her mouth to retort when a ball of brown and white fur came hurtling in through the door, dragging a foul-smelling mouthful of something very dead.

"Never mind," said Moss, his odd-coloured eyes narrowing to slits. "I remember now."

* * *

Frances worked steadily for four hours, collecting and transporting bags of rubbish from the studio to the back of her car. The previous tenants had apparently used the studio for what looked like "found art" assemblages. Or at least that's what she supposed from the odd assortment of half-finished sculptures made from milk bottles and rusted bits of wire. One of them, a bizarre amalgamation of old horseshoes, baler twine and plastic netting, twisted into the rough approximation of, according to Moss, a fertility goddess caught his eye and was given pride of place in his Collection.

"It reminds me of my glory days," he'd said, gazing wistfully off into the middle distance.

Frances had sense enough not to inquire further.

After clearing out all of the unwanted rubbish, Frances spent the next two hours helping Moss scrub the walls and floor with a solution of hot water, vinegar and baking soda. The windows, which had been the selling feature of the space, had been washed and polished with vinegar and old newspapers.

Another selling point in the studio was a large wooden table that the estate agent had assured her was of ancient vintage - possibly Iron Age - to which Moss, perched as he was at the time on the outside pocket of her satchel, had barely suppressed a barking snort of laughter. Faulty historical timelines aside, it was a gorgeous piece — solid oak, bearing the scars and dents of years of service. It was too big and heavy to be moved and so was a permanent fixture of the space.

"I do believe the Iron Age peoples simply built around these treasured pieces of furniture," the estate agent — Miriam was her name — had said with great authority, twinkling her exquisite manicure in the vicinity of the table. She seemed to be one of those people who would brook no argument, no matter how ludicrous her statements, so Frances merely smiled and nodded, not wanting to risk her chances of getting the lease. This had been the only suitable place she could afford, and even then, barely. She'd very specifically wanted to be on the outskirts of the village, for various reasons.

One of those reasons was still worrying the foul-smelling item he'd found in the substantial rubbish heap behind the studio.

"I bet Miriam would call that a midden. Eh, Angus?" said Frances, to the smiling face of her Jack Russell terrier. "Probably Norman-era and that's very likely the cast-off garment of a genuine country serf."

"Plague-victim, I should think," muttered Moss, skirting a wide berth around the little dog, as he lugged his own lumpy bundle up onto the counter of the kitchenette. He'd claimed the large enamel bread bin as his own. With faery magic, the bread bin had taken on dimensions far larger on the inside and was already home to his Collection and the assortment of scavenged sheep's wool and scraps of linen that he used as a bed. "We'll all be erupting in boils next."

"Oh, stop bullying him," said Frances, looking fondly at Angus. He wagged his stump of a tail and cocked his head sideways in the way he felt to be most charming. It had saved him from his own indiscretions many times over.

"Why should I?" retorted Moss. "If it wasn't for him and his horrible behaviour, we wouldn't have been evicted from our flat. Our nice, warm and dry flat that had a proper stove and…"

"You know fine well that we weren't evicted," snapped Frances, her nerves starting to wear thin. The phone call from Sophie, combined with the amount of work it had taken to clean up the studio, only to have it still looking bleak and dingy, was wearing on her nerves.

"Oh? And what would you call a note pushed under the door with the words 'Be out by the end of the month', if not an eviction?"

Moss had dropped his bundle and stood, his hands on his hips, flashes of blue light sparking in the air around him - a vision of otherworldly ire.

5

Angus whined and came to sit on Frances' foot. He'd been on the receiving end of Moss' temper more than once - the stump of his tail still itched where Moss had tied a posy of nettles to it the week before.

Frances swallowed hard, feeling tears sting behind her eyes. She'd been trying so hard to forget the events of the past month. Everything had unraveled so quickly. She took a deep breath and scrubbed a hand across her face, leaving a smear of dust and dirt.

"Let's not fight, Moss, please? Besides, no-one said you had to come with us."

Moss straightened himself to his full twenty inches of height, his expression turning from anger to pure haughtiness.

"A brownie of House Briar never, *ever,* leaves his post. Even when that post moves from a warm cosy flat to a damp hovel. A house brownie is, above all, loyal and true, no matter how undeserving his chosen mistress. Which, I may be forgiven for noting, you often are. Now, shall we have tea?"

* * *

Moss had, in his usual way, managed to conjure at least *some* comfort from the sparse surroundings. He'd dragged a couple of old wooden milk crates in from the rubbish heap, or rather, midden as they'd decided to now call it, and arranged them in an inviting fashion around the electric fire that the previous tenants had left behind.

"We'd do well with a sofa of some kind," he said, smoothing a crisply ironed linen cloth over an upturned galvanized planter. "I'm sure we could find one at one of those marvelous car boot sales."

Frances eyed the little brownie. For all of his impeccably pressed clothing, superior manners and high society tastes, his fondness for rummaging through other people's cast-offs gave him away as a true creature of his kind. She knew he was simply angling for a scavenging trip.

"I don't think you can buy sofas at car boot sales," she said, accepting the steaming mug of tea that he offered. "How would a sofa fit in the back of someone's car?" She purposely didn't look at him, suppressing a smile as she sipped her tea.

Moss was silent for a moment, pausing as he poured his own tea, his lips pursed in careful consideration. He shot a glance at Frances who was finding it increasingly difficult not to smile. Scowling, he made a point of placing the teapot carefully on the tray then fisted his hands and placed them on his hips.

"It would behoove you to treat me with a little more respect, Frances," he said, his voice full of remonstrative hurt. "You've uprooted me from a very comfortable situation and now I'm expected to perform my duties to the standard to which we are all accustomed," he spared an imperious glance for Angus who was busily gnawing away at one of the twice-baked biscuits that Moss made for him. "To continue to that standard," he went on, "in, I think we can all agree, far reduced circumstances. And why is that, I ask myself? Ah, yes. Because you have let the delusional opinions of one self-important upstart derail your entire career path and that," he pointed at shaking finger at Angus, "can't be left on its own without barking the house down."

Frances took a deep, steadying breath. They'd had this exact argument approximately thirty times since she'd announced they were leaving the flat in the city.

"It's not that simple, Moss, and you know it," she replied, her voice soft. She gripped her mug in both hands, keeping her eyes on the steaming tea. "I just need some time to get some money together so I can pay back what I owe then I can find us a place in the village. This is temporary."

"And your painting?" said Moss, softening his shoulders and his tone. He placed some lavender shortbread on a small flowered plate and held it up to Frances. "Will you be going back to your painting?"

Frances hesitated, then reached out and took one of the offered biscuits.

"No, Moss. I can't."

"Can't or won't?"

"Leave it, Moss. Please? I'm tired and not in the mood."

Frances rubbed her hand across her eyes, feeling the grit of her skin. The studio had started to seep into her pores.

Moss regarded her, feeling his resolve weaken. For all of the strength it had taken her to pack them up and move them here, leaving far more behind than just a warm and well-appointed flat, she was still so fragile. Humans in general, he mused, were surprisingly delicate creatures.

He reached out a long-fingered hand and patted her arm. She offered him a grateful smile.

"I still think we should venture into the car boot sale," said Moss, having a dainty nibble of lavender shortbread. "I hear there are some people there who have a passion for antique buttons, and I'm told you can even find entire boxes of old photographs of folk that aren't even family. Can you imagine?"

Frances looked at the brownie, his green-blue eyes were sparkling with genuine wonder. She would find him a sofa; surely Sophie would know someone. It was the least she could do.

"Amazing, isn't it?" she replied and let his excited chatter dull the sharp pang of unease that had taken up residence in her stomach since the day everything had come unraveled.

* * *

Frances awoke to the sound of the rain pattering on the roof of the studio…and the distinctive sound of water plinking into a metal container. Groaning, she rolled off the hideaway bed that she'd tucked into the back room. It was meant as extra storage space, but she found it fit her camp-bed just perfectly. She'd already built a story around why she had a bed in there, in case anyone asked discomfiting questions.

"Oh, sometimes I stay up super late working and then have a need for a quick cat-nap in the afternoons," she would say, breezily, dismissing further questions with a vague wave of her hand. "It's just easier than trekking all the way back to the flat."

Angus jumped down beside her, his bottom wiggling madly in anticipation of breakfast. He started his low-pitched 'wuff' that would invariably rise in volume and octave if it went unacknowledged.

"Don't you start," Frances grumbled. "Just because we're out here in the back of beyond doesn't mean you can carry on with your awful habits. We need to fix that if we've any hope of returning to civilized society."

Angus' response was to bark more loudly.

Frances sighed.

She pushed her feet into a pair of tartan slippers and padded out into the main area of the studio, where she found Moss

9

busily arranging saucepans to collect the drips that were coming from above.

"Oh dear," she said, scrubbing a hand through her hair.

"Yes, you might say that," muttered Moss, dryly. "I would have put the kettle on but as you can see, my presence was otherwise required."

He glanced sideways at her disheveled appearance.

"Sleeping in our clothes now, too, are we? Tsk. Tsk. How the standards have plummeted. Tell me, did you have to pay extra for the aerated ceiling?"

"Your sarcasm is wasted on me," said Frances, walking past him to the door to let Angus out. "It's pelting down and this is an old building, it's only natural to expect a few quirks."

She unlatched the bottom of the dutch door and was just struggling with the top half when Angus nosed the bottom open and shot out into the rain. Swearing softly, Frances jiggled the upper latch without luck.

"Angus!" she shouted. "Don't you run off!"

"Because of course he's going to listen to you," said Moss, folding his arms, an expression of world-weariness creasing his angular features. "When has he ever done as he's told? He's an exasperating creature and ought to be sent back to where he came from. There was obviously a reason why he had two other homes before you were conned into taking him."

"That's enough!" snapped Frances, fear and frustration in her voice. "You could at least help me…"

The air crackled briefly and the latch on the top of the door popped open. Frances flung it wide and ran out into the pouring rain, calling for Angus.

Moss shook his head.

"And not a word of thanks," he muttered, stalking off in the direction of the kitchenette. Frances had filled the kettle the night before and so all he had to do was climb the conveniently placed stack of boxes onto the chipped Formica counter and switch it on. He busied himself spooning tea into the pot and moving mugs onto a tray. He put two slices of bread into the toaster and dragged the butter dish over to the tray. The last of the lavender shortbread and a packet of chocolate biscuits made their way onto a plate, as well as a jar of honey. He was just contemplating the severe lack of appropriate breakfast food - they would have to do a proper shop - when Frances burst back through the door, hair plastered to her head, dripping onto the floor.

"He's gone!" she wailed. "I can't find him. I've called and called. Oh, Moss! What will I do? He could be anywhere. There's just miles of fields and hedges, he could be chasing a rabbit and lose his way and...."

She broke into a gulping sob.

All of the events of the past month welled up and overflowed. Losing Angus was simply the last straw.

Moss carefully lifted the whistling kettle, pouring the hot water into the teapot.

"There now," he said, his voice taking on a sing-song quality. "Go and get yourself a towel and dry off or you'll catch your death of cold and then what use will you be to that silly little dog, eh? Moss has made the tea and the toast has just popped; let's just have a sit and sip and get ourselves together, shall we?"

France nodded her head, sniffling loudly. She went obediently into the bathroom and dried her hair. Then she peeled off her wet clothes and pulled on a pair of paint-splattered jeans and a much-darned navy pullover.

11

When she emerged, still sniffling, Moss had set the tray on a little wheeled cart and trundled it over to the edge of the counter, where Frances dutifully picked it up and carried it over to the rickety card table that was serving as their dining area.

She pulled up a stool for Moss and a slightly wobbling chair for herself.

"There now," crooned Moss. "Isn't that better?"

Frances nodded, wrapping her hands around the steaming mug of tea. Moss had buttered her a slice of toast and was applying a liberal layer of honey to his own.

"There's naught to be gained with hysteria," he said, patting her hand fondly. "You know the little blighter knows where he's well-off. Just wait and see, he'll be scratching at the door and barking any minute now. He hasn't even had his breakfast, after all, and his tummy clock is very punctual."

Frances managed a weak smile.

"Thank you, Moss. I'm sorry I shouted at you. I think it's all catching up with me, you know? I had to hold it all together to get us moved and now I think it's starting to finally sink in."

Moss tilted his head and smiled, genuine affection in his expression.

"It'll all work out just fine, you'll see. You just need a week or two to get back on your feet, that's all. Besides, maybe a sojourn in the country is just what that aggravating little bast…"

"Moss," said Frances, warningly. "You were doing so well there, weren't you?"

Moss sighed and shrugged his bony shoulders.

"It near killed me," he said. "But surely I get points for the effort?

12

Frances grinned.

"You do, my friend, you most certainly do."

* * *

Later, after washing up the breakfast dishes, in an effort to not think about Angus and when he might return, Frances set about organizing her art supplies.

She'd already set up her drafting table, formerly known as the Iron Age artifact, next to the largest window and had wheeled her trolley full of paints and inks into place beside it. She unpacked brushes and pens and set them in old baked bean tins and empty honey jars. Next came sketch pads and loose-leaf watercolour paper, which she stacked in an antique magazine holder which she'd placed on an old plant stand that had belonged to her grandmother.

Feeling quite pleased with her progress, she turned her attention to the last three boxes and the large portfolio that still leaned against the table.

Pausing, she bit her lip and frowned, hesitating slightly before opening up the first box.

It was full of acrylic paints and her larger paintbrushes, canvas stretchers and bottles of primer and sealant. She closed it up again and shoved it under the table, right to the back.

The next box was all pre-stretched canvases and she slid that one under the table as well.

The third and final box was large and very heavy, too large and heavy to be shoved under the table. She paused, her hands hovering over the top.

"Go on," said Moss, softly. He came to stand beside her and placed a gentle hand against her leg. "Maybe it's time you had a look at them again. It'll do you good."

Frances sighed. She looked around the room and spied a large metal cabinet against the back wall that she hadn't noticed yesterday.

She took a deep breath and pulled the tape off the top of the box. Without looking, she plunged her hands in and picked up a framed painting, marched it over to the cabinet and stuffed it inside. She did the same with each of the large paintings that were in the box, followed by the rest of the portfolio. Then she slammed the metal door closed and dusted her hands on her jeans, flashing a grim smile at Moss.

"Or you could just shove them in the cupboard and refuse to deal with it," muttered Moss, shaking his head. "Typical."

"Oh, shut up," said Frances, good-naturedly. He scowled and went back to his dusting.

Just then the latch on the door jiggled and a soft whine sounded.

Frances whirled around.

"Angus?" she said, crossing the floor in three swift, jubilant strides. "Where've you been you naughty…"

She pulled the door open and stepped back in surprise.

It was Angus, but he wasn't alone.

Chapter 2

He has the most startling green eyes, thought Frances, quite inappropriately.

A red-faced, white-haired man stood in the doorway of her studio, brandishing a carved walking stick.

"Can you not control that useless hound of yours? Have I not told you afore, you cannae let the beast run amongst my ruddy sheep!"

The man, although clearly of an advanced age, was slim and straight and strong.

He carries that walking stick more like a weapon than a mobility aid, thought Frances, desperately wracking her brain to remember where she knew him from because he was clearly of the opinion that they'd already met. Not only that, they'd discussed some transgression of Angus'. There had been so many of those sorts of awkward exchanges in the last few months, none of them that she particularly cared to remember.

"Well?" he demanded, "What're you going to do about it this time?"

"Um. Oh, dear. I'm ever so sorry, you must believe me," said Frances fervently. "It's just that he has a fondness for sheep. I'm sure he thinks they're just large, fluffy dogs."

Frances giggled nervously.

"He doesn't mean any harm to them; you must know that. He wouldn't hurt a flea. Really, he wouldn't."

The old man glared at her without speaking.

Frances shifted uncomfortably under his sharp, emerald gaze. Angus sat at her side, a model of obedience.

"Um. Would you like to come in for a cup of tea? I've just boiled the kettle, and I've some nice lemon-drizzle cake from the bakery in the village. Perhaps you'd have a slice by way of an apology?"

"Skelly," he said, pushing past her into the studio.

"What?" she said, startled, closing the door behind her.

"You forgot my name again." He turned to face her; his eyes bright in his weather-beaten face. His hands, roughened and gnarled, gripped the walking stick tightly.

"Um, well, yes actually. I'm terribly sorry, I seem to have a hard time holding it in my head, for some reason," she said, smiling weakly. They'd very obviously met before. She felt an odd, dissociative feeling at the lack of memory.

He nodded.

"That's because I hadn't given you the right one."

* * *

Frances placed the sturdy brown teapot on yet another folding card table that Moss had salvaged from the pile of rubbish behind the building. It was sturdier, he insisted, than the last one. She'd been momentarily torn, not certain whether she should entertain her guest at the kitchen table or go for the more formal, sitting room location. Not that the sitting room was anything like formal and she worried that the elderly farmer might have trouble negotiating the upturned milk crates that were serving as seating. In the end, she decided on the kitchen table, which was where her strange guest was now perched.

Moss had insisted they use the small electric fire; to ward off the damp, he'd explained, but between its suspicious safety rating and pure economy, she doubted she'd ever turn it on for her own purposes. Still, it was a nice focal point and helped the place look less utilitarian. So, in a fit of extravagance she flipped the switch and was rewarded with creaky ticking noises and the smell of burnt dust.

Digging in the basket next to the sink, she unearthed two mismatched enamel mugs that were reserved for company. Moss nodded approvingly from behind the bread bin where he was hiding. He had very high standards when it came to entertaining and had gone to great lengths to try and convince Frances that she ought to have 'guest' mugs. That they were from a car boot sale was a concession on both sides.

Moss leaned out to get a look at the visitor. He had a habit of offering snide commentary about anyone who ever visited her old flat and considering her company was usually composed of fellow art students and their assorted oddities, he'd had plenty of material. Frances gave him a pointed look, trying to silently communicate that he bugger off but Moss was staring at Skelly. Frances looked over at her elderly visitor, who looked back, raising a shaggy white eyebrow enquiringly. His gaze traveled over the kitchen, his eyes narrowing slightly as they rested briefly on the bread bin before drifting elsewhere. Frances turned back to Moss who had paled visibly. She was about to reboot her pointed glare, but he'd already withdrawn into the clutter of boxes that still took up most of the kitchen counter.

Frances breathed an inaudible sigh. Mustn't be feeling well, she thought. Small mercies. Despite not being visible to the general populace, Moss had, on occasion, enjoyed a bit of poltergeist mischief along with his cutting comments.

"Why haven't you made your own mugs?" asked Skelly, as he perched on the wobbly three-legged stool that was slightly too tall for the table. The effect was one of a sharp-eyed bird peering down at her from above.

Frances smiled, glancing over at the unused pottery wheel in the corner.

Shrugging, she said, "Oh, that? It actually belongs to my friend Sophie. We both had the brief notion that we'd go into the handmade tableware business when we were still in art college. It was only ever a whim - just a hobby, really. Then Sophie decided to open up her book cafe and I…well, I just couldn't justify the time."

"What good is any of it if you can't enjoy it your own self?" he asked, reaching for the tin plate that held the biggest slice of lemon-drizzle cake.

Frances had her cake resting on a clean rag she'd taken from Moss' pile. Two mugs she could justify, but two plates had seemed like an unnecessary extravagance. The everyday plates were still somewhere in the boxes on the counter.

"I don't know. I suppose I was always so focused on having to make a living and painting seemed the better option. It's what I liked most, anyway."

She laughed, a hollow, bitter laugh.

"Not that that really went according to plan either," she muttered, breaking off a corner of cake.

"Anyway, art is only ever on loan to the artist," she said, reaching into her bag of condescending philosophy that she

18

saved for such conversations with, as she and her art college friends referred to as, 'muggles'. "There's no point in getting attached to it, much less clutter up the place with it. My art has to pay its way."

"And does it?" he asked, leaning towards her. "Do your paintings earn their keep?"

Frances startled, sloshing tea from the pot as she poured it into the two mugs. She willed herself to not get defensive, which was her default response to such impertinent questions.

"Actually, they don't. If you must know. Why else would I be slumming it in this arse-end of a place if I was making pots of money?"

So much for not getting defensive, she thought, hardly daring to look at Skelly.

"And that's why you do it then?" he asked. "To make pots of money?"

Frances frowned.

"No, of course not. I mean, yes I have to make a living, but…."

"But you'd still do the painting if you never made a penny?"

Frances gazed down at her hands. The creases of her fingers were permanently etched with leftover paint. She was sure to go mad eventually, the side-effect of some vile pigment. She sighed, a deep heart-weary sigh. The past few months had certainly tested that theory.

"Yes," she said, with a small smile. "I suppose I would."

"Good!" he said, slapping his knee with great emphasis, as if a point had been made clear. "It's good to know we're on the same page, like."

"Oh?" said Frances, faintly. She felt the conversation was veering out of her control. Why aren't we discussing my dog's anti-social behaviour, she briefly wondered.

Skelly nodded.

"Most people haven't got a nose for the magic," he said, matter-of-factly. "Most people think the world goes around on schedules and scorecards and collecting as many bits of tat as they can get their grasping little hands on. You ones with the creative streak have a much better grip on it."

"It? What? The magic, you mean?"

He nodded, wordlessly, and tucked into his slice of cake, washing each mouthful down with a large gulp of hot tea.

He seemed disinclined to continue the conversation. Frances, however, was reeling ever so slightly. Bewildered, she broke off another piece of cake and sipped her tea. It was really an excellent combination. In the spirit of the current randomness, she made a point of saying so out loud.

Skelly stopped chewing and tilted his head, regarding her with a piercing gaze.

He really *is* like some sort of bird, thought Frances, a sudden, uncomfortable feeling of being scrutinized washing over her. She hid her face behind her mug and took a deep drink. The tea felt warm and sweet, chasing away the chill of the dismal studio and her even more dismal prospects.

"Why are you here, lass?" he asked, a spray of yellow crumbs flying from his mouth.

Frances giggled from behind her mug.

"Do you mean that in an esoteric, existentialist, way? Or why am I in this horrid, damp, and miserable building?"

Skelly frowned. He glanced around the studio - the piles of clutter, bleary windows and damp walls; he took in the shelves for drying canvasses, the paint-splattered rug and the crooked easel. His gaze came to rest on the tall, narrow, cupboard at the back.

"What about the ones in there?" he asked, pointing a gnarled finger.

"Oh, those? They're nothing…"

Frances' eyes widened.

"Wait, how did you…"

Suddenly, Skelly reached over with his walking stick and rapped it hard against the edge of her stool.

Angus leapt up with a frightened yip and Frances spilled tea down her jumper.

"Listen and listen well, lass. I've been here for a good while. Long enough to know the way of things. When you truly want the answers you're looking for, you know where to find me. I have a tale that needs telling and I'm thinking mebbe you're the one that needs t'hear it."

With that, he was up off the stool and halfway to the door, twirling his stick like a baton before Frances could mop up the spilled tea and quiet a whining Angus.

"And keep that feckless hound away from my sheep!"

* * *

"I don't want to talk about it," said Moss, folding his arms and jutting his jaw mulishly.

"But you always have something to say," said Frances, putting the mugs and plate into the sink. She turned on the tap then jumped back as a reddish-brown jet of water burst forth. "It's one of your more endearing qualities."

"Your sarcasm is wasted on me," replied Moss. "And you have to let it run for a minute before you put the plug in. Apparently, it needs to purge itself of the bilge that's

21

accumulated in the pipes."

"Don't change the subject," said Frances, wincing visibly at the colour of the water. "And besides, it's not bilge. I'm sure it's just the iron content of the spring water. We're on a natural spring, you know?'

"Iron? Wouldn't that be perfect?" scowled Moss. "More reasons to hate this wretched place." He shivered, wrapping his arms around himself.

"Are you alright?' asked Frances, frowning down at the brownie. His usually green-brown skin looked pale and his eyes had dark smudges beneath them. "You look a little peaky."

Moss snorted.

"Probably the iron-infused plumbing," he muttered. "Anyway, I'm fine. Just a bit tired that's all. It hasn't been easy for me you know."

His lower lip trembled slightly. Frances bit back a giggle. He had a great flair for the dramatic. Still, the move and everything that preceded it had been very upsetting for the little man. She felt a stab of guilt. It had taken her a very long time to adjust to his presence in her life but once she had, she tended to take him for granted.

"I know, my friend," she said, smiling fondly at him. "Why don't I make you a cup of tea and you go and have a lie down, eh? There's plenty of lemon-drizzle left and there's still tea in the pot. It'll be nice and strong, just how you like it."

"Leftovers, is it?" he asked, a pool of tears brimming in his large, round eyes. He sniffed dramatically. "Is that what my dedication is worth? The cast-offs from some glam…" He broke off in a fit of coughing. He held up a hand and shook his head as Frances started towards him. The coughing subsided and he wiped his streaming eyes.

"Could I have honey in my tea?"

Chapter 3

"Coo-eeee!"

The sound of the door latch rattling was drowned out as Angus launched into a full-scale "intruder alert" stream of loud barks. His stump of a tail vibrated back and forth at high speed and he was jumping up and down in place.

"Ah, so not an axe-murder, then," said Frances, not bothering to shout at him to be quiet. Experience had taught her that there was simply no point. She wove her way through the shrinking towers of boxes to open the door.

Angus shrieked and hurled himself past Frances to greet his best friend in all the world who had been gone for years. Or so you would think by his level of enthusiasm.

"Angus!" said Sophie, giggling as she tried to fend him off, a feat made difficult by the large bags she was carrying. "Has it really been two days? I thought we'd never see each other again."

Frances grinned at her friend and reached over to relieve her of her baggage so that she could pay the appropriate levels of attention to the frantic terrier. One of the things she loved about Sophie was that, instead of being critical of Angus' bad behaviour, she happily went along with it. Even, to the point of encouraging him at times.

"It's his natural temperament to be boisterous," she had been known to say. "I wouldn't crush another human being's spirit by expecting them to dim their light, why would I do it to a poor defenseless creature?"

Frances had already predicted that Sophie and Stuart would have a herd of tangle-haired, barefoot children with names like Tarquin and Meadow. When she'd told Sophie that, she'd just laughed and waved a bangled arm, gesturing at the tiny, cluttered shared digs they'd all lived in at college. "Now where on earth would we put a herd of children?" she'd said, as if that were the only obstacle to the idea. Her eyes had shone, though. A herd of barefoot children would be just about right, especially as it would be another sod-off gesture to everything that Sophie's social-climbing family stood for.

Eventually, the ritual of greeting over, Sophie waded into the studio. She glanced around, assessing the situation.

"The light is surprisingly good," she said, noting the large, yet still slightly bleary windows. "And what a darling little fire! Does it work? It'll be just the thing for the damp. These old building are so lovely, but they do seem to wick up all the moisture from the earth. And the wee kitchen! How clever!"

Frances felt a lump of tears forming at the same time a wave of gratitude washed over her. She knew that Sophie was trying to be supportive, despite how she really felt about the situation. Which only made Frances feel like a bigger idiot.

She sighed.

"You don't have to say nice things," she called out to Sophie's retreating back. "It's a hovel, I'm well aware."

From somewhere in the vicinity of the corner, a tiny snort erupted, quickly disguised as a stage-snore. She gritted her teeth and glared at what appeared to be a haphazard heap of old paint rags, but which was actually 'a carefully curated collection of repurposed cloth'. Moss was obviously doing an inventory.

Sophie returned from her little tour, her face a picture of concern. Her brown eyes were filled with something that wasn't quite pity but close - more of confusion and a desperate urge to understand why her best friend would refuse all offers of help and instead settle for living the stereotypical life of a starving artist. Complete with her very own damp, and very probably, drafty garret.

"Please, Fran," said Sophie, all pretense of jollity suspended. "Why don't you take Jack up on his offer of the studio space? It's a far better situation. And wouldn't it be nice to be with the old gang? Remember our salon nights? And if you didn't want to live in the city, you could easily stay with Stuart and me. The bus stops right across from the cafe. Wouldn't it help to be among people who understand? Who are doing the same thing as you instead of holing up here by yourself? I worry, Fran. This isn't a healthy response."

Frances shook her head and turned away. She busied herself filling the kettle - blocking Sophie's view of the taps' initial eruption. She swallowed hard, pushing down the clog of tears. She'd faced lots of things in the last few months without so much as an outward quiver, but Sophie's genuine concern was undoing her.

She took a deep breath and turned to face her friend.

"I can't tell you how much it means to me that you're doing this. I know Jack and Yvette would rather not have me there and they're only offering because you're shaming them into it."

She smiled at the look of mock horror on Sophie's face. She'd even gone so far as to put a shocked hand to her chest. Her minor in theatre wasn't being wasted. The slight comic relief eased the last of her emotional distress, just as Sophie knew it would.

Frances held up her hand to ward off any further protestations.

"Look, Soph, I've accepted that this is the way things need to be for now. If you think about it, I'm being very sensible. That gallery debacle pretty much derailed any chance I have of making a living selling paintings. Thurgood was right. No-one wants to buy pictures of faeries unless they're sparkly and twee. There's a reason that Disney changed the whole faery aesthetic. The real thing…" she paused, her face reddening, "The old, mythical style is too dark for public consumption." If only people could see what I've seen, she thought, shivering slightly. "And I won't change my style so it's better that I just move in another direction."

Sophie folded her arms across her ample bosom, looking for all intents and purposes like a disapproving hen. But she kept silent as Frances talked on.

"At least I'm not giving up on art altogether," she said, waving her hand at the studio. "Let's face it, I could've packed it in and got a job in an office somewhere."

They both paused to consider that. Reaching the same conclusion at the same time, they looked at each other and grinned.

"The horror!" they cried at the same moment and burst out laughing.

* * *

An hour later, they were perched on the rickety stools around the card table, drinking their third cup of tea and munching their way through a plate of assorted pastries that Sophie had brought from her cafe.

"Mmmph," mumbled Frances, chewing with rapt delight some sort of gooey, fruity macaroon-ish confection. "These are absolute heaven!"

"Aren't they? said Sophie, beaming. "I get them from this darling old girl who bakes out of her little cottage in the next village. I found her through another lady who attends the same church and apparently Mrs. McTavish wins the summer fete baking contest every year. And isn't it marvelous that I can support a local person? And a senior citizen at that. Imagine those poor dears trying to live on the pittance of a pension they get. Well, I'm just glad she agreed to sell me stuff. And it's done wonders for the traffic at the cafe. People heard that I'm selling her baked goods and they come in just for that reason. I mean, it's only a small selection and Gary makes up the rest but …"

"But you're giving the old girl something to liven up her day and make her feel not quite so pointless? Honestly, Soph. They'll be nominating you for the sainthood before long. And I suppose the ones that follow the trail of macaroon crumbs fall in love with the place - and you - and leave with a pile of books and a stack of notecards?"

Sophie grinned, blushing.

"Well, sometimes, yes. I suppose they do. But it's the fruit bars that keep them coming back!"

Frances reached across the table and squeezed Sophie's hand.

"Have I told you how deliriously happy I am that all of this worked out so well for you? Analogue Daze is the perfect reflection of all of the things that are wonderful about you. You are the most deserving person I know."

Sophie cast her eyes down, nodding.

"I know you're happy for me, Fran. I just wish you'd let me help you. I could stock some prints. Maybe you could let me have your paintings from the show? I could hang them in the cafe - you know, attach tiny cards with giant price tags?"

Frances shook her head.

"No, Soph. I can't. Besides, it'd bring the tone of the place down. All those…how did he put it? 'Grim and dreary depictions of a dark fantastical underbelly'. And that was just the nice bit of the review."

She laughed a small, bitter laugh.

"I think what bothered me most was that he obviously didn't get it at all…he didn't see…"

"What you see?"

Frances glanced quickly at her friend. She'd spent months after first meeting Sophie, trying to decide if she ought to tell her about the strange affliction, as she thought of it, that she'd had ever since childhood. The idea of being able to see faeries was something out of fiction. But the sheer ridiculousness of it stopped her. It was too 'mad artist' and the last thing she needed was to be misunderstood or disbelieved. But the more she got to know Sophie, the more she realized that she was probably the only person she could ever trust with her secret. And so, she'd told her and Sophie had not only believed her, she'd been delighted and curious and had made Frances sketch her a drawing of Moss so she could see what he looked like. Moss, for his part, adored Sophie. Not only was she from a Good Family, but she said all manner of flattering things

29

about his housekeeping and his obvious style.

Sophie smiled at her.

"You see the magic in the world, Fran. And everyone knows that magic isn't all rainbow dust and sparkle. You can't let the jaded and unimaginative opinion of Spencer Thurgood, who everyone knows is a raging git, stop you from making your art. He's one person in a sea of even more stupid opinions. The things he criticized are exactly what make your paintings so *real*. It's like I can almost *see* them. You make people believe that there really *are* pixies at the bottom of the garden and dryads in the streams and that perhaps they don't always like us very much at all because of what we've done and how we go on…"

Frances gave a tight smile. She heard another snort from Moss and made a mental note to ask him if he had a cold.

"…and why would they? We're quite horrid. We've done this planet no favours at all. This is what art is for, to hold up a mirror, right? And there's nothing twee or sparkly about what we've done to the world."

Sophie put her mug down on the table and folded her hands in her lap. She took a deep breath.

"So, and please don't take this the wrong way, because I'm the very last one to judge another person's life choices, but Fran, wallpaper design? Really?"

Frances stiffened.

"It's not just wallpaper," she said, "it's textiles and house-wares. And, I might add, it pays well and like I said, it's better than typing and filing papers. As long as I can be making a living from my art — and this can certainly be considered art — then I don't see what the problem is. Plus, I can work from home and that's probably the most important thing because Angus has a meltdown if I leave him. My brief stint at the art supply shop proved that. I'll only need to stay here until the contract pays and then I can find somewhere a little less…rustic. I just have to get out from under the massive debt I went into devoting a year of my life to that giant failure."

Her voice cracked slightly but she forced a smile.

"And besides, I wouldn't be the first artist to have to hunker down in a moldering garret to serve her art. Maybe I'll revolutionize textile design and make a giant fortune. I could have my own line of accent pillows."

Sophie frowned and glanced around the studio. She got up off her stool and walked around the partition at the back where Frances had put the trundle bed.

Frances cringed, knowing what was coming next.

"Are you seriously LIVING here?" exclaimed Sophie, a look of abject horror on her face. "Surely not! Frances!"

She put a hand over her mouth, in genuine disbelief this time.

"Oh my goodness, this is worse than I thought. You can't possibly…it's a…"

"Hovel? Dive? Yes, possibly all of those things. Although I'm not finished cleaning it up and unpacking yet. And like you said, the electric fire is darling. I feel like there's a tartan sofa in my future as well. These stools aren't at all comfortable."

"Oh be serious, Fran!" said Sophie, waving her hand impatiently. "This is no time for jokes."

A look of realization crossed her features.

"Wait. Are you even *allowed* to be living here? Is it zoned for that? Oh, I bet it isn't. No-one could seriously try to pass this off as suitable for human habitation. I bet the bloody cows were happy to see the back end of it."

Frances bit her lip. Sophie was right, of course. The estate agent had even made a distinct point of warning her against any possible ideas of this becoming a "flop house" as she'd called it. 'You artist types are prone to that sort of thing' were her exact words. But Frances had argued with herself - and Moss - it was only temporary. She just needed time to get herself back on her feet. Not to mention, it would be difficult finding a place where Angus' propensity for loud, incessant barking wouldn't be a problem. This studio surrounded as it was by nothing but hedges, laneways and sheep pastures was absolutely ideal.

Frances told Sophie those exact reasons.

"But you're not *allowed* to live here, Fran. What if someone finds out? What if some random official happens to drop in, how will you explain the obvious habitation?"

"Because of course, random officials are very likely to wander in off the bridle path," retorted Frances. She held up her hand, because of course she'd already thought of how she'd react. "I'll simply plead the intense and slightly lunatic tendencies of an artist. That, when seized by wild inspiration, I work late into the night and then am required to put my head down for an hour the next afternoon. And I also like my work-space to look homey and lived-in."

Sophie's shoulders sagged.

"I'm not going to convince you, am I? Honestly, I had no idea. I thought you'd found a place in the village. Then again, I don't remember you mentioning it," She clasped a hand to her forehead. "I'm sorry, Fran. I've been so distracted and obviously very remiss. Are you *sure* I can't lure you to the relative luxury of our flat above the cafe? You'd have the tiniest, most cramped and uncomfortable box room to sleep in, barely enough room for your camp bed. You'd have to share a kitchen and a loo with two other people. Such overcrowding as to be barely humane. And Stuart has a terrible habit of clipping his nails into the sink. It would be pure torture. It would perfectly suit your aesthetic."

"Nice try, Soph," said Frances, walking across to take her friend into a giant hug. She squeezed tightly and whispered into the tangle of Sophie's sandalwood-scented hair. "I love you for caring and love you even more for letting me just get on with it."

Sophie nodded and squeezed back.

She took a deep breath and whispered,

"You have to use a privy, don't you?"

France nodded.

"Oh my god. I think you're mad, you know," she said. "Utterly mad."

Frances pulled away, smiling.

"There's solid evidence to prove that theory," she said. "Now, what else have you got in those bags you brought."

* * *

The two women spent the next hour unpacking various delights from Sophie's studio-warming packages. There were the requisite candles — beeswax; several large boxes of tea — Yorkshire; and a bundle of sage.

"What's this for?" asked Frances, giggling as she pulled out the large wad of tightly wrapped, dry but very pungent herb.

"I thought you might like to recharge the energy of the place," explained Sophie, looking around with a small frown. "You know, clear out the previous tenant's vibe. You wouldn't want

33

it interfering with your curtain patterns."

She grinned and winked as Francs opened her mouth to protest.

Frances grinned back.

"True," she said. "Although now I'm channeling an inspiration to make a throw rug in the pattern of found objects. I'm seeing a repeating series of old pram wheels and discarded fishing tackle."

Sophie burst into laughter.

"See? There's always a silver lining, eh?"

Frances sighed.

Sure, she thought, I'm nothing if not optimistic.

* * *

"Right, my dear," said Sophie, folding her reusable bags into a tiny square. "I really ought to be getting back. I left Melinda in charge of the cafe and I think the prospect was terrifying her. The after-work crowd will be coming soon."

Her shoulders sagged.

"Are you sure you're going to be okay? It's not too late. It'll take me less than ten minutes to put sheets on the rollaway bed in the box room."

Frances shook her head.

"I so appreciate the offer, Soph. And I promise if it all becomes too much I'll take you up on it. But you're forgetting one rather important reason why I simply can't move in with you and Stuart."

That important reason was currently working away on the knuckle bone that Sophie had pulled out of one of her bags. His tail stump wagged as he chewed.

Sophie looked down, fondly, at the little dog.

"He really is a bit of a menace, isn't he? Maybe he needs to see a doggy psychiatrist or something. To find out why he barks so much, apparently at nothing."

Frances chuckled.

"Something like that." She dismissed the sum total of Angus' behavioural problems with a casual wave of her hand. That was a can of worms that no-one wanted to open.

"Oh! Speaking of which, I can't believe I forgot to tell you. We've already been in trouble with the neighbours because of the little menace. I had some irate sheep farmer banging on my door because Angus was trying to play with his sheep. So, you see, it just wouldn't be a good idea to come into the village. He can't even behave himself out in the wilds."

"Oh, Frances!" Sophie's face creased with worry. "Why didn't you say? Oh no, was he horrible? Some beefy, red-faced fellow wearing big wellies and smelling of sheep dip?"

"Ha!" laughed Frances, thinking of the slender, white-haired man with his battered overcoat and walking stick. "Quite the contrary, but similarly disturbing."

She went on to tell Sophie the story, leaving out the part where Skelly had asked about the paintings in the cupboard. She was still trying to sort that one out in her head. The whole visit had been packed into a mental box and put on a shelf at the back of her brain to be dealt with later. Much later. That shelf, she mused, was getting very full.

Sophie was shaking her head as she shoved her bags into her capacious handbag.

"This doesn't make me any more confident in the sanity of this idea," she said, rummaging for her car keys. "That old boy could be the one to tell on you if he thinks Angus is going to

35

be a problem. Worse still, he might take matters into his own hands. Farmers are very no-nonsense when it comes to their livestock. What if he tries to shoot him or something?'

The occurring thought sent a shiver down Frances' spine. She shook her head, refusing to entertain the option.

"He didn't really seem the type, Soph. And it's not as if Angus was trying to eat his sheep. He just sort of, well, frolics."

Sophie frowned.

"Even so, upsetting them is just as bad, I'm sure. Makes their wool curl the wrong way or something. Anyway," she said, brightly. "It's an easy thing to avoid. Why don't you just tie a long rope outside the door? That way Angus can have a bit of freedom while you're working but you don't need to worry about him wandering."

"That's a grand idea," said Frances, happy to grasp at a simple solution that stopped Sophie and her prophecies of doom. "And you're right. It's easy to thwart further aggravations. I just need to be more careful, that's all."

Frances rubbed a hand over her eyes. She loved Sophie dearly and was so glad that she'd come to visit — bringing her lots of lovely things — but what she really wanted was to be alone. There had been far too many things unearthed with her visit; annoying facts, upsetting feelings and very real problems that she'd safely buried away.

"You're tired," said Sophie, putting a hand on her friend's arm. "I'm going to get out of your way. Why don't you have a rest? It's been a long few days for you. You see, that's where the tartan sofa would come in handy. You could just put your head down for an hour and if some council busybody was to wander by it would be the perfect vision of artist-at-work. Maybe I should organize a studio tour. You could be the keynote destination."

Frances managed a small smile, knowing Sophie was only partially kidding.

"Oh! I almost forgot! I've got some post for you. It was forwarded to me at the cafe."

"Is that alright?" asked Frances. "I had to send it somewhere until I can sort out having it held at the post office for me to pick up."

Sophie interrupted her by waving the stack of letters.

"Absolutely, it's the very least I could do. Besides, it gives me an excuse to visit and for you to come into the cafe. We can't have you becoming a hermit out here!"

* * *

Frances stood outside and waved Sophie off, Angus beside her, safely tethered to his leash. He whined softly.

"I know, I know. I miss her terribly, too. I miss them all, really. But everyone is off doing their own thing now and we can't let ourselves get all nostalgic for the heady, carefree days of art college."

Angus wuffed, softly, and tugged the leash.

Frances followed his gaze.

A pair of pixies were gathering flowers in the hedge that ran along the lane leading down to the road. They glanced towards Frances and her dog. The taller one nodded slightly but the smaller one made a rude gesture and flung a plump rosehip. It bounced along the gravel path and rolled towards Angus.

He barked.

Frances sighed.

"And people think *you* need a psychiatrist. They'd have a field day with me." She paused to watch the pixies as they went about their work, purposely ignoring the continued rude gestures which had turned into something of an obscene mime performance. "Still, it's nice to see them. It's been quiet since I stopped painting. Then again, maybe Spencer bloody Thurgood did me a favour after all. I mean who needs to look at that?" She shot a meaningful glare at the rude pixie who simply increased his efforts.

She bent down to smooth her hand over Angus' ears. He whined and licked her hand, his brown eyes twinkling merrily before he turned his attention back to the hedge.

The pixies were gone.

"Come on," said Frances, tugging the leash. "Let's go and have a nap *then* we'll go out for a nice long ramble."

* * *

A restless hour later, Frances was boiling the kettle for a post-nap cup of tea. Moss, bless him, had tidied away the detritus of Sophie's visit and set up the kettle and a mug. He'd also finished unpacking the box of goodies that Sophie had brought from the cafe and placed a square of apple tart on a saucer and covered it with a cloth. She smiled and looked around so she could thank him.

"Before you get all gratitudinous," he said, appearing from behind the bread bin, "I took the liberty of securing a few of the tastiest selections for myself."

"Why do you do that?" said Frances, wearily.

"Do what?"

"Utterly negate the pleasantness of your actions with some

snarky comment or gesture? I mean, it would've been enough to just accept my gratitude. I never would've known you'd cadged all the best bits."

"I'm not good with gratitude," said Moss, sulkily. "It's one of your disturbing human habits and not something we faeries bandy about willy-nilly. Gratitude means obligation. And you don't ever want to be obligated to a faery. If you'd ever bothered to learn anything about my people, you'd know that."

Frances cast her eyes towards the ceiling.

Moss with injured feelings was only slightly more exasperating than Moss denied the first pick of pastries.

"And considering the company you're keeping, you might do well to brush up on your faery lore."

He folded his arms and glared at her. He was still a bit pale but had lost the peaky look of earlier.

"Glad to see you're feeling better," said Frances, choosing to ignore his line of dialogue. He was fishing for an argument and she just wasn't in the mood to indulge him. She poured boiling water into her mug. He had obviously cracked open the box of Yorkshire tea, no doubt relieved to be saved from having to use the cheap store-brand bags that economy had required.

Moss snorted, turning away and heading back to the bread bin.

"I thought you might set yourself up in the corner over there," said Frances. "By the warmth of the fire. What's with the bread bin hideaway?"

Moss turned back, all huffiness gone from his features. He picked at the hem of his tunic, fingers plucking nervously.

"I wanted something a bit more secure," he said.

Frances raised an eyebrow. He stopped plucking his hem

and straightened up, scowling.

"There seems to be a lot of traffic coming and going it and I don't want anyone mistaking my cleaning things for rubbish or something. Lady Sophia was itching to tidy them up. She kept looking over. So, I'm keeping everything in the bread bin. Is that alright? If you need one of my cloths, you'll just have to ask."

Frances shrugged but looked at him with concern.

"Are you really alright?" she asked. "You don't seem yourself."

Moss sniffed, assuming an air of haughtiness, but the hint of a smile crooked at the corner of his mouth.

"I'm fine!" he said. "Not that you're all that bothered. As long as there's a tea bag in your mug and your paintbrushes are washed…"

He disappeared behind the bread-bin, muttering as he went.

"Thank you!" called Frances, giggling as he responded with a loud banging of the metal sides of the bread bin.

I really need to get a more comfortable chair, thought Frances, as she perched on her rickety stool. This simply won't do.

Along with her mug of tea and apple tart, her stack of mail and a sketch book lay on the table. She'd been kidding when she'd made the comment about a pattern of found objects, but it had prompted the idea to incorporate bicycles into a design.

She doodled idly as she sipped her tea, letting her pencil travel over the paper in loose strokes. Before she was aware of it, she was sketching the outline of the studio window with the view of the hedge opposite. The faint figure of the rude pixie began to appear.

The sound of a loud metallic bang of Moss clattering around

the bread bin made her startle, the pencil skidding across the page in a bold streak.

"Dammit," she muttered, more to herself than Moss, scribbling over the vague figure, turning it into a large elderflower.

Sighing, she put down her pencil and took a bite of apple tart. Naturally, it was like heaven wrapped in pastry. Gary, Sophie's pastry chef/cook was nothing short of genius. The simplest things turned to magic in his ovens.

She turned her attention to the pile of letters. Most of it was junk - some art supply store catalogues, an offer for window replacements. I might wish I had better windows come winter, she thought ruefully. After the sorting, there were only three valid pieces of mail — a postcard from their friend, Lois, who was off restoring old paintings in a castle in Belgium and two official-looking envelopes that sent a stab of cold chills down her spine.

She bit her lip and picked up the first one. It had an anonymous-looking return address on it. Taking a deep breath, she opened it. Her stomach made an uncomfortable gesture as she scanned the contents. It was a demand letter from the bank; they wanted her to start paying back the money she'd borrowed. Her mouth ran dry at the proposed monthly payment - how had she ever thought she'd make that kind of money? Oh yes, she reminded herself bitterly, she thought she'd have sold her paintings and been on the fast-track to art world fame by now.

A small brown hand appeared and rested on her arm. She looked up, teary-eyed, to see Moss's concerned face peering at her.

"Are you alright, pet?" he asked, worried creasing his forehead. "What's in that letter? Did someone die?"

Frances laughed through her tears, sniffing loudly.

"No, and you're right," she said. "It could be a lot worse news."

She shrugged.

"It's the bank," she said. "They're calling in their loan. As I knew they would. Only I expected to be able to pay them off all at once, you know, with the pots of money I made from my paintings."

Moss pursed his lips and glanced towards the letter. He opened his mouth to speak but Frances put a gentle hand over his where it still rested on her arm.

"Please don't lecture me about making deals with untrustworthy forces. I know it's not done lightly in Faery, but I'm not a faery and I needed money to live on for that year while I poured my heart and soul into my paintings. And yes, it was a gamble and yes, I lost. Badly."

Moss clamped his mouth shut and nodded, patting her arm.

Frances sniffed again. A large, immaculately pressed, lavender-scented hanky appeared in Moss' hand and he passed it to her. She wiped her eyes then blew her nose.

Moss cleared his throat softly.

"Would it be impertinent to suggest that you just try again? With the paintings, I mean. Why not take Lady Sophia up on her offer to hang them in the bookshop? It can't hurt and it'd be better than having them sit in a damp cupboard for all eternity?"

Frances shook her head.

"I can't, Moss. I can't face them not selling. They're just too personal - they're more than paintings to me. It was probably a huge mistake to put them out there. I should've stuck to my design work. Which is exactly what I'm going to do now. I've learned my lesson."

Moss sighed.

"I suppose you know what you're doing," he muttered.

"Thank you for your vote of confidence," said Frances, reaching for the last letter. She ripped it open and her face broke into a smile.

"See? It's a sign," she waved a sheaf of papers at him. "It's the specs for the design contract. If I work really hard, I can have it done in half the time, pay off the balance of the loan in full and we'll be home free."

She rummaged through her pen case and pulled out a pen. With a flourish, she signed the contract and held it up to show him.

"There! Done! I'll pop it into the post tomorrow and it'll be official. I can't tell you how much better I feel. Don't worry, we'll be back living in civilization before you know it."

Moss remained unmoved.

"If you're so happy about this," he said, reaching for the empty saucer where the apple tart had been. "Why aren't your eyes smiling?"

Chapter 4

This is madness, Frances muttered to herself as she clambered over the dilapidated stile into the sheep pasture. Angus bounced ahead, having squeezed through a gap between the stone wall and the shed.

Why would I ever think that Angus would lead me to the old man's house? That sort of thing only ever happens in films with desperately intelligent dogs that have made rescuing half-witted humans from themselves their life's mission.

Angus, however, was delighted with the idea that, not only was he no longer tied up outside the studio, but that his kind mistress was actually *escorting* him to play with his woolly companions. He was quite certain that he was the luckiest dog to ever walk the earth.

"Right," said Frances. "Which way now?"

Angus cocked his head, inquiringly. The pasture was dotted with sheep, their heads down grazing on the lush, green, grass. As far as Angus was concerned, they had arrived.

Frances glanced around, shielding her eyes from the early morning sun. After four days holed up in the studio, drawing bicycle wheels and random swirls she was in desperate need for diversion. She and Angus took daily walks down the lane and into the village, but she felt it was time for a longer, more exploratory ramble.

"I've earned it," she told Moss as she made sandwiches and put a packet of crisps in her satchel. After a moment's thought, she added some of Angus' favourite biscuits; the ones she used when she really needed to divert his attention from something more interesting.

"But why go looking for *him*?" asked Moss, wringing his hands. "Give the Lady Sophia a ring. Maybe the two of you could go somewhere. Take a trip into the city, see the sights."

She'd given him a withering look.

"The city? Really, Moss? It's only the absolute last place I want to be right now. Maybe ever. Besides, Angus has been so patient with me, working the hours that I am, he deserves a jaunt as much as I do."

At the mention of his name, Angus had wuffed and wagged his bottom vigorously.

"And," continued Frances. "I'm just curious about this man. That whole exchange was so very bizarre. He's been lurking at the back of my mind ever since he visited."

"I bet he has," murmured Moss, picking at the sleeve of his tunic.

"What was that?"

"Oh, nothing, nothing." He flapped a hand and heaved a world-weary sigh. "I don't know why I'm even bothered," he said. "His kind don't want to be found unless they want to be found."

Frances raised a querying eyebrow.

"What does *that* mean?"

Moss's eyes widened and he put a hand to his mouth.

"Moss?"

He pulled his hand away from his mouth and smoothed

45

down a wayward spike of hair. He was wearing the apron Frances had made for him out of a scrap of fabric he'd found in a pile of discards - one of her college roommates installation projects involving vintage Liberty print fabrics and strings of twinkle lights. It was the apron he wore when he was planning an especially deep clean.

"Well, he struck me as a sort of hermit type, that's all. You know, all patched overcoat and lack of social etiquette. I mean, he probably doesn't have a lot of human interaction while he's out chasing sheep across the fields."

Frances narrowed her eyes.

"You're doing that thing where you're not fibbing but not telling me the whole truth, either," she said. "I can tell by the babbling accompanied by the tic of your left ear twitching."

Moss blushed, turning his green-brown skin a mottled shade.

"I have no idea what you're talking about," he said, jutting his lower lip. "I'm merely expressing a concern that you're probably not going to find him anyway."

"Hmph," snorted Frances, deciding it would be less effort to just abandon the subject. "Be that as it may, we'll still have a lovely outing. Even if we just enjoy the walk."

She tucked her sketchbook in beside her sandwiches started to buckle the strap of her satchel.

"Are you sure you won't come with us? You could maybe see some…friends, or do some foraging?"

"Emphatically, no," said Moss, shaking his head vigorously. He gave a little shudder.

"Alright, alright," said Frances. "There's no need to be so dramatic about it. I just thought you might like the fresh air. You've been cooped up indoors for long enough. It's not like you, that's all."

She slung the satchel over her shoulder and bent down to clip Angus' leash onto his collar. The little dog was writhing with excitement.

"Wait!" said Moss, suddenly remembering something. He disappeared into the kitchen and came out with a lump of something wrapped in wax paper.

"Just in case you do find him," he handed her the package.

She sniffed it and smiled.

"Lemon drizzle!" she said. "Of course. It's a good thing I've developed an addiction to it."

"Well, he seemed to enjoy it. Last time he was here."

Frances reached over and kissed Moss on the cheek.

"For all of your curmudgeonly ways, you have a heart of gold, you know that? Always the gracious host."

Moss scowled over the smile that spread over his features.

"It's just my nature," he said, primly.

* * *

Frances followed the lane down to the road, such as it was. It was really no more a farm track, used more by tractors than vehicles which was nice as she didn't have to worry about cars whizzing by. If Angus had been any other dog, she could have let him off his leash. Pausing briefly, she looked up and down, trying to decide which way to go. It occurred to her that she actually had no idea where the old man's farm was. She racked her brain, trying to remember things they'd passed on their way in from the city.

I cannot, for the life of me, remember seeing a farmhouse or yard or anything, she mused. It can't be far, though. He walked to the studio, after all.

Angus tugged at the leash, whining.

"Oh, for heaven's sake, Angus," said Frances, "just ignore them. The more you react, the more likely they are to keep teasing you."

She scanned the hedgerow, assuming there was some faery creature taunting the little dog but could see nothing.

Sighing with exasperation, she bent down and took Angus' face in her hands. He whined softly and licked her nose.

"Do you suppose you could show me where your sheep friends live?" she asked, stroking his wiry head. "Would that be just the most ridiculous idea I've ever put out into the world?"

Angus wriggled his bottom and squirmed out of her grasp. Frances stood up.

"Alright," she said, letting the leash go slack. "Lead the way." She made a shooing gesture with her hands and Angus set off at a smart, meaningful trot with Frances scurrying behind to keep up.

After an hour of walking, pleasant though it certainly was, Frances was beginning to think they'd never find the old man. She had been certain that Skelly would be out tending his flock. Everything she knew about farming and livestock pointed to desperately early starts in the day. They'd passed plenty of fields, dotted with sheep, but not only was Skelly nowhere to be seen, neither was any sort of building which may have suggested either a barn or a house.

At some point, she'd grown tired of being towed along by Angus and unclipped his leash. She was now regretting that decision as she'd slipped into a daydream and lost track of him.

"Angus? Angus?"

There was also no sign of the little terrier.

"Oh for heaven's sake!" muttered Frances. "Where can he possibly have gone off to?"

"Mebbe he's looking for trouble,"

Frances almost leapt out of her wellies.

"Mr.Skelly!" she cried, as the wiry, white haired man, stepped out from a gap in the hedge. "I'm terribly sorry. I'm not meaning to trespass. It's just that when you left the studio last time, you said….and then I realized that I didn't know exactly where you live…. I fancied a walk …thought Angus might be able to find you."

Frances stuttered and blushed, suddenly finding the whole idea ridiculous and questioning her sanity at expecting her well-meaning, but essentially useless dog to lead her any-where.

"Aye, well. I'm not the sort to go around leaving a calling card, am I?" said the old man, squinting across the pasture at his charges.

Frances followed his gaze, frowning. She didn't remember there being sheep there a moment ago. She shook her head. I really must stop daydreaming, she thought. One of these days I'll step off a cliff or into the path of an oncoming bus.

He reached up with his walking stick and tilted back his tweed cap. His bright, green eyes were laughing at her, crinkling pleasingly at the corners and with a twinkle that was contagious.

Frances sighed in relief. He wasn't angry with her. In truth, she found the queer old man rather intimidating. He was the sort that you were never sure if he was joking or serious and she found those kinds of people rather unsettling.

49

Narrowing his eyes, he leaned in towards her.

"I've two questions for you."

"Yes, of course. Anything."

"Number one - where *is* that fecking dog of yours and number two - is that a lemon-drizzle you have wrapped in that satchel?"

* * *

Skelly led Frances through the gap in the hedge and into the field beyond. From there, they walked to a small hollow on the far west side of the sheep's pasture. There were several large stones strewn about, like a giant's game of jacks, mused Frances, and they settled themselves down on two of them. The morning sun was pleasingly warm and the stones had held the heat of yesterday. Angus had materialized almost instantly after Skelly's inquiry, saving Frances the task of hunting him down over acres of pasture and rabbit warrens and wooded copses and heaven knew what — all of which would have entertained him for days had he been left to himself. After making his ecstatic introductions, he took off again before Frances could clip on his lead. Rabbits and weasels aside, the faery folk were merciless in their teasing of him and would lead him a merry dance in which he was always more than happy to oblige. Frances sighed inwardly, trying not to think about what he might be doing.

Skelly produced a large metal flask from one of the over-sized pockets of his coat.

"I always have my morning tea with the sheep," explained Skelly. "And I happened to fancy you might be turning up today, so I brought the big flask. I also fancied you might have a bit of cake and I'm glad I wasn't led wrongly."

He smiled widely; his teeth were extremely white in his sunburned face.

Frances unbuckled the satchel.

"I have some sandwiches, too," she said, "And packets of crisps."

"Lovely," said Skelly, "I love a cheese sandwich and they go lovely with a mouthful of crisps."

He unscrewed the cap of the flask. A pair of tin mugs materialized from his capacious overcoat pockets and he poured into one, handing it over to Frances who took it gratefully. She took a sip of the steaming brew - it was sweet and milky but gloriously strong; a bold builder's as Sophie would say.

"Sorry, they're only cheese. I haven't had a chance to go shopping since we moved." Frances fumbled with the wrapped bundles, passing one to Skelly, without looking up at him. How did he know they were cheese, she thought, quelling a twinge of unease? Did I say they were cheese? She couldn't remember. She was also trying to avoid thinking about how he would've guessed either her intentions to find him, or that she'd be bringing cake. She decided to dismiss the cheese and that he was just saying he knew she was coming to be clever and he'd made a lucky guess about the lemon drizzle. Feeling better about it all, she pulled out the packet of crisps and set it between them on the stone.

"No complaints here," said Skelly, tucking into his sandwich. "It's been a long time since breakfast and I was finding myself a bit peckish. I thought you'd never get here."

Frances didn't quite know what to say to that, so she concentrated on her sandwich. She realized she was starving.

They must have been walking for hours. She looked down at her watch, which appeared to have stopped. Sighing, she tapped, uselessly, on the face.

"Time pieces don't work out here," said Skelly, through a mouthful of crisps.

Frances looked up, startled, but Skelly was gazing past her, into the distance.

Never mind, she thought, just ignore it. He's doing it to off-balance me. He's just a mad old sheep farmer who probably doesn't have much human contact.

Skelly made a sound that may have been a chuckle or may have been food stuck his throat. He shoved the last bite of his sandwich into his mouth, chewing thoughtfully.

"Don't fret," he said, "Your dog is on his way back," He nodded his head towards the distant hedge. "Been getting hisself into mischief, I don't doubt."

Frances looked over towards the boundary of the field but could see nothing. She narrowed her eyes and squinted, still nothing. She shrugged, shaking her head.

Dusting the crumbs off his overcoat, he looked pointedly at the satchel.

Frances blushed, dropping her sandwich into her lap. She retrieved it and set it aside on the rock.

"Are you ready for some cake?" she asked, musing that if Moss had been here, he would've already had some waiting.

Thinking of Moss she said, "I remembered that you'd quite enjoyed it last time you…er…visited. So, I thought I would bring you some as an additional apology for Angus' bad behavior. And then you find us tramping all over your meadow like trespassers…. I'm so terribly sorry."

"Never mind that, lass. You spend far too much time

apologizing for things that are naught to be given a second thought. Now, give us a lump of that cake, will you?"

Frances sawed off a generous slab of cake with Skelly's pocket knife - procured from yet another overcoat pocket; it was a rustic affair with what looked like a bone handle. She handed it to him then offered up her tin mug for a refill of tea.

They sat in companionable silence for a time - munching on the cake and sipping the sweet tea. Frances marveled at the view — the sea glittered in the far distance.

"I hadn't realized you could see the ocean from here," she remarked. "I didn't know I had come quite that far west,"

Skelly smiled, but his eyes were sad.

"Aye, I chose this meadow for just that reason. I miss the sea and even having a wee glimpse keeps my old heart from breaking."

"Oh?" said Frances. "Are you from the coast? Why don't you live out on one of the islands? There's lots of people have sheep out there."

Skelly's face clouded over.

"Never mind that," he said, his voice a soft whisper. "My time with the sea has been long over. I have my duties here and I'm grateful for what I've got in them."

Oh heavens, thought Frances. I've gone and upset him. There's obviously a reason why he's not there. Why, oh why, do I open my mouth without thinking?

"I'm sorry, Mr. Skelly. I truly am. That was thoughtless of me."

Skelly waved a gnarled hand dismissively.

"Don't be daft, lass. When you've walked the earth as long as I have, you learn to let go of things past. There's nothing that holds a body prisoner than wishing for things gone by."

Frances nodded, not really knowing how to respond. She felt like she ought to mention a reason for her visit, for invading the peace of his sheep and his morning's work, but she found herself having difficulty remembering why exactly she'd decided to come. She frowned, trying to retrace her thoughts.

Skelly smiled again and nodded at nothing in particular.

"That's alright, then," he said, enigmatically. "Just as I thought."

He poured the dregs of his tea onto the grass and wiped out the cup with a large, blue-and-white checked handkerchief that appeared from yet another pocket of his overcoat.

Standing up, he dusted the crumbs of lemon-drizzle cake onto the ground where Angus had been patiently waiting for them.

"Angus!" said France, startled. She hadn't even noticed him return. Why was he being so quiet and well-behaved?

"Come on then," said Skelly, leaning on his stick. "If you've finished feeding your face, I've a few bits of things to show you."

After Frances had packed up her satchel, she slung it over her shoulder and looked, questioningly, at Skelly. Despite their cozy meal sharing, she was still a little wary of him.

"I have to be back by five o'clock," she said, pulling the time out of the air. "I have a friend coming to visit. I wouldn't want her to turn up and me not be there."

"And how will you know the time, then?" asked Skelly, tilting his head and glancing at her wrist at the non-functioning watch.

Dammit, thought Frances. I forgot about my sodding watch.

"Aren't you one of them modern young people who carry

those eejity phones with them all over the place?"

Frances frowned.

"As a matter of fact, I do not have one of those eejity phones. I don't actually believe in them."

Skelly chuckled.

"How can you not believe in a thing that's right there in front of you?" he asked, narrowing his eyes.

Frances was taken aback. His expression was challenging.

"Well obviously I believe in their existence," she replied, defensive. "I just don't believe in including them in my life. They're intrusive and annoying and I get along just fine without one. I have a plain, old-fashioned mobile and it serves its purpose."

I also often leave it on the table instead of putting it in my satchel, she thought, once again quelling a frisson of unease.

"Hmph," he said, nodding. "This way, then. And don't worry, you'll be back in plenty of time for, what was it? "he paused, shaggy eyebrows waggling. "Right, you're expecting a friend."

He winked at her and set off across the meadow.

Frances scrambled after him, calling pointlessly to Angus who had already run ahead.

Chapter 5

"As you seem to be a one for having great thoughts on believing, would you be of a mind to believe in magical things?" Skelly had asked, breaking a long silence.

They'd been walking for about fifteen minutes, to look for a missing sheep - or so Skelly had told her. There were sheep dotted all around the meadows but obviously none of them were the one in question.

Frances glanced over quickly. She'd been trying to keep an eye on Angus, who was tearing about the fields like he'd been confined to a kennel for weeks, rather than already having spent the morning doing goodness-knows-what.

Skelly watched her reaction. His green eyes crinkling at the corners. Frances wasn't quite certain if he was serious or just having her on.

"Oh, I meant the question, lass. I meant it true enough."

How did he know what I was thinking, thought Frances, her mind racing. Or did he?

"Ach, an old trick of mine," he said, smiling at the confused look on her face. "It's a knowing of things that we have, you see."

"We?" she asked, distracted.

She had lost track of Angus. He had darted off into a patch of brambles after what may or may not have been a rabbit and not returned.

"Do you believe in the Good Folk?"

"What?"

Frances felt a jolt of something hot and cold all at once shooting up her spine. Her forehead broke out in a clammy sweat and her tongue cleaved to the roof of her mouth. Breathe, she coached herself. Just breathe. She cleared her throat and aimed for a look of complete nonchalance.

"What, you mean, like faeries and brownies and that sort of thing?" she asked, anxiously scanning the horizon for Angus. The sun was climbing higher in the sky and she was feeling uncomfortably warm. And very, very uneasy. The conversation was veering into extremely dangerous territory. What if this Skelly character was some sort of dangerous crackpot? She was out here alone, with no mobile and no-one knew where she was.

He erupted into a deep, sonorous, laughter.

Frances blushed. *Surely,* he didn't know what she was thinking?

"Ah, not so much *exactly* what you're thinking, you see. Just a general feeling it is that I have."

He cocked his head to one side, his eyes still laughing.

Frances tried to concentrate on not tripping over hummocks of grass. Her thoughts were racing in unhelpful circles.

"Well?" prodded Skelly. "Are you inclined to answer my question?"

"I…I'm not sure what to say, actually," she replied, settling on honesty but not meeting his eyes. "To be entirely truthful, I'm feeling a bit out of my depth."

"Not to worry, lass. I'll leave the question with you for a spell, shall I? We've got a bit of a hill to climb here and we'll need our wind for walking, not for chattering,"

Frances nodded, still unsure how to respond. How does one respond to an old man who can apparently read your thoughts and wants to know if you believe in magic? If she were a normal person there'd be no problem answering the question. When did life get so complicated? She looked ahead at the hill they were going to climb, and realized, with a sinking feeling, that not only had she lost Angus, she had no idea where she was.

Skelly's firm hand squeezing her elbow sent a quiet warmth up the length of her arm.

"Don't you worry, lass. I've not been dangerous for about three hundred years."

* * *

They were climbing the longest hill in Creation, of that, Frances was quite certain. It wasn't exactly steep, but the slope was steady and relentless. She had wracked her memory, trying again to decipher exactly where they were, but she could think of no large hills and no ocean view within walking distance of either the studio or the village. Twice she had asked Skelly where they were and twice he had only grunted in reply. In the end, the exertion had overcome her ability to speak and they trudged on in silence. Angus, to Frances' extreme relief had reappeared and, his every dream apparently come true, ran back and forth, tongue lolling and stumpy tail in a state of constant motion.

Finally, they reached the summit. There was a scattering

of boulders, oddly familiar but nonetheless convenient, and Skelly gestured for her to sit, which she was only too happy to do.

I really must make a point of getting more exercise, she thought, leaning her elbows on her thighs.

Skelly pulled the flask out of his pocket and poured two mugs, handing her one.

"That flask's a bit like the TARDIS," commented Frances wearily, not wanting to know why it seemed to still be full, despite them already having enjoyed a large mug each.

Skelly grinned. "It is that, lass. Grand to know you're catching on."

He winked conspiratorially and settled himself in to taking extravagant swigs of the steaming beverage.

Frances shifted on the boulder, not quite knowing whether she ought to demand answers to the purpose of this exercise or to keep a low profile and hope it would soon be over. The two options warred heavily in her mind. Despite the strangeness of the whole morning, she was deeply curious. Adding to everything else that was odd about the day so far, the faery people activity on their trek had been immense. It had taken every ounce of self-control on her part to not startle every time a wood elf or talking hedgehog popped up. It was no wonder that Angus was haring about like a mad creature.

She sneaked a glance at her companion, who was gazing off at nothing in particular as he swigged mouthfuls of tea. Everything about Skelly had developed a surreal quality. It had been a long while since she believed him to be just an elderly sheep farmer with a few odd quirks.

"Now, then," he began, swiveling his attention abruptly and alarmingly back to Frances. "Let's get down to the business, shall we?"

Frances nodded, clasping her mug to keep her hands from shaking. She had no idea what 'business' was going to entail but she wanted to keep her wits about her. Her immediate thought was that she was sure she could outrun him if need be. A trio of pixies trooped by in procession, holding aloft a burdock leaf, piled high with thistledown. One of them stuck its tongue out at her as they passed. She flicked an annoyed glance before quickly focusing back on Skelly.

The hot-cold stabby feeling came back as she saw him looking at her with a raised eyebrow and a smile quirking at the corner of his mouth. He looked pointedly at the pixie procession and then back at Frances. It took every ounce of self-discipline to not follow his glance at the faery people. She raised her own eyebrows and leaned forward, feigning indistracted interest in what he was going to say next. She firmly suppressed the rising panic in her chest. *He doesn't see them*, she told herself. *He was just wondering why I was staring. People do that all of the time around me. I shall claim artist's daydream like I always do. Just breathe.*

Skelly lowered his gaze for a moment and took a deep breath, nodding his chin to his chest.

Dear lord, she thought, *he's going to drift off.* Frances opened her mouth to speak, intending to prompt him but his head snapped up again and he fixed her with his unnerving green gaze.

"Tell me about the paintings in your cupboard."

Frances sat with her mouth open for a split second. That wasn't at all what she was expecting. She realized that she didn't actually know what she was expecting but was sure that wasn't it.

"I, er..." she floundered, casting about for a calm and collected thought. In another split second, she felt a wave of irritation pass over her. None of your damn business, she thought.

Skelly snorted.

"Actually, lass. It's every bit my business."

Frances scowled, her annoyance allowing her to ignore his disturbing mind-knowing habit for a moment.

"No, actually," she said, emphasizing the words. "It's not. My paintings are my own concern and at this moment in time, seeing as how they're locked in a cupboard, they are especially none of your business. In fact, I'd be extremely curious to know how you're even aware they're in there. Have you been snooping around when I'm not home?"

Skelly snorted again.

"And when might that be, lass? You haven't left yon building since the day you moved in. Is it the hermit life you're after then? Because I can tell you from experience, it's not all it's cracked up to be, aye?"

Frances blushed.

"Also, none of your business."

She took a nerve-steadying sip of her tea, silently willing Angus to come back so they could leave. She briefly considered just getting up and marching back down the hill but didn't want to go without her dog. She filed this, yet another, behavioural transgression, in her mental Angus File. She promised herself for the thousandth time that she would never, ever, ever let him off his leash again, no matter how much she knew he enjoyed romping around with rabbits or sheep or faery folk.

Speaking of the faery folk, out of the corner of her eye she

61

saw several wandering over to where she and Skelly were sitting. Little bastards, she thought, furious. They're doing it on purpose. To her mounting alarm, there were more of them coming, popping up from behind clumps of heather and around stones. They seemed to be settling themselves in a circle, sitting down, cross-legged, chins resting on hands.

Why don't they bring deck chairs and a picnic, thought Frances, forgetting herself and glaring at them? Sod off, you little menaces.

"I asked them to come," said Skelly, breaking into her silent tirade.

She was too shocked to respond, her mug of tea hung, poised, halfway to her mouth as she grappled with what he'd just said.

"They're here because I asked them to come," he repeated, as if perhaps she didn't hear him the first time.

"I heard you," she whispered, her mouth struggling to make the words. She lifted her mug all the way and drained her tea, trying to moisten her tongue from where it had become lodged again to the roof of her mouth.

"You see them, I knew that from the beginning," he explained, waving a gnarled hand, dismissively. "It's no secret so you can stop making yourself batty trying *not* to look at them."

Frances cleared her throat and swallowed. Trying to sort out what it all meant. She felt a faint, light-headed feeling wash over her in a queasy wave.

"Deep breaths," said Skelly, reaching over with his flask to top up her mug. "Have a bit swig o' that. It's strong and sweet."

Frances obeyed, taking a large gulp. She coughed, her eyes watering, when she realized it wasn't tea. Instead, it was a slightly thick, honey-tasting liquid that burned pleasantly on the way down. It had the desired effect, though, and she felt her head clear. There was no point in questioning any of it, she decided, she would just get through whatever waking nightmare this was and deal with it all later. In her mind, she conjured another box to contain the morning's events on the shelf in her brain.

"Right," said Skelly. "Now that we're all gathered like, you can tell me," he paused, inclining his head toward the circle of faery folk, "tell *us*, about the paintings in the cupboard."

Frances stared at him, dumbfounded. He took persistence to all new levels. She cast her eye around the circle of expectant faces. They were mostly familiar, pixies and naiads and other forest folk; she'd seen some variety or other of all of them for her entire life. In fact, many of them appeared in those paintings that Skelly was harassing her about.

She knotted her fingers around the empty mug in an attempt to stop them from trembling, and wished for the thousandth time that Moss was here or that Angus would stop behaving like a sugar-addled toddler at a birthday party and come and sit beside her, pressing his little warm body against her leg, anchoring her to the earth.

There was no choice, she finally decided. I'm never going to get away from here if I don't tell him.

She glanced up at his face. His features, although weather-worn, had a softness to them. His startling emerald eyes, sparkling from under his bushy white eyebrows were expectant, but kind, and the sparrow-tilt of his head further reinforced the vision of warm, grandfatherliness. All of a sudden, she was filled with the urge to unburden everything. To finally set down the load she'd been carrying for all these months.

Skelly nodded, encouraging, and the little people leaned in.

And so she told him everything.

Chapter 6

"I majored in graphic design and minored in painting," she started, thinking that it only made sense to start at the very beginning. "But at some point, towards my third year, I got the mad notion that I'd like to switch my major so that I could do a series of paintings for my final year project."

Skelly nodded.

"Did you realize you were liking the painting better than the other lot, then?"

Frances shrugged.

"Oh, I always knew that," she said. "I always wanted to paint, but it made more sense to focus on graphic design as my degree."

Skelly blinked, his face still questioning.

"Because I had to do something that would translate into an actual marketable skill, you see. There's not much money to be made in painting."

"And that was the important thing?"

Frances narrowed her eyes and glared at him, searching his face and tone for signs of accusation or judgement. His face remained open and curious, so she accepted it as a genuine question.

"Only in that I've always known that I wanted to be able

to make a living with my art. The thought of having to do some other, mundane job to support myself is practically unbearable."

She flapped a hand, waving away any protest before it arose. Although, she realized afterwards, there wasn't any coming.

"I know, I know. Lots of people support themselves and their art with 'day jobs' and it works for some of them. I just know it wouldn't work for me and believe me; I've tried. I'm practically unemployable. I once had a summer job in a garden center and I spent half my time chasing flower faeries out of the hanging baskets and the other half secretly sketching them."

A ripple of high-pitched laughter went around the circle of watching faeries. Frances shook her head, suppressing a smile.

"It was the same no matter where I worked," she explained. "They tended to follow me around and were either causing trouble or distracting me. I've lost more jobs for vague and poorly explained reasons…anyway, I don't blame my employers, I was a terrible employee;"

She paused and fixed Skelly with a questioning stare of her own.

"Well, *you* must understand," she said. "You can see them too and you've obviously found an occupation that gives you some peace and freedom to deal with it all."

Skelly grunted but didn't reply.

"Anyway, graphic design was the most sensible option. It's still something that I enjoy, and it means I can work freelance, which ticks all the necessary boxes."

"But you wanted to do the painting," prodded Skelly, turning the conversation back.

Frances nodded.

"I don't know why I switched my major. I suppose it was the heady euphoria of being in art college, surrounded by all kinds of people doing marvelous, creative things without any agenda other than following their inspiration."

She smiled, remembering.

"I suppose I got caught up in it. Plus," she added. "My friend Sophie was a terrible enabler and she convinced me that I should've put equal effort into my painting. And she was right, in a way. Graphic design was going to be my version of a 'mundane' job, but without it being actually mundane. I'd done enough of the course already that I would've been able to go freelance without anyone questioning my qualifications."

"So, you went back to the painting?"

"Yes, I did. And then after I'd got top marks for my final project, I made the lunatic decision to keep going with it. One of my supervising teachers arranged for me to have a gallery showing and so I spent a whole year painting. I immersed myself for an entire year, painting this lot," she gestured at ring of faeries. "Going into massive amounts of debt along the way. I had to borrow the money to live on, but I simply assumed that I'd make it all back when I sold my paintings."

She fell silent, turning her mug over in her hands. They were clean, for the first time in months. There was no ink embedded in the creases of her fingers, no half-moons of paint stuck in her cuticles.

"And then?"

Frances sighed. He was adamant to pull it all out of her. She gave a resigned shrug.

"And then it was a complete disaster. There was this very well-respected and important art critic at my opening —

because it had been so widely publicized, thanks to my art college friends and my supervisor who, bless her heart, was a disillusioned as I was. This person, who's name won't actually pass my lips without it making me want to vomit, tore me to shreds. He ruined everything."

Her voice broke. She swallowed hard and blinked.

I will not cry, she thought, furious with herself. I will not act like a big, blubbering baby. She sniffed loudly and took a deep breath.

"His opinion — and let me be quite clear when I say that he considered me and my paintings to be absolute rubbish — has a lot of clout in the art world. To get that sort of review is basically career-ending. Believe me, there's no recovery from that sort of annihilation."

There was more silence as the whole nightmarish event flashed through her brain in a montage of shame and mortification.

"So you see," she said, finally, glancing around at the faces in circle. "That's why I'd rather just forget they even exist. They're a constant, glaring reminder of my utter humiliation and my very public failure."

Skelly unscrewed his flask and leaned over towards her, beckoning for her to hold out her mug.

"I hope it's tea this time," she laughed, weakly. "Whatever that last stuff was, it's leaving me with a pounding head."

Skelly chuckled.

"Nay, lass. It's the relief of getting it all off your heart," he said. "The ache will ease now. And aye, it's tea."

Lifting the steaming mug to her lips, Frances breathed in the familiar, grounding scent. There was a reason why people made tea in times of crisis. It had the unique quality of pausing time and letting things settle into perspective. As she sipped, she reflected on the fact that the unloading of her accumulated shame had indeed eased the dull ache that had been lodged in her chest and behind her eyes since everything had come undone.

"And so this chap," said Skelly, returning to the subject at hand. "The one who wrote the review, he's in charge of what the rest of the world thinks, is he?"

Frances startled.

Skelly's tone had a sharp edge to it and his emerald gaze, this time, was challenging.

She blushed, feeling a stab of irritation collide with something that felt, inexplicably, like guilt.

"Of course not," she retorted. "And don't bother with *that* angle. I've been over it a thousand times with Sophie and everyone else who had to witness the whole mess."

"There's no need to get uppity, lass. It's a fair question. Only that it seems you're putting an awful lot at risk just on the opinion of one person. Who sounds, by the way, like the worst kind of bloated git as you would ever come across."

Frances smiled, briefly, at the startling accurate description of the art critic, although the only thing bloated about him was his ego, tending as he was, towards an aesthetic of malnourished chic.

"I don't know what you're talking about," she said, "I've not put anything at risk. I'm simply returning to my original plan, that's all."

"But you're not painting?"

"Not at the moment, no. But I will. Eventually, I'm sure. I'm in the rather difficult financial position of needing to make a lot of money fairly quickly. After my debts are cleared, I can think about picking up my brushes again."

"And you'll go back to painting my," he broke off, coughing. Frances eyes widened in alarm and she reached over to steady his small frame. That strange warmth rippled up her arm when she touched him.

He shook his head and straightened.

"Sorry, lass. I've a bit of a chest going on. The perils of old age, aye?"

He smiled, his eyes crinkling merrily but there was a hint of something else beneath it.

"As I was saying," he said, pulling a large spotted handkerchief out of his overcoat and wiping it across his face. "You'll go back to painting the wee folk?"

Frances frowned and shook her head, emphatic.

"Oh no," she said. "Absolutely not. I've learned my lesson there. The one thing that horrid man did get right was the fact that no-one wants to look at paintings like mine. People want sunshiney, jolly things. They want their faeries to look like Tinkerbell."

Skelly scowled.

"And why do you suppose that is?" he asked, glancing around at the circle of faeries that did absolutely in no way resemble the Hollywood version.

Frances shrugged.

"I suppose it's just what they're used to."

"And you don't think they need to know the truth?"

She shrugged again.

"What difference would it make?" she asked. "Besides, they can't see them anyway so why disillusion them? It's a far easier thing to imagine a faery as being sparkly and full of innocent mischief rather than dark and capable of actual menace."

Skelly sighed.

"Have you ever seen a wee person who looks like yon Tinkerbell character?"

Frances laughed and shook her head.

"No, absolutely not."

"And why do you suppose that is?"

"Um, because Tinkerbell doesn't actually exist?"

Skelly nodded.

"And yet folk think that's what faeries look like? That's what they'd be inclined to believe?"

It was Frances' turn to nod.

"Of course, but that's only a problem if you happen to paint the real…. well, the sort that we can see. It's fairly well documented that it's human nature to not like the things we aren't familiar with."

Skelly gestured towards the circle of observers.

"And these folk, as we can both see, do exist."

He tilted his head again, an expression of expectation on his face. He waited.

Frances looked between him and the faeries and back again, unsure of what he wanted her to say. She said as much.

"How do you think people are going to understand — and *believe*," he paused, putting more emphasis on the word. "How will they learn to believe in the wee folk if they don't know what they properly look like?"

Frances shook her head in confusion.

"I honestly don't know what you're getting at. What difference does it make? Why does that even matter?"

She looked at Skelly, trying to decipher if he was actually being serious or just having her on.

"Why does it matter if people believe in faeries?"

A whisper of shock ran through the circle and several of the faeries leapt to their feet, disappearing from view behind the boulders.

"It matters, lass," said Skelly, his shoulders slumping with fatigue. "Because if people don't believe in faeries, then they, and the magic that created them, will disappear from the world."

* * *

The sun was starting to slide down the horizon as they made their way back down the steep hill. Angus seemed to have finally run out of energy and was trotting happily at Frances' side.

Where were you when I needed you, she thought, smiling fondly at the little dog. She loved to see him happy, even if it meant having to put up with occasional naughtiness. It was, she supposed, the root of her failing as a dog guardian.

The conversation with Skelly had left her more confused than ever. The box of untended thoughts in her mind was becoming uncomfortably full. She knew she'd have to unpack it eventually, but the events of the day had been unsettling. Even for her, used to the appearance of the faery folk in her everyday, the level of otherworldly influence surrounding the funny little sheep farmer veered towards mildly disturbing.

"Penny for them," said Skelly, squinting over at her.

Frances shrugged.

"It would be a poor investment," she joked.

"Och, not likely lass. I've given you a big lot to think about this day. I don't want to think you burdened by it all."

Frances snorted, tripping over a hummock of grass.

Skelly reached out a hand to steady her, the flash of warmth jolting up her arm as he touched her.

"What *is t*hat?" she said, giving in to the frustration of so many unanswered questions. All semblance of politeness and respect for an elder fell away. "Why do I get this weird jolt every time you touch me?"

Skelly waved his hand, dismissing the whole thing.

"'Tis just a thing I have," he said, which explained nothing. It may as well have been an explanation of his stiff joints or other physical complaint.

"A thing?" she replied, incredulous. "After all that you've told me, after all that I've told you, you're going to blow me off with that sort of answer?"

She stopped walking and stood, folding her arms. Skelly was forced to stop or else keep going without her.

"I'm not going another step until you tell me exactly where you belong in all this."

"What do you mean, lass?"

She waved an arm in gesture, taking in the meadows and the hill.

"We are miles away from the sea," she said, ticking points off on her fingers. "There are no steep hills within walking distance of Thistlecrag or my studio. We have seen exactly zero sheep since we started walking."

She glared at him.

"Shall I go on?"

Skelly shifted his weight. He leaned on his walking stick and peered at her from under his bushy eyebrows, a twinkle of mischief danced in his eyes. Finally, he seemed to come to a decision.

"So, you'd noticed then?" he said, smiling.

73

"Of course, I bloody well noticed!" Frances voice had almost reached shriek level. Angus whined and pressed himself against her leg. She reached down and smoothed a comforting hand over his ears.

"Well, I suppose you're as clever as I thought you might be then," he said, starting to walk down the hill.

"Really?"

Frances was indignant. She stayed where she was, fuming.

"Aye," he called back. "Now if you've finished with your sulk, mebbe that brownie of yours will have the kettle on and a bit of something to eat. I might be inclined to do a bit more talking if I could get something in my belly. It's been an age since those sandwiches."

Frances suppressed a scream and started walking. She marched purposefully past him and stayed ahead of him, all the way back.

* * *

Walking up the lane towards her studio, Frances felt her anger and frustration seeping away. It was hard to stay angry surrounded by such beautiful, calming scenery. The lane was bordered on both sides by a beech hedge. The copper leaves flickered in the breeze, giving the impression of flames. She supposed it had been trimmed and maintained once, but it had been many years since that had been a regular occurrence. Elder and hawthorn had inserted itself into the hedge, along with a promising tangle of bramble. The idea of blackberrying right outside her door filled Frances with giddy delight. There were wild roses, too, and the drooping remains of spring daffodils, planted in clumps in the long grass that bordered the rutted track. Cow parsley waved gently, and purple thistle nodded drowsily in the warmth of the afternoon sunshine. Because surely it was late afternoon by now, thought Frances, glancing down at her watch which had started working again. Unfortunately, it was moving on from the point at which it had stopped. Nine thirty-five, somewhere around when she'd agreed to go walking with Skelly.

Skelly. Hmph, she thought, a tingle of embarrassment rising in her at the little tantrum she'd had. Well, what could anyone expect? He'd been cryptic and evasive, and it had unbalanced her. Talking with him left her feeling vulnerable and uneasy. Not feelings she enjoyed.

Her pace slowed as she walked up the lane. Angus had bounded ahead again. Despite their ongoing feud, Angus knew that Moss would always have something tasty waiting for him in his dish. A nice large biscuit, or perhaps a soup bone. He disappeared around the bend and Frances heard him yapping, summoning Moss to let him in.

Moss.

How was she going to explain all this to Moss? Her thoughts raced ahead. Obviously, Skelly could see him, and had probably seen him when he'd visited the first time. Why hadn't Moss said anything? Surely, he would've been aware. Frances frowned. It was very unlike the little brownie; he had loud and definite opinions on every subject and another person with the Sight was certainly valid material for discussion. Frances mentally shrugged; she had very few resources left for puzzling out her companion and his complicated system of slights and offences.

She arrived at the open door of the studio and turned around, not expecting to see Skelly. She'd been walking very purposefully, and rudely, she realized, cringing to herself. But there he was, rounding the bend, his stride long and certain, belying the need for the walking stick he carried with him.

Sighing, she pushed the door open and called out to Moss in the dim coolness.

"Moss! We're home!"

There was no answer, although Angus was slurping merrily at something in his bowl and the fragrant wafting of freshly brewed tea floated from the kitchen. There was also the delicious aroma of freshly baked something.

"Moss?" she called, setting her bag on the chair and walking around the partition into the kitchen. She tapped gently on the enamel bread bin.

"Go away," he replied, his voice a fierce whisper. "I've got a thumping head and I just want to be left alone."

"But you've made us tea and everything," said Frances, bewildered. "How did you do that with a bad head?"

"Sudden onset migraine," he replied, his voice dripping with ire. "it's a thing."

"Alright, alright," replied Frances, too weary to argue. "Can I get you something? Some willow-bark tea, maybe?"

Moss snorted.

"I've got some, thank you all the same," he said. "I wasn't just going to boil the kettle for the likes of…well, for you, you know."

Frances sighed. There was no point in bringing up the freshly baked somethings or the treat in Angus' bowl. If Moss didn't want to be bothered, then it was best to let him have his sulk. She was sure she'd hear all about it later.

"Okay, then. If you're sure. Mr. Skelly came back with me. I'm going to give him tea and whatever delicious tidbits you've left." A little flattery never went wrong with Moss. "And then if he's not gone in an hour, and you're feeling up to it, can you please do something to make him want to go? I've about had my fill."

Moss could never resist an opportunity for mischief, she was certain that would illicit a response. Still, there was no answer from the bread bin, so she gave it an affectionate tap and turned her attention back to her guest.

* * *

"These are grand," mumbled Skelly, through a mouthful of macaroons. "Your wee man make these?"

Frances winced at the reference to Moss. She was so used to having to try and hide his presence from people, to have someone casually mentioning the little brownie was strange and off-putting.

She took a sip of her tea, and nodded, hoping the line of questioning would end. She made a point of studying the pattern on the oilcloth that Moss had draped over the card table. It was a reproduction William Morris.

"Does he do your shopping as well?"

Frances looked up, a sharp retort bristling on her tongue but Skelly was grinning, his straight, white teeth, startling in his wizened, sun-brown face.

"Sorry, lass. You were looking a bit ragged, like. I just wanted to see if you still had your sense of humour."

Frances held a brief inner battle. Part of her was truly fed up with the peculiar and exasperating man and would have liked nothing more than to never have to see or talk to him again. But the other half was strangely consoled, to know that

77

there was someone else out there that had similar experiences as her. She always stopped short of calling her Sight a gift, because it seemed to bring her more trouble than not. Either way, she had never imagined there was anyone else who could see the faery folk, much less that she'd be having her millionth cup of tea of the day with him.

Comradeship won out and she smiled.

"I'm sorry," she said. "I'm a terrible hostess. It's just that this whole day has been a bit of a shock. I mean, I never in my wildest dreams thought there was anyone else out there like me. You know, who sees them."

Skelly nodded, reaching for another macaroon.

"There are actually lots of you," he said. "Although, most of the other lot don't actually see the wee folk with their eyes."

"Oh?"

Frances' thoughts had begun to run wildly towards support groups and networking; opportunities to talk with other people who understood what it was like without sounding like a nutter.

Skelly shrugged.

"No, it's more of a *sense* of the magic that they have."

Frances sagged in her seat, the support groups vanished before her mind's eye.

"So, they're not actually like you and me?" she said. "They don't truly *see* them."

"Och, they see them alright. Just without their eyes, as such."

Frances bit back a snide remark. He was being cryptic again.

"So, what exactly does that mean, then? How can you know that those people, what was it, sense the magic if they don't actually see it? I mean, who are these people?"

Skelly smiled.

"Folk just like yourself," he replied, belching loudly.

Frances winced. Moss would be mortified.

"Artists, writers, poets, makers, musicians," he continued, ticking off on his fingers. "Some of your ones who build the bridges and cathedrals. Not many of them, mind you. There's only a handful of those ones left that have the sense of the magic. Too much influence of the brain and the money bags these days."

Frances sat, bewildered once again. Just when she thought he'd said the most outlandish thing possible, he came up with something even more so.

Skelly chuckled.

"It's not so mad as all that," he said, wagging a gnarled finger at her. "The faery folk have always been drawn to the creative types. The wee ones love music and art, it attracts them like bees to flowers. And when they come, they bring their bit of magic with them. So, for instance, the more a musician plays, the more magic there is for him, or her, to tap into. And not just him, you see. Because the magic feeds on itself and so when he composes a tune and plays it for other folk, then *they* get the gift of the magic as well and so it goes." He waved a hand as if that was sufficient explanation.

Frances fiddled with her tea spoon, a thousand questions running through her head. But also, an uncomfortable feeling of recognition, a realization that what he was saying was true.

"And it's the same as when folk go, say, to an art gallery or a museum, or even a wee gift shop and look at cards and woven things and boxes of tiny biscuits. If they look at something that really touches their soul, like, gives them that certain feeling of it being made just for them, it's because they've taken in the magic and so that stays with them and they carry it away as

79

they go about their day."

Frances gave an exasperated sigh.

"This is all very jolly and full of the good vibrations and everything but if this is some sort of complicated, and hugely outlandish, ploy to try and get me to paint again, you're wasting your time." said Frances, suspicious and slightly embarrassed to have been taken in by his story. "Did Sophie put you up to this? Because I really don't know why it's any concern of yours. If what you say is true, and trust me, I'm holding it all very lightly, there are plenty of artists and musicians and poets in the world to keep the magic circulating. What's the big deal if I'm not painting? I'm still making art, aren't I?"

"Are you asking me that question, or yourself?"

Frances flushed.

"That wasn't the point of my question, and you know it," she said, getting up from her stool. She started to gather up the tea things onto the tray. Maybe if she made a point of tidying up, he'd get the hint and go.

There was a sudden movement and Skelly was standing beside her. Frances stared, shocked. How had he moved so quickly? She took a nervous step back, holding up the tea tray as a sort of shield. He reached out and gripped her arm. That same warmth she'd experienced out on the hill, shot up her arm, but it had a slight undercurrent of electricity this time. It was strange, but not altogether unpleasant. Her vision blurred for a split second and it came to her in a realization that crept up her spine in a chill prickle.

He's one of them, she thought, her eyes widening in recognition.

Skelly nodded, letting go of her arm. Frances put the tray

back on the table and leaned against it for support.

"Aye, lass. That I am."

"But, who…"

He held up his hand.

"None of that matters, lass. And you'll not remember it, either. Because it makes no difference in the end what or where any of us come from, all that matters is that we don't disappear."

Frances squeezed her eyes shut, trying to dispel a sudden fuzzy feeling that passed over her. She was having trouble gathering her thoughts. Shaking her head, she returned her attention to the conversation at hand.

"And what do you mean, disappear?" she continued, picking up her thread of thought and gesturing towards the door. "There's clearly no shortage of them, you saw that out on the hill. I can't move for tripping over some aggravating little creature or having it hurl rosehips at me."

Frances was recovering from the shock of his explanations and moving swiftly back into incredulity. This was all getting to be a bit much. This is absolutely the last thing I need, she thought.

Skelly shook his head, an expression of immense sadness crossing his face.

"No lass, that's not true. It might seem like there's a lot of the wee ones, but that's only because these ones are a bit less, well, dependent on belief to survive. Like your wee brownie. His kind have lived with humans for centuries. Besides, when they know you can see them it just encourages the devilment so they're more inclined to gather."

His eyes twinkled, briefly, and then clouded over again as he continued.

"I'm sure you know all the old stories," he said. "About how humans used to have the great belief in the Good Folk and would leave out the dishes of milk and maybe a wee dram of whiskey if they wanted a bit of help with things, or to be in their good books."

He tilted his head, questioning.

"I'm guessing that's how you found your wee man?"

Frances nodded, blushing. It was true. The everyday things had got a bit desperate at one point during her third year of college and, on impulse, she'd tried to lure a house brownie, not really believing it would work. Well, it had. Although not as she thought it would. The old stories could do with a bit of refinement, she thought. She couldn't recall any mention of them being opinionated tyrants of etiquette.

"Anyway, that's all gone now. Your people don't have the same connections to the magic anymore. It comes, in part, from being connected to the land, to the natural rhythms of things and there's naught but a handful of folk who have any serious interest in that these days. Not enough to keep us going, anyway."

France took a deep breath, steadying her patience and her nerves.

"Let me get this straight. You're telling me that because people, humans, don't believe in faeries and magic like they used to, and because we're not all planting turnips and knitting our own yogurt, that faeries are becoming, what, extinct?"

"You think that's unreasonable?" he challenged her, his green eyes flashing. She caught a brief glimpse of something very ancient in his face and it left her breathless for a moment.

"I don't know," she said, suddenly deflated. She was just so very tired. She placed the tray back on the table and put her hands up to cover her face. She rubbed them over her eyes before looking back at Skelly, who looked, for all the world, like an elderly man in a patched overcoat.

"I just don't understand what any of this has to do with me. I'm obviously a believer, so I'd say I'm doing my bit."

"Mebbe," he said. "But had you noticed, during the time you were working on the paintings in yon cupboard, that things were a wee bit different than they are now?"

He held up a hand and she opened her mouth to reply.

"Think on it, careful like, afore you answer. I'll leave it with you, shall I?"

Without waiting for further response, he was halfway to the door. He turned back to look at her, a half-smile on his lips, the smile that never quite reached his piercing green eyes. He tilted his head towards her in goodbye and left.

Chapter 7

Frances stood and looked at the closed door for several minutes before willing herself to move. Mechanically, she finished tidying up the teapot and mugs, turning on the tap to fill the dish pan with sudsy water. Washing dishes was a form of moving meditation for her and she wanted to quiet the million thoughts and questions that were galloping around her brain.

"He's gone then?" said Moss, emerging from the bread-bin. He walked across the worktop and hopped up onto the tea caddy, perching there with his legs crossed and his hands on in knees.

Frances nodded, feeling quite unable to speak.

Moss watched her washing the mugs, spinning the dish cloth around and around and around inside each one.

Finally, she spoke.

"You knew?"

Moss shifted uncomfortably on his perch. He examined the hem of his tunic with great consideration before nodding.

"Why didn't you tell me?"

Moss shrugged.

"He has a bit of power," he replied. "That sort of thing makes a humble brownie such as myself a bit nervous."

Frances nodded.

"I can understand that," she said. "He makes me nervous and I'm not a faery. How do you suppose he got that sort of power? I mean the whole thing with the flask of tea and the asking the faeries to come? Is that because he's old? He's had a lot of practice?"

Moss frowned and squirmed on the tea caddy. He slid down and stood, leaning with an air of casualness against it. He folded his arms across his chest.

"What, um, what exactly did he say about it, himself? Did he mention what...erm, where he was from?" he asked.

Frances looked up from the tea spoon she was giving a thorough scouring.

"I never asked, actually. He was too busy blowing my mind with other revelations. Why?" she asked, narrowing her eyes. "What else do you know that you're not telling me?"

"Nothing," said Moss, avoiding eye contact, "that I'm sure won't come up again. Eventually, that is."

Frances carefully placed the teaspoon in the drying rack and turned to face Moss, folding her own arms across her chest. The dishcloth dripped down her jeans.

"And was that, perchance, your 'faeries-can't-tell-an-untruth' clause kicking in?"

Moss' green-brown skin darkened in a blush and he clamped his lips tightly, refusing to look at her.

"Moss," said Frances, her voice weary. "If there's something else I need to know about, please will you tell me? I don't think I can cope with anymore trauma right now. I've just been told that I apparently have some bizarre and completely outlandish role in keeping the flow of magic in the world. Or some such lunacy," she waved a hand flinging water from her dishcloth as she did so. Moss flinched and edged back towards the bread bin.

"Honestly, this whole day has felt like the discarded script of a discount-bin children's film. The more I think about it, in fact, the more ridiculous it seems. Should I be clapping my hands or ringing bells? Honestly, I'm beginning to wonder if that silly old man isn't a bit unhinged. And if so, is this a result of him embracing the whole 'I can see faeries' thing, as he obviously has? Which further leads me to the utter certainty that I'm doing exactly the right thing by abandoning the whole bloody lot entirely."

With that, she flung the dishcloth onto the tap and stalked out of the kitchen.

"I'm going to lie down for an hour," she called over her shoulder. "Then I'm going to get to work on something that will both pay the bills and *not* make me lose my mind."

* * *

Two hours later, and Frances was blissfully engrossed in sketching what was to be a repeating pattern of marigolds and daisies. The repetitive nature of the task was both pleasant and calming. She had her headphones on, listening, on the advice of Sophie who believed wholeheartedly in these things, to some brainwave augmenting sound patterns, overlaid by rain and thunder. It was just the ticket to soothe her ragged nerves. She felt calm and focused for the first time in months.

See, she thought, holding up her sketch pad at arm's length and feeling very pleased with her efforts. This was absolutely the right decision; it's far better for my mental health than wrangling with otherworldly mischief and the replays of my weird dreams.

That last thought stuck, unwelcoming, in her mind, niggling at her memory. She tried to ignore it, turning up the sound on her brain music and putting pencil back to paper.

She sketched for a few minutes more, adding a bit of light shading to the daisy petals. None of that would translate into the final design, the specs sent by her contractor were for simple, geometric sorts of patterns, but the attention to detail was for her own benefit. She could erase it later when she transferred it all to her computer. Ever since learning of her decision to go commercial, Sophie's Stuart had been trying to convince her to switch entirely to digital art, arguing that it was far more efficient and she could skip many of the steps she had to take by doing all of her designs on paper first. Ever the accountant, she knew he was only trying to help, but she far preferred the tactile nature of traditional art. It was her one concession to leaving the painting behind, she supposed. It left her something of it, anyway. Besides, she'd never really got on with technology, it had a habit of either seizing up or blowing up, although she had a sneaking suspicion that had something to do with Moss.

Unwanted thoughts crept back into her concentration and she sighed, crossly, putting down her pencil. She gazed out of the window at the fading light. The sun was setting, and a blaze of burnt orange was tinging the midnight blue of the late afternoon sky. She picked up her pencil and scribbled on a scrap of paper. It was just the hue she wanted for the marigolds. Curled up in the basket under her desk, Angus whined, softly.

"Yes, yes," she said to him, looking under the table and smiling fondly. "I know, I need to take a break."

At those words, Angus leapt out of his basket. He knew that 'break' and 'walk' were essentially the same word and were often followed by a biscuit afterwards. Frances chuckled at his enthusiasm, following him to the door. He stood, bottom wriggling, glancing expectantly up at the latch, then back at Frances, as if to remind her how it all worked.

"Oh no you don't," she said, reaching down to clip his leash onto his collar. "I'm not going to be charmed. This is a brief jaunt up and down the lane, for leg-stretching and head-clearing purposes only. I have no intention of chasing you across the fields when it's about to get dark."

Angus wuffed, apparently unfazed by the accusations. Frances smiled again, her heart bursting with affection for the little dog. He'd caused her so much trouble, and yet she couldn't help but love him to absolute pieces.

She unlatched the door and stepped out into the cool evening air. The quiet washed over her like a soothing balm. There were only the rustlings and chatterings of birds in the beech hedge, settling themselves in for the night. Frances found it all very comforting. After years of living in a large city, she had worried she'd find the country life too quiet, but she was realizing very quickly that it was entirely the opposite. Not that she had any choice in the matter, she thought, ruefully. Still, it was good that her time here wasn't akin to purgatory.

They strolled on, pausing from time to time as Angus sniffed and investigated the smells in the grass along the hedge.

Somewhere, in the distance, a fox screamed, causing her to startle. She laughed at herself as the prickle of adrenaline subsided. All at once, she was filled with a warm burst of gratitude. Despite all that had happened, she was content and back in control of her situation. Things had been difficult, but she was working towards a solution and that pleased the orderly part of her brain. It was simply a matter of getting on with the tasks at hand. She would work hard and finish up her contract so that she could pay off her loan. Then, hopefully, the company would be so pleased with her work, they might have something else for her. She could expand a bit, perhaps take Stuart up on his offer to set her up with a website and do some smaller bits of things like logo designs. All of it added together would bring in a decent income and then she could move into a proper flat. Or maybe there was a cottage she could rent, somewhere else in the area. She was, after all, very much enjoying the seclusion of the countryside.

She was still happily mulling over these thoughts when Angus started barking, with that slightly hysterical note that suggested faery activity.

Frances heart sank. She'd been doing so well, not thinking about any of it at all. She glanced around, but the light was getting so dim, it was all blackness in the hedge. She swore, softly, wishing she'd thought to bring a torch. City slicker mistake, she admonished herself.

A sudden rustle to her left revealed two figures, one supporting the other.

Frances pursed her lips. It was a bit early for them to be legless, she thought. If she'd been out at dawn it wasn't unusual to see drunken sprites and dryads staggering and weaving through the undergrowth. If there was one thing they were all consistently skilled at, it was having a good time.

Angus' barking faded into excitable whining. He strained at his leash, nose pointed forwards as he sniffed.

"Never mind, Angus," said Frances, pitching her voice to carry. "It's just a pair of drunken louts getting an early start on the evening."

As the words left her lips, she winced. She sounded like a disapproving elderly aunt. Where was her sense of fun ?

Instead of fading back into the hedge, the two figures emerged to stand on the edge of the lane. The one was clearly incapacitated as his friend struggled to carry him, shifting weight and securing an arm across a shoulder. Frances frowned. Something didn't seem right. Angus agreed, his whine had changed from excitement to confusion.

Knowing she'd regret it later, Frances took a step towards the pair of faeries to take a closer look. There was always the chance that this was just one of their tricks and she was going to get pelted with rosehips or unripe blackberries by a posse of their friends hiding deeper in the hedge.

"Is everything alright?" she asked, leaning forward. The light really was fading fast.

The upright faery started chattering in a language she didn't understand. She soon realized, however, that she didn't need to know what the words meant to grasp that the little creature was agitated. He gestured towards his friend, who hung limply against his shoulder, head down, ropes of hair hanging over his face.

"I'm sorry, I don't understand what you're saying," said Frances, feeling helpless. "Is your friend ill?"

More chattering and gesturing; an arm waved towards Frances and then swung out down the lane.

Just then, the limp faery moaned softly and the one trying to communicate with Frances switched his attention back. He pulled at his friends' tunic and jabbered, a frantic note rising in his voice. Frances took another step forward which only caused more shrieking, so she stumbled back, watching in confusion and horror as the ill faery started to flicker and flash. She blinked, thinking it must be a trick of the fading light.

The stronger faery let out a cry and started to wail, lowering his friend to the ground. Sure enough, the prone creature seemed to be phasing in and out of sight, like the picture of an old television or a radio station that wasn't quite tuned in properly.

Angus had stopped staining at his leash and was sitting, pressed against Frances' leg, letting out the occasional soft whine. Frances crouched down to put her arm around him. A sudden tremble ran through his little body. She looked up just in time to see the flickering faery wink out of sight. His friend stared at the ground where he had just been for a moment, before letting out an ear-piercing shriek.

Frances stood up and stepped back, not certain what she was seeing. The little creature moaned, hands pressed over his face.

Frances cleared her throat.

"Is there something I can do to help?" she asked, still a bit bewildered at what had just happened. Had the little creature been pulled into another dimension or just called home by an irate spouse? It was so hard to tell with faeries sometimes. They all seemed to have a penchant for the theatrical. Moss was famous for his hysteria over seemingly small things. This could either be a catastrophe or nothing much at all.

The little creature stopped his wailing for a moment, fixing Frances with an unnerving glare. His strange, otherworldly face was streaked with tears and she was suddenly struck by a very intense feeling of dread creeping up her spine. She tightened her grip on Angus' leash, silently willing him to pay attention so they could make a run for it if needed.

Suddenly, the little man exploded into a torrent of what Frances could only assume was abuse. The arm waving and hand gestures, the unmistakable fury on his face, made it abundantly clear that he was not at all pleased. She took an involuntary step back, more out of shock than fear, and he followed, stabbing a finger at her and continuing his verbal assault.

Finally, he seemed to run out of steam. The flow of words stopped, and his little shoulders sagged. He still glared at Frances, but the anger seemed to have abated. She felt like she ought to say something, but between the language barrier and genuine confusion as to what exactly had transpired, she really was at a loss.

She was just about to offer assistance again, when the little man burst out with one last barrage of words, flung something at her feet, and disappeared into the hedge.

Frances stood for a moment, letting it all sink in. She had absolutely no idea what she'd just witnessed. She shook her head, trying to dislodge an irrational feeling of guilt that the angry faery had left her with. What did she have to feel guilty about? She was merely an innocent passerby to the whole drama. A large rosehip spun lazily against her welly where it had landed.

Angus was obviously over it as he was tugging at his leash again, eager to continue with their ramble. The rosehip has come dangerously close to bonking him on the nose and he had no desire to wait around to see what might be next. The evening chatter of birds had faded to the occasional call and the rustling in the leaves of the beech and elder and hawthorn was the work of a light breeze and not the comings and goings of faery folk.

Uneasy, Frances shivered then allowed Angus to lead her down the lane.

* * *

The studio was in quiet darkness when they returned from their walk. Angus merrily received his biscuit and settled himself under the desk to crunch. Too unsettled to work, Frances busied herself making a sandwich to eat for a late supper. Moss was nowhere to be seen and, for once, she wished he'd pop up and start criticizing her sandwich making skills or badger her about getting back to work so they could move back to civilization. The whole experience with the disappearing faery had left her more rattled than she had first realized.

She also realized that she wasn't even hungry so she wrapped the assembled sandwich in one of Sophie's beeswax cloths and set it aside to eat later. Sighing, she picked up her sketchbook, wished for the hundredth time that she had a sofa to sit on and walked around the partition into her 'bedroom', switched on her little lamp and lay down on her bed. The scrabble of toenails on the flagstone announced Angus, who, never wanting to miss out on the opportunity of a shared nap, hurled himself onto the bed and settled in beside her. Smiling, she reached down and smoothed his wiry hair, drawing comfort from his small, warm presence.

* * *

The wind tasted of salt and seaweed. It whipped a fury around

93

them, sending Frances' blonde hair flying in a wild tangle around her cold-reddened face. The beach was deserted, other than Frances and her companion. She turned to look at him, a tall, dark-skinned man with raven-black hair that came to a sharp widow's peak. He smiled, a wolfish grin that made her stomach lurch and wobble, not entirely unpleasantly. He inclined his head towards the churning surf, the ghost of antlers rising from his forehead. For some reason, the sight of them wasn't anything out of the ordinary and Frances turned to follow his gaze. A red-haired girl knelt at the water's edge, her hands digging into the wet sand. She turned to look at Frances and seeing her, smiled, lifting her hand in a wave. Frances started to raise her own hand but then the girl was gone and, in her place, stood an old man, no, a young man - tall, with ropes of blue-green hair. The wind flung salt-spray into her eyes and she blinked, trying to clear the sting. A firm hand on her elbow turned her away from the water's edge and led her through a door into her old studio space. It was night and the string of fairy lights around the window illuminated the easel that stood in the middle of the floor. The raven-haired man pointed at the easel, and Frances walked towards it. It was half-finished — paint and pencil lines, but definitely hers. She leaned in closer to look, recognizing it; it was one she hadn't finished in time for her gallery showing. Turning back to question the antlered man, thunder crashed overhead, and the roar of the ocean filled her ears as lightning tore the sky.

"What the…"

Frances blinked in the glare of a torch. She sat up, her sketchbook sliding off her chest onto the floor. Angus snored from his nest of blankets at her feet. She looked at her watch -

it was past nine, she must have fallen asleep.

"The lights aren't working," announced Moss, shining his torch around the room as if to illustrate. "Are you already not paying the bills?"

"Don't be such a turd," muttered Frances, crossly. She felt disoriented. Was that a dream? Why did it feel so real? "There are no bills to pay, the electric is included in the rent. I imagine it's the storm, it must have knocked the power out. It's not like living in the city, you know."

"What weather? It's perfectly clear," retorted Moss, placing his free hand on his hip, shining the light into Frances' face.

Just as he finished, thunder reverberated overhead, sending Angus bolting out from under the blanket.

Frances only just managed to suppress a grin at the look of confused suspicion on Moss' face.

"Just think," she said, getting up from the cot, "Now you can use those lovely candles you've been hoarding."

"I haven't been hoarding, as you so indelicately put it," snapped Moss, jumping down off the bed and stalking into the kitchen. "I've been curating a collection of the finest faery-made beeswax candles for just such an occasion as this. If it was up to you, we'd be sitting in the dark until the lights came back on."

"Good thing it's not up to me, then, isn't it?"

* * *

Frances sat at the card table, sipping a mug of hot cocoa that Moss had made for them on the wheezing Aga. She'd refrained from mentioning that if they'd had a modern electric stove, they wouldn't currently be enjoying a nice mug of something hot on the cool, damp night. She'd eaten the sandwich she'd made earlier and now just sat, sipping, as the storm crashed around them. Not a great fan of thunder, Angus had taken himself back to bed, burrowing under the blankets as if to try and drown out the noise of the wind and rain.

She was still confused about the dream, or what had seemed like a dream. Who was the black-haired man? And the red-haired girl? She seemed to have known both of them. And where was the beach? It wasn't one she recognized. And then the strange shift back to her old studio space in the city. A thought squirmed its way into her conscious mind and she immediately tried to dismiss it. No, it couldn't be. Or could it? Shaking her head, as if to rid herself of the thought, she turned her attention back to her sketchbook. With her mug in one hand, she flipped through the pages with the other. Page after page of sketches glowed in the light of the candles, eventually giving way to the more simplified line drawings she'd been working on earlier. She flipped back, smoothing her hand over the pages with old style depictions of rue and lavender. She'd forgotten she'd done those. Perhaps she'd show them to Sophie; her uncle Phineas was always after Frances to do illustrations for his *magnum opus*, a vast tome of the area's natural history. She'd resisted until now, but it was another possible income stream and she preferred drawing proper plants to stylized geometric ones.

Her mind drifted back to the strange encounter by the hedge, of the irate faery and his disappearing friend. She frowned, her fingers tapping on the page. She glanced over at the tall cupboard against the wall and then looked away. A flash of lightning lit the room, illuminating the sparsely furnished space, forcing her to look around.

Frances sighed.

She got up off the chair and walked to the narrow cupboard. The latch was stiff, and she had to wiggle and jimmy to loosen it. Oh, but it was all ripe with metaphor, she mused. Giving the door a sharp tug, it opened. Frances winced at the smell of damp that seeped out of the darkness. Moss was partially right. The moldering darkness probably wasn't the best place for the paintings.

She pulled out a stack of canvasses. Most of them were the finished pieces from her gallery showing, others had been abandoned when the threads of the dreams and images that sparked them drifted out of her remembrance. When everything fell apart, she'd just bundled everything large and painted into a box. These, she thought, with a hint of unwelcome rebellion as she ran her hands over the familiar feel of canvas, *these* were her art. Not designing cushions that matched the sofa.

Flipping through them she found the one she was looking for, the one her dream had made her remember. One of the unfinished ones — she couldn't remember why she had stopped. It had emerged from another dream she'd had and was the image of a beautiful, young, girl, standing to her knees in a wild sea. The white-capped waves were alive with creatures of legend - sea elementals with sinuous, fish-like bodies and fronded fingers, water-horses with savage teeth and blood-soaked muzzles. In the dark sky above, she had sketched in two images - barely visible. One had the look of a man with antlers rising from his forehead and the other...

Frances leaned in, daring herself to see what she already knew, in her heart, was there.

He looked much younger, and only half-drawn, of course.

But rising against the storm-leaden sky, arms raised against the antlered man, was, unmistakably, the blue-haired figure from her dream and, without understanding how she knew it, the creature she now knew as Skelly.

Chapter 8

"And that's when I think I started to lose my mind over the whole thing."

Frances sighed and stared down at the mug she had cradled in her hands, shoulders slumping with fatigue.

Sophie reached across the space between them and patted her arm. They were sitting on a large, squishy tartan sofa. Sophie had found it in one of the storage sheds out behind Analogue Daze. It was where she'd stored all of the things she'd salvaged when she was furnishing the bookshop cafe. In due course, it was heading for Frances' studio but at that moment, it was in the cobblestone yard at the back of the bookshop. It seemed the perfectly obvious solution on a glorious sunny morning when the cafe was full of the village Knit and Natter ladies and a quiet spot was needed for a strange conversation.

"So, you think that the faery man in the painting is actually this elderly sheep farmer fellow who you've been meeting for rambling, tea and lemon drizzle?"

"Well when you put it like that is sounds even more ridiculous," said Frances, groaning. She flung herself back into the welcoming tartan cushions. "I know how this sounds, even more mental than the things I usually tell you. But I'm almost positive it's him."

"Even though your one Skelly is an old fellow and your chap in the painting is some luscious sky faery?"

Frances groaned again.

"Please don't say 'luscious'," she begged. "It's incredibly off-putting. The cognitive disconnect is too immense."

"Cognitive disconnect?" said Sophie, throwing her head back in a peal of laughter. "Frances, darling. Everything you've ever told me in regard to your little friends requires gargantuan leaps over the yawning chasm of cognitive disconnect. You *do* know that anyone else listening to the things you tell me would've had you committed by now?"

Frances gave a small smile, nodding.

"Which is why I think you should stop trying to understand all of this and simply allow it to exist alongside everything else."

"But…"

Sophie placed a be-ringed hand on Frances knee.

"But nothing," she interrupted. "Your strength has always been your willingness to entertain the possibilities. It's what makes your art so real. Speaking of which, you said you had something to show me. Tell you what, why don't you come into the cafe and have a bit of lunch, on the house."

Frances had opened her mouth to protest. There were absolutely no spare funds for eating out and she didn't want to be taking advantage of Sophie's friendship.

"Well, not exactly on the house," continued Sophie, fully aware of Frances' inner battle. "I've started the most inspired scheme you see. We have so many lovely regular customers and because I'm wanting to expand the gallery space and local artisan wares I came up with the glorious plan of offering what I'm calling 'patron sponsorships.'"

Frances smiled more widely this time. Sophie was the perpetual encourager. All through art college, she'd been the one bringing meals and snacks to her friends so they could immerse themselves in their projects. All while somehow producing her own huge body of work.

"It's all voluntary, of course. I've set aside a couple of tables and called them creative zones. People have the option to direct an extra tip into a patron fund which sponsors a few hours at a table. The artist who benefits gets a meal and an endless pot of tea to fortify them while they work. The other customers get to feel good about supporting the arts and they get to watch a creator in action. Additionally, the artist gets to spend a few hours in, what I flatter myself to think, is an inspiring space without having to worry if they're going to get tossed out for stretching one cup of tea for three hours. What do you think?"

Sophie's enthusiasm was infectious. Frances felt, as she was sure was Sophie's intention, the weight of worry lifting from her shoulders. It would be lovely to just sit and sketch for a while. She could finalize her first set of designs.

"It's genius, Soph," she said, blinking back some unexpected tears. "It's absolute genius and I would be honoured to benefit from the largesse of your wonderful customers."

* * *

An hour later and Frances was engrossed in a pattern of bicycle wheels and plant pots. Inspired by the pile of rubbish behind the studio, she was working on what she hoped classified as "everyday delights" as per the list of requirements from her contract specs. She'd polished off a bowl of leek and potato soup and toasted cheese sandwich. It felt ridiculously indulgent to have such an exotic, hot meal and she felt a stab of something unwelcome piercing the armour she'd constructed around how absolutely okay she was with living in her reduced circumstances. It wasn't that she wanted or needed a fancy place to live, it was more that the studio wasn't actually meant to be lived in, as such. She'd pushed that thought swiftly from her mind, however and poured herself another cup of tea. At some point, her bowl and plate had been cleared away and another plate, holding a selection of fruit and biscuits had materialized. Genius, she thought again, absolutely genius.

She put the final touches on a stylized geranium and put her pencil down, leaning back in her chair for a stretch. Looking around the cafe she was pleased to see it was quietly busy. Analogue Daze was everything Sophie had always dreamt of, everything she'd talked about since the day the two girls had met, in an Intro to Art Business class. Part bookshop, part cafe and now, apparently, part artisan's gallery, the former hairdresser's shop on Thistlecrag's high street was unrecognizable. Gone was the acrid tang of setting solution and in its place, the smell of baked goods and whatever Gary had concocted for the lunch menu that day.

Everything in the cafe had been salvaged or repurposed. Sophie had spent months scouring antique markets, car boot sales and estate auctions for everything from the tables and chairs (vintage 50's Formica from a salvage yard specializing in restaurant fittings) to the squashy armchairs beside the wood-burner that sat in the stone hearth, which had been built using reclaimed stone that she'd commissioned from a local mason. Every single detail was Sophie — the care and delight she took in people and their skills as well as her exquisite stewardship of the planet reflected her values and choices. Even Gary, her shaven headed, tattooed, Cockney chef had come to Thistlecrag from a prison outreach program. He'd taken a pastry chef course from inside a London prison for crimes as yet unspecified and Sophie had taken one bite of his blackberry turnovers and hired him on the spot. Gradually, she'd convinced him to expand to lunches and cream teas and he'd grudgingly risen to the occasion, only to discover a true passion for producing meals that both nourished and comforted people with their traditional familiarity and fresh, local ingredients. That was Sophie all over, thought Frances. She somehow managed to zero in on talents and passions that people didn't even know they had and bring it all to the surface.

"More tea, Frances?"

Frances was jolted out of her musings by Melinda, the soft-spoken local that Sophie had hired as her right-hand person. Shy and awkward, an aspiring librarian, Melinda had seemed an unlikely candidate, the complete antithesis to Sophie's exuberance and Gary's loud and vaguely menacing manner. They were an odd trio, that was certain. Somehow, though, in true Sophie fashion, it had all worked out. Melinda had thrived on the bustling but gentle atmosphere of the cafe. Her passion, of course, was for the books and Sophie had put her in charge, far earlier than might have been advisable, of curating the stock they had for sale. It worked. Immersed in the glory of what she loved, Melinda's confidence had grown, and she was now chatty and engaged. She knew the regulars and was often seen, mousy-haired head bent over holiday snaps or scrapbooks of grandchildren's visits. She'd organized book clubs and letter writing nights and apparently had a very popular video channel that discussed all things bookish. When it had come time to apply for the library science program, Sophie had helped her fill out the forms and given her a glowing reference. That was the other thing, mused Frances, even though being accepted into the program would probably mean losing her, Sophie had delightedly encouraged Melinda. Utterly selfless. If Frances didn't love Sophie with all her heart, she might actually find her sickening. Frances grinned inwardly at the thought.

"That would be lovely, thank you Melinda," she replied, "Although I might float away if I drink too much more."

Melinda smiled. It was a genuine smile that lit up her plain features, illuminating the fact that she was truly quite pretty.

"I find that just having a full teapot beside me when I'm working inspires me, even if I don't actually drink it."

"I think you might be on to something there," said Frances, passing the expired teapot. "There's nothing that says settling into a creative session like a steaming teapot. It has definite inspirational qualities, doesn't it?"

Melinda nodded, beaming.

"Yes, it's like a vote of confidence."

"Are you still working on your novel?"

Another nod, this time accompanied by a slight blush. Melinda had only confided in her co-workers and Frances about her novel-writing efforts. She insisted it was just a hobby and had no aspirations of publication, but they had all cheered her on. Gary, especially, was convinced it would be a bestseller someday.

"Little bits, here and there," she said, "When I have time. It's been busy at home as well as here, so I don't always have the energy."

"And the application? Have you heard back?"

"Nothing yet," said Melinda, her eyes downcast. "But the deadline was only a couple of weeks ago, so I suppose it takes a while to sort through them. Anyway," she made a fuss of arranging the fresh teapot on the table, smoothing the cloth and turning the plate of goodies around. "Like I said, I've lots to keep me occupied."

"You'll get in," said Frances, reaching out to pluck Melinda's hand-knitted sleeve. "I have every faith, and so do the rest of your friends."

Melinda gave a quick smile, averting her eyes.

"I'll let you get on, shall I?" she said. "I just remembered I have to tell Gary about a party coming in for a cream tea on Saturday."

Frances frowned at the retreating figure, wondering at Melinda's odd behaviour. She shrugged to herself, just nerves, she thought. It can be an alarming thing finally getting what you've always dreamed of. Not that I'd know, she added bitterly. That's enough of that, she immediately remonstrated, you've got lots to be thankful for. This glorious macaroon for starters.

* * *

"Excuse me, miss?"

A small, high-pitched voice cut through Frances' concentration. She was trying to figure out how to incorporate pineapples with palm trees in a way that was 'exciting and new'.

She looked up to see a small red-haired girl standing beside her table. The girl clutched a notebook to her chest, a worried sort of expression on her face. She wore a star-spangled hair band and her vibrant green leggings paired with a cornflower blue sweater created the impression of a small, brightly coloured flower.

"Yes?" said Frances, peering past the child, wondering if there was an adult attached to her. Children weren't really her area of excellence. Their inherent unpredictability made her slightly uncomfortable.

"Don't worry," said the girl. "Sophie knows I'm here. My mum drops me off when she goes to into the city to do the shopping. She says I'm allowed to stay as long as I sit quietly and don't bother the other customers. My mum, that is. Sophie is far more pleasant."

Frances toyed with pointing out the ongoing violation of her terms but decided to hold it in reserve, amused by her turn of phrase. She absolutely belonged in a bookshop. Also, she had a sort of charming earnestness about her that suggested she was one of those peculiar children who weren't likely to suddenly demand a doll's tea party, or a story read aloud.

"Are you an artist too?" asked the girl, gesturing towards Frances sketchbook. "Only I saw that you were drawing and you're sitting in the creative corner. This is where I sit too."

The girl looked expectantly at Frances, her eyes widened, and she leaned in slightly. Frances amazed herself by catching the hint.

"Ah, so then you must be an artist also," she said, smiling. "And to answer your question, yes, I am in fact an artist."

The little girl beamed.

"My name's Fiona," she announced, climbing up on the chair opposite Frances'. "Oh don't worry, I won't stay. I can see that children make you nervous. I was just wondering if maybe I could ask you a question. You know, artist to artist?"

Frances bit back a grin, schooling her features into a state of bland seriousness.

"Of course," she said. "How can I help?"

"Well," said Fiona, placing her notebook on the table between them. It was a simple, spiral bound sketch pad that could be found in discount shops everywhere. It was the sort that Frances had used up by the dozen when she was a child. The paper quality was suspect, but she'd filled them so fast with her "endless scribbling" as her mother had called it, it was the most economical option. The cover was purple and depicted what looked to be a frantically happy unicorn. "I was hoping you might give me your opinion on something."

Oh no, thought Frances. She'd better not ask me if I think she's good at drawing or something. That feels like a potentially life-altering question. I could be responsible for either false hope or utter obliteration of her dreams. Good grief listen to me. When did I get so jaded?

She took a long draught of her tea, reached for another macaroon and smiled.

"Sure. What's on your mind?"

"Do you believe in faeries?"

Frances spluttered; a fine spray of coconut flew from her lips as she choked slightly on her macaroon.

Fiona waited while she took another gulp of tea, her little face tilted, eyes serious.

"Do I believe faeries?" repeated Frances, dabbing her streaming eyes with a vintage linen napkin. She felt that repeating the question might buy her some time.

Fiona nodded.

"It's just that *I* do. Because they're real, *obviously.*"

Frances nodded, thinking if she could encourage Fiona to talk, she might forget she asked the question. It may have been rhetorical anyway, as the child seemed to have already formed her own opinion.

"And I'm not talking about Tinkerbell or that sort of thing," explained Fiona, earnestly. "Because *I've* never seen a faery that sparkles, have you?"

Frances shook her head, smiling at the thought, then stopped, suddenly aware she might be giving away her hand. She cleared her throat.

"Well, I suppose the Disney artists needed something that would be appealing to small children," she offered as an explanation, hoping it sounded full of industry detail and artistic camaraderie. "Sometimes, as working artists, we have to follow specific instructions. You know, like when you're at school. Maybe you have to do what your art teacher tells you?'

Oh, she thought. That was a good answer.

"Your faery drawings don't look like Tinkerbell," said Fiona, crossing her arms and leaning back in her chair. "That's why I thought you'd be the right person to ask."

Frances opened her mouth to reply, but nothing came out. She frowned.

Fiona leaned forward again, whispering.

"Sophie showed me the leaflet from your art show," she said, conspiratorially. "I know I'm not supposed to mention it because you're a bit touchy about it, but I need you to take my question very seriously. Besides, I think your paintings are magnificent. I want to be able to paint like that someday."

Frances remained speechless, a thousand thoughts chasing themselves around her brain. Her first was that Sophie must have sent Fiona to try and guilt her into displaying her paintings. She immediately dismissed that option but quickly moved on to other, equally ridiculous conspiracy theories.

"So," persisted Fiona. "Do you believe?"

"Why does it matter if I believe?" said Frances, rallying with avoidance. "Belief in magic is a very personal thing, you know. And whether or not a person believes has no bearing on whether or not a thing is true."

As the words left her mouth, she felt the wrongness of them. It wasn't just the strange and maddening conversations she'd had with Skelly, it was the simple fact that she knew her statement to be untrue. When it came to magic, it mattered very much that she believed.

Fiona clearly agreed. She scowled and pushed her unicorn notebook across the table towards Frances.

"I think we both know that's not true," she said, "so please stop talking to me like I'm some tea-party-playing little girl."

Frances blushed. How did she become the person who spoke down to children like they were of lesser intelligence?

"I'm sorry, Fiona. I'm not very good with children and I don't want to say anything that might upset you. Or your parents."

"Thank you for your honesty," said Fiona, primly. "But you've no need to worry. I'm quite grown up for my age, you see. And I only have one parent and she's far too busy trying to keep a roof over our heads to worry about whether or not I believe in faeries."

"I do see," said Frances, stifling her smile again. She was receiving a disturbing amount of detail about Fiona's life. "I'm sorry, Fiona. Please accept my apology. And now that we've got that awkward bit out of the way, let's return to our artist-to-artist discussion, shall we?'

Fiona grinned, her gap-toothed smile returning her face, ever so briefly, to that of a small girl who simply enjoyed wearing a plastic tiara.

"Agreed. Now, I was hoping you might write me a note to give to my teacher. She's under the impression that dragons don't exist."

* * *

"So you see," explained Fiona, pointing to the drawing of an eastern dragon, "I went to the library and found a book about the different types of dragons so I could practice this sort. I'm not sure how I feel about them. I rather prefer our traditional, British dragons but then that might be a bit narrow-minded of me, do you think?"

Frances was enjoying herself immensely. Fiona was a charming and obviously very creative child, and her passion for filling sketchbooks reminded her very much of her own younger self. She found herself wondering when she'd started questioning the things she drew and how she drew them. There was an expansive joy in how Fiona had filled page after page with what she clearly considered serious study of her subject. The only thing she seemed to lack was any self-consciousness. The fact that her teacher had challenged her only made her more determined to seek out proof that she was the one in the right.

"I think you've done absolutely marvelously," said Frances, meaning it. "Eastern dragons are definitely a lot different, but I think they have a certain appeal. They're far more graceful, I think. Almost like sea creatures that would fly through the sky."

Fiona's face lit up.

"That's exactly what I thought!" she said, grinning. Then her face clouded over.

"What's the matter?"

"Well, it's just that I'm not really allowed to be drawing them," she said.

Frances frowned.

"What do you mean? No-one can tell you what you can and can't draw," she coughed slightly, choking a bit on the irony of her statement. Other than yourself, she thought.

"You can think that because you're a grown-up," replied Fiona, closing her notebook and tracing a finger over the spiral binding. "Grown-ups think they know everything," she added, with a touch of out-of-character bitterness.

"I think you and I both know that's not true," said Frances, leaning towards Fiona. "We grown-ups might *think* we know everything, but I can tell you for certain, that we absolutely have very little idea, a lot of the time."

"Is that why you won't let Sophie hang your pictures?" asked Fiona. "Because you don't think she knows what's right?"

Frances ignored the question, bringing the line of conversation back to Fiona's problems.

"Who told you that you can't draw dragons?"

"My teacher."

"Not your art teacher?"

Fiona shook her head.

"No, he's lovely. He lets me do extra work when the other kids are dripping paint everywhere."

Frances smiled.

"No, my regular teacher. We're doing a unit on medieval

times and we have to decorate our folders with scenes from castles and things. I was so excited because I know exactly what mine's going to look like. It'll be like a scene from King Arthur's court."

Her face lit up as she described what she had in mind, but then clouded over again.

"Then she made a very loud point of telling us that there weren't allowed to be dragons because they don't exist."

Frances felt a surge of extreme and unexpected rage at the nerve of Fiona's teacher. What sort of children's educator actively discouraged creative expression?

"Well!" she said, a breath of indignant air exploding from her nostrils. "I'm not sure I've heard anything more ridiculous. I think…"

She paused, suddenly aware she was talking to an eight year old child.

"What does your mum think?" she asked. "Only, I don't want to get you into trouble with my outlandish opinions."

Fiona shrugged.

"Like I said, I don't think she has time to worry about it. I didn't want to bother her with this, you see. She's tired a lot and I don't want to upset her."

Fiona's lower lip trembled dangerously. She was obviously very bothered by this flagrant assault on her belief system. And by a person who was supposed to be supporting and encouraging her! Frances realized, with uncomfortable clarity, how much she related to what Fiona was going through.

"Well, as long as you don't think it'll get you into trouble with your mum - we artists must be mindful of the people who love us, you see, because they always just want the best for us." She glanced over to where Sophie stood, chestnut head together with Gary's bald one, discussing some item of the menu, her heart full of warmth for her friend. She turned back to Fiona, whose wide eyes were bright with tears, hanging on her every word. "but everyone else is fair game. I think you should always draw the things that bring you joy. Always. There's not much point in it at all if you deny yourself that. And if someone wants to tell you what's real and what isn't, then the best way to challenge that is to carry on doing exactly what you're doing."

"Really?" breathed Fiona, her face shining with the possibility of it all. "So, I should draw dragons on my folder?"

Frances hesitated. She wanted to encourage Fiona to be brave and daring but also was aware that she was, in fact, still a child.

"I think you should draw a dragon on a separate piece of paper and then clip it to the inside of the folder. That way, whenever you have to hand it in to the teacher, you can unclip it so she won't see it, but you'll have it there whenever you're working."

Fiona pursed her lips, mulling over the suggestion.

"You'd be practicing a form of art rebellion, you see. But in a way that won't get you into trouble with your teacher. Then, when you're older, you can do whatever you like!"

Frances ignored the inner shouty voice that questioned her last statement.

"And it will still count?" asked Fiona. "The dragon will still count even if it's not actually on my folder?"

"Absolutely!" said Frances. "As long as you put it onto the paper, you will have made your point."

She paused, wondering if she was brave enough to pursue the topic further. This conversation with the small girl had brought up a whole lot of her own baggage, her current situation notwithstanding. She even wondered if things might have turned out differently for her if she'd had an older, arty influence in her life who supported and encouraged her. Maybe if the idea that art wasn't a worthy pursuit hadn't been seeded so widely in her childhood, she might be braver and more defiant. Making art her life had seemed, for the most part, an uphill battle. And the terrain hadn't levelled off much in the last year or so. She took a deep breath.

"And," she said, leaning in and lowering her voice. Fiona's eyes widened and she leaned forward. "I have it on very good authority that when we draw the magical creatures, it helps them to stay alive in the world."

Fiona's rosebud mouth pursed into a round 'oh' and her eyes sparkled.

"Really?" she breathed, wriggling in her seat with barely contained excitement. "Is that true?"

Frances nodded, filled with an unexpected warmth to see the little girl so clearly taken with the information. Children were always so ready to believe in things. It was no wonder the faery folk spent so much time around them. She felt a brief pang of hypocritical guilt and pushed it firmly away.

"So I'm told," replied Frances, winking. The dark cloud of guilt persisted however, over her delight in the reality she was creating for the child. A pang of conscience, perhaps? More like hard-won wisdom, she conceded. Or would that be cynicism? "But it's probably not something that you should go around telling other grown-ups. There aren't a lot of us around, you see. Who know about this sort of thing, I mean. And because you're still young, I'd hate more than anything for you to get into trouble or…"

"Get made fun of," finished Fiona, nodding sagely. "That happens to me a lot already."

Frances winced, visibly. Good grief, she thought. Here are all of my own childhood traumas come rushing back.

She bit back all of the unhelpful advice she'd been given over the years and nodded her understanding.

"It's not easy being an artist, is it?" asked Fiona, her features composed in a thoughtful frown. "I mean, I always think it's going to be the best thing in all the world, but I suppose there are hard bits to it as well?"

Frances cleared her throat. There was an unusual constriction building that felt suspiciously like tears. She nodded again, not trusting herself to speak just at that moment.

"Fiona Mary Reed!" exclaimed a harried sounding female voice. "What have I told you about bothering people? Sophie very kindly lets you stay here with your pencils and the last thing she needs is you harassing her paying customers."

A tall, blonde-haired woman in her early thirties came bustling up to the table, her hands clutching the strap of her handbag tightly. Her face, although exquisitely made-up, had that pinched, worried look of someone who always felt three steps behind without ever hoping to catch up. Frances felt a surge of compassion for the woman she assumed, correctly, was Fiona's mother.

"Oh she's not really a paying customer, mum," explained Fiona, her own eyes worried. "She's Sophie's good friend, Frances, and she's in the patron's corner so she's here on sufferance, just like me."

Sufferance? Frances suppressed a smile. Fiona's mother closed her eyes for a moment, summoning strength, no doubt. She turned to Frances and smiled, holding out her hand.

"Hello, I'm Alice, Fiona's mum. I'm terribly sorry if she's been pestering you. I told Sophie she needn't have her here. There's no reason she can't come and do the shop with me."

Frances shook her hand.

"Hello, Alice. Please don't be cross with Fiona. We've been having a lovely chat, actually. She's helped me immensely."

"Have I?" asked Fiona, beaming. She clutched her unicorn notebook to her chest.

"Indeed you have. I've been muddling over a problem and I think that chatting with you has given me a sort of solution."

"Really? Is it something to do with, you know, what we talked about?"

Fiona attempted to wink. It was more of a grimace, but Frances got the point. She winked back and put a finger up to the side of her nose in the universal gesture of mutual understanding. Fiona grinned and hopped down off her chair.

"Thank you again, for putting up with her," said Alice, reaching out to grasp her daughter's offered hand. "She's a good wee girl, really. Always with her head in that notebook, though, drawing fairies and dragons and things. I don't know if it's at all healthy but it makes her happy so what can I do?"

Frances smiled, thinking of her own eight-year-old self.

"You can tell her she's clever and talented and will make a great difference in the world with her art someday."

Alice blinked, stepping back slightly and Fiona giggled, gazing up at her mother.

"Oh mum, aren't I though?"

Frances blushed and fussed with her sketchbook.

"Sorry," she said. "That was a bit odd, wasn't it? It's just my parents were never very understanding of my wanting to be an artist and it's just really lovely to see how you're encouraging

Fiona."

Alice offered a quick smile, looking down at Fiona who was beaming at Frances.

"Yes, well," said Alice, "I suppose there are worse things. Right come on pet. Let's get on. I don't want the frozen things to melt. We'll have a fish supper, shall we? I'm gasping for a cup of tea."

She turned back to Frances.

"Thanks again for talking with my girl. I hope she wasn't a bother."

"Not at all," Frances assured her, then, directing her words at Fiona, "Remember what we talked about, yes?"

Fiona nodded, the glittery stars on her hairband bouncing.

"I must draw the things that bring me joy," she said, grinning. Then, adding in her wink-grimace. "And also, be an art rebel."

Frances darted a glance at Alice, but she was already rummaging in her handbag for keys and hadn't heard the last bit.

She winked back at Fiona.

"Exactly."

* * *

It wasn't until later, as she and Angus walked along the lane after their evening meal that it came to her. It was a sinking feeling that crept up, like a slow, dawning realization. She was a hypocrite. She'd been so free with her advice to Fiona, encouraging her to draw the things she wanted to draw, to believe in faeries and dragons and to defy the people who would naysay her. But what had she done?

"I'm a complete failure," she said, aloud.

Angus ignored her; he was investigating the underside of a particularly dense stand of brambles. "I've been kidding myself all this time. Even worse, I'm a coward."

"You might say that."

Frances jumped, a shriek escaping from her lips.

"Moss!" she hissed. "How many times have I told you not to sneak up on me like that? Angus, I'm not impressed. You ought to have warned me."

Angus wagged his bottom and went back to his explorations, unraveling the extended leash all the way to the end.

"You were saying?"

Frances scowled at the brownie. He was dressed in what he referred to as his 'evening attire' - which meant he was going foraging. He hadn't attended a revel in the whole time Frances had known him, proclaiming them to be the province of thieves and scoundrels. He had standards to uphold. Still, he always dressed the part, even if he was just going to collect dew or blackberries or a bottle of summer wine. There must be a market on.

"You mentioned failure and cowardice, I believe," prodded Moss. "That warrants further exploration, don't you think?"

Frances slumped, all of her irritation with Moss deflating into a heavy sigh. She told him about her conversation with Fiona.

"So, you see," she finished. "I was basically the world's greatest hypocrite during that whole exchange."

Moss nodded, his arms folded. He had three bags slung about his person and it gave him the air of a disgruntled messenger.

"And what, then, are you going to do about it?' he asked, a moccasin-clad toe tapping.

118

"What do you mean?"

"Well, you seem to have a situation that needs remedy. And only you can fix it. Surely you know the answer?"

France frowned down at the handle of Angus leash. Of course, she knew the answer. She nodded.

"Yes," she said, slowly. "I suppose I do."

"And….?"

"And, I really don't think I'm up for it, to be honest. I keep banging on, telling everyone - including myself - that I'm living my dream life, supporting myself as an artist when I'm really only doing half-measures. I'm playing it safe and, quite frankly, I'm not happy with myself for being like this. But I really don't see any other option right now. My version of living the full-measure dropped me into a very deep hole and my only job is to dig us, me, out of it."

Her voice caught and she coughed.

"Anyway, you have things to do," she said, brightly, gesturing at his empty bags. "And I really want to get Angus home. See you later?"

She set off down the lane, shoulders squared, willing herself not to burst into tears.

Chapter 9

"You've a new sofa," remarked Skelly, as he stood in the doorway of the studio. For a small man, he seemed to take up the entire opening; backlit, he created an almost ominous, towering presence.

Frances blinked, momentarily confused that there appeared to be a hulking great man looming in her doorway. She shook her head, sorting it out; just a dubious looking old fellow then.

"Mr.Skelly!" she said, pasting a smile on her face. "Yes, my friend Sophie…. will you come in? I just switched the fire on, it was a bit chilly this morning."

He nodded his head, a curiously regal gesture, and crossed the threshold. The pockets of his patched overcoat were bulging, and Angus' sudden excited whine drew her attention to them.

"Oh!" exclaimed Frances. "You've got lambs in your pockets! How darling."

Skelly smiled, looking down at his coat.

"Aye, lass. It seems I do."

Frances waited, assuming there'd be an explanation, but none seemed forthcoming.

"I was just about to put the kettle on…"

"Aye, lass. I thought you might. 'Tis why I chose this

particular moment to stop by. I've a great thirst."

Frances squashed a pang of annoyance. His persistence in conjuring up the air of mystery was so obviously transparent. She sighed. He's just a lonely old sort, and with a grand imagination.

She heard a what sounded like a snort from Skelly but when she turned, he was arranging himself on the tartan sofa. He adjusted the cushions to accommodate his bulging pockets-full-of-lamb and leaned back, sighing happily.

"Do they need anything?" she gestured towards his pockets. "A bowl of milk or something?"

Moss was lurking behind the bread-bin and poked his head out long enough to give her a withering glare.

"What?" she whispered at him.

He rolled his eyes.

"Not really a country girl, are you?" came Skelly's question.

"No, actually, I'm not."

"Thought so."

"Why do I feel like I should be ashamed of that? Would I make fun of you if you'd visited me in the city?"

Frances scowled, plopping strawberry scones onto a plate. Sophie had sent a box full of them when she'd sent the sofa. It grated on her slightly that she had to share them with that wretched man.

"I've no judgement, lass," he responded, his voice soft and lilting. "There's no need to get your dander up."

"Sorry," said Frances, carrying the plate over to the sofa. She'd found a wobbling wooden table in the rubbish heap behind the studio. With a bit of canvas glue, she'd secured the rickety leg and it served well as a coffee table. It wasn't quite up to Moss' standards, but he'd attacked it with his homemade furniture polish and it had a rustic, farmhouse-chic feel to it and said less 'transient rubbish' than the upturned galvanized tub.

"New table as well?"

Skelly gestured at the scarred surface.

"Yes, as a matter of fact. The sofa needed something to make it complete. I suppose you're going to mock me for that as well? Something to do with my city ways?"

Skelly grinned, transforming his odd features into a crinkling beam of warmth. Frances reluctantly felt her irritation melting away.

"Nah, lass. It's a fine bit of furniture indeed. So's the sofa. Very comfy."

He patted the cushions, still grinning.

"You're turning this little place into a right homey sort of affair, aren't you?"

Frances stiffened.

"It's not a home," she said, "It's a studio. But it's nice to have somewhere to relax when I'm brainstorming or doing my invoices and things."

She tailed off, realizing how feeble her lie sounded but Skelly nodded.

"That's a good one. Very believable."

He winked and reached for a scone.

"If I were a busybody sort who was wondering what the young lass with the dog was doing in this studio - if she might be breaking the law and actually living here - I'd be totally convinced she wasn't."

He took a large bite of scone and nodded at the sofa and table.

"This is obviously just the young lass trying to liven up

the dismal old place and besides, a person who was actually charging money for this moldering ruin is the one who might be in danger of breaking laws."

He beamed through his mouthful of scone.

Frances managed a small smile, her heart banging like a drum in her chest. She felt very off balance. He seemed to have that effect on her and she resented it. No wonder Moss kept out of sight. She swallowed the rising feeling of panic and widened her smile.

"Good," she said, brightly. "I'm glad to see you understand how things are. Now, let me get that teapot."

In an attempt to turn the tide of the conversation, she called back to him.

"Was there another reason for your visit?" she asked. "Other than needing your elevenses? I've been very diligent about keeping Angus on his best behaviour. I'm sure you've no further reason to persecute…um, question his activities."

"As a matter of fact, there is a reason for my visit. And no, yon wee doggie hasn't been harassing my sheep." replied Skelly, accepting the steaming mug of tea. He dusted scone crumbs from his beard and took a large sip.

Frances winced. Surely it was too hot, but he seemed unfazed.

"Ah, that's grand, that," he said, sighing happily.

She sat at the far end of the sofa, perched on the edge, her mug held firmly in her hands. She waited.

"I was just coming to see if you were ready to take me up on my offer."

Frances blinked.

"What offer? I don't remember an offer of any sort."

Her tone was probably sharper than it needed to be, but

she was tense and on edge. His strange manner, almost passive-aggressive, she was sure Sophie would say, left her feeling always on the brink of making a blunder or having forgotten something important. Like possibly an offer he'd made that she was supposed to be considering. She decided that confident assertiveness was the best way to proceed.

Skelly took another mouthful of tea and leaned over the dozing lambs to take another scone.

"These are lovely," he said. "Your friend must be doing a great trade."

"She is, thank you," replied Frances, stiffly. "Sophie works very hard and is brilliant at what she does."

Skelly nodded, chewing thoughtfully.

"What about you, then? Would you call yourself a hard worker?"

The change of tactic only unbalanced her further and she fought the inclination to get up off the sofa and busy herself elsewhere. Anything to escape that piercing green gaze.

She cleared her throat.

"Actually, I would," she said. "I'm not at all afraid to tackle what needs doing." She waved a hand in the vague encompassing gesture that included the studio and all that it entailed.

"Oh, I didn't ask if you were afraid," he said, matter-of-factly, "Although I might argue that mebbe you are."

He tilted his head slightly, but then shifted his gaze down to the lambs. His eyes softened and he placed a gnarled hand on the head of the one who had poked its head above the opening of his pocket.

Angus, who had sat himself on Skelly's feet, whined softly, wriggling as close as he could. He was desperate to get to the lambs. France put a warning hand on his wiry head, and he looked at her briefly, licking her hand as if to assure her that he was using his very best manners and turned back to stare at the lambs.

Skelly remained like that for a moment or two, seemingly lost in thought. Frances scrambled for something to say, the silence weighing down was unbearable.

"You will have seen them vanishing, then."

Skelly's voice was soft. It was more a statement than a question and it served to send Frances reeling once again. Why was he so unsettling? She found herself getting irritated.

"Seen what vanishing?" she retorted, although she knew fine well what he was talking about. Moreover, she knew that he knew that she knew.

Skelly remained silent, his hand resting on the lamb's head. He raised his eyes to hers and blinked slowly.

Exasperating man, thought Frances, bleakly. Her shoulders slumped.

"Yes, yes, yes. I saw one little fellow blink out of sight when I was walking Angus along the lane the other night." She waved a hand again, dismissing it as nothing very much important and certainly nothing to do with her. "What does that have to do with anything? He was probably late getting home and his irate wife called him back. His friend had to hold him up, he was obviously paralytic with the elderberry wine or something."

Skelly offered a small smile.

"Aye, the wee fellows have a taste for the wine. But that's not what happened and I'm thinking that you know that."

"Really?" said Frances, her loss of patience winning out over her unease. "And how do you know that I know that? Are you

125

reading my mind again? Because I have to tell you, that's rude and intrusive. And I'm fairly certain it's a breach of etiquette or something. Besides, it's doubly offensive because you're not one of them."

"Is that so?"

Skelly took a deep breath, put his mug down on the table and proceeded to gently extract the lambs from his pockets. They wriggled and squirmed, feeling their legs free of the coat. Angus was beside himself and pushed his nose at them, whining and wriggling just as much as they were. Skelly placed them on the floor, and they tottered a few steps on wobbly legs. Angus bowed an invitation to play but the two lambs were more interested in nibbling on Skelly's bootlaces.

Frances couldn't help but smile. The lambs were truly adorable. It made it difficult to imagine Skelly was all that horrid when he clearly cared for his charges.

"Angus," she warned, as he executed a mock charge that never failed to win over doggy chums into a game of chase. "I somehow don't think they're interested in playing with you."

"Och," said Skelly, smiling down at them. "Give the wee souls a minute to get their legs. They're keen for a caper once they know how to work them."

"Are they orphans?" asked Frances.

Skelly shook his head.

"No, not as such. They're both the weaker twin of a set. And latecomers, at that. Their stronger siblings weren't letting them have much time at the bag and I find it's better just to look after the wee things myself than fuss about. It's easier on the ewes anyway. Mebbe not what most would do, but it's how I like to manage things. I've not got a big flock so it's no hardship."

Frances nodded, feeling a twinge of empathy. She smiled down at them as they started trying out their legs. Angus wuffed encouragement.

"Angus is delighted to have someone to play with," said Frances. "I told you he fancies them as strange woolly dogs."

Skelly laughed.

"Aye, you did that."

There was a long silence as they watched the game unfold. Frances felt a wave of peace and contentment wash over her. Everything was as it should be, she thought, as a pleasant warmth filled her.

"You'll take up the painting again, aye?"

Frances sighed. She was feeling magnanimous. Watching the lambs gambol around the room, with Angus following closely, waiting for his chance to join in, she suddenly wondered what she'd been fussing about all this time. Of *course* she would go back to painting. It was the right thing to do and the only thing that would truly make her happy.

She was just about to say so and had a beaming grin on her face at the prospect when a sudden clatter from the area of the kitchen startled her.

She frowned, gooseflesh rising on her arms. Looking up, she saw Skelly regarding her with an odd look in his eyes. His gnarled hands were gripping his corduroy knees and he leaned forward slightly. Another bang from the kitchen and Frances stood up. Moss was in one of his moods. She put out a hand to steady herself, she felt slightly light-headed.

"I'm sorry," she said to Skelly who had sat back on the sofa, scowling. "There's some sort of difficulty in the kitchen..."

Her voice trailed away; she'd forgotten why she was standing up. What was the matter with her? She needed to eat something that wasn't a pastry, she decided. She was eating far too much sugar. Was she just about to say something? She glanced over at the locked cabinet and then back at Skelly. He was still scowling but directing it towards the kitchen. She followed his gaze. Moss was standing in front of the bread bin, his arms folded crossly. A large wooden spoon was tucked into the crook of one elbow. A stack of enamel tea plates had slid out of their pile, explaining the loud noise. He was glaring at Skelly who glared back.

"Aye, then," whispered Skelly, his voice low and flat. "I see how it is."

Moss inclined his head slightly, the arrogant tilt of his head taking on an even more self-satisfied look.

Skelly nodded and stood up, with surprising nimbleness for a man of his age and a sofa of such soft and enveloping tendencies.

"Are you going?" asked Frances, feeling slightly stupid, but not entirely disappointed. "I was just going to say something…did you ask me a question? I'm sorry, I feel a bit odd."

Skelly nodded.

"Could be the mould," he said, starting for the door. "Sometimes it gets into the brain, aye? Turns you funny."

Frances's jaw dropped, her eyes widening. She hadn't thought of that. Oh, wait. Was he kidding? It was so very hard to tell. But he wasn't smiling. Reaching for the latch, he turned slightly.

"I'll leave you to it, then. Thank you for your hospitality, I'm grateful."

His voice had a formal intonation and if she'd been feeling less addled, she might have wondered more. As it was, it was all she could do to stand straight. She leaned against the back of the sofa for support.

"Think on it, lass. Think on it hard."

"I will," she assured him, brightly, but without having any idea what she was meant to be thinking about.

He was out the door before she could gather the question.

"Oh!" she called after him. "Mr. Skelly! Your lambs!"

The pair were embroiled in a sort of lolloping game of bounce around the room, with Angus trotting gleefully beside them.

A high-pitched whistle came from outside and the two lambs stopped their aimless capering and fell obediently into line, trotting across the floor and out of the door. Angus started to follow but Frances lunged at him, the first organized thought she'd had in the past five minutes and scooped him up before he could join the train. She stood in the doorway, watching the old man walk down the lane, the two lambs trotting behind him.

* * *

"Well I don't know that you needed to be quite so rude about it," said Frances, re-stacking the tea plates. She'd found them in a box in the storage room and thought they'd be handy if ever anyone came to visit. Not that anyone really did, nor was she planning on inviting anyone. She paused for a moment, wondering what had given her the thought in the first place. She shook her head, it didn't matter. They were lovely to look at — that off-white with navy blue trim. They reminded her of her grandad's allotment and the mugs of tea she'd make for them in his little potting shed after a morning digging up potatoes.

"I had to act quickly," said Moss, his arms folded and his tone huffy. "He was putting a compulsion on you. Didn't you feel it?"

"A compulsion? Are you even serious?"

"Yes, I'm serious. I told you, he has power."

Moss said the last part in a hushed whisper, even going to far as to glance over his shoulder.

"How can he have power?" asked Frances, folding her own arms. "Next thing you'll be telling me is that he's a wizard or some such nonsense."

Moss blushed.

"He's not a wizard," he replied, scowling. "But he isn't what you think he is either."

"Well then what is he?" said Frances, exasperated. "If he's such a menace, why won't you tell me the details? Surely I'd be better able to handle myself in his presence if I knew."

"I can't."

Moss turned abruptly and stalked to the length of twine that Frances had tied to the cupboard handle. He set about shimmying down to reach the kitchen floor.

"And why not?" persisted Frances.

"There are rules about such things and I'm not of an inclination to break them."

"Well I suppose that settles it then," said Frances, reaching for Angus' leash. The little dog leapt up from where he was curled up on the sofa, somehow intuiting that an adventure was to be had, despite not being able to see Frances reaching for the leash.

"How do you mean?" asked Moss, narrowing his eyes. He had gathered up his feather duster and cloth, no doubt settling for a polishing session.

Frances shrugged.

"You won't tell me what the problem with Mr.Skelly is so I shall continue to interact with him. He's odd but as far as I can tell, quite harmless. He's probably just lonely, lots of elderly people are. Besides, he must be a good person at heart, look how he cares for those little orphan lambs. I think you'll find that you're just overreacting to this whole thing."

She bent down to clip on Angus' leash. He spun and wriggled with delight, making the simple task rather more difficult.

"I'm going to walk into the village to pick up the post. I'll probably stop in at the bookshop so don't expect me back too soon."

Moss muttered something under his breath.

Frances turned to glare at him.

"Sorry, I didn't quite catch that?"

"I said, I think you'll find that his name doesn't require an honorific."

"Meaning?"

Moss sighed with exaggerated effort and rolled his eyes.

"His name isn't *Mr.* Skelly. It's just Skelly."

He gave her a meaningful look, as if trying to telegraph some important information.

Frances frowned.

"I don't know what that means."

Moss groaned.

"No, I don't imagine you do. Give my regards to the Lady Sophia."

* * *

Frances enjoyed her walks into the village. It wasn't a short trip, probably about a half hour on foot, but it gave her time to think and to enjoy the scenery. It also offered up an opportunity for exercise, which she found she craved after sitting at her work for hours on end. Angus clearly enjoyed the outings as well, as they offered all manner of possibilities in the sniffing department.

The mostly-beech hedge gave way to a greater assortment of standard hedge-fare — elder and bramble, interspersed with hawthorn and wild rose. As they walked further, it enlarged to include bigger trees — elm, oak and hazel. She made note of the abundant blackberries, ripening to plumpness, thinking to come back and fill up a basket or two. A clump of blackthorn was weighed down with shiny, purple-blue jewels. Money would be tight this year, a bottle or two of sloe gin would make excellent gifts for Christmas. Sophie was especially fond.

The late summer hedgerow was a place of immense bounty, mused Frances. With Moss to forage for them, they might not starve after all. A faint rustling and a movement out of the corner of her eye alerted her to something in the dense shade of the bushes. Angus particular interest in it assured her that it wasn't anything that she wanted to be involved with and she averted her eyes from whatever faery creature was lurking there.

"Other people see hedgehogs or rabbits in the hedges," she said out loud, directing it to Angus but meaning it for her otherworldly companion to hear. "They're happy to know that robins are nesting there. How nice it would be to be so innocent of the less-than-savoury inhabitants."

A high-pitched chittering burst out from the hedge, followed by a thrashing of waving branches.

"Temper tantrums do nothing to endear you to us," said Frances, eyes straight ahead on the path. "I suggest you take your mischief elsewhere."

Several rosehips rained down on them at that point, one of them hitting poor Angus sharply on the top of the head. He yelped loudly and clamped his tail down. Frances bent down to retrieve the tossed fruit and spun to face the hedge. She pelted them back into the depths of the shrubbery, not expecting to hit anything. She was rewarded by a piercing shriek and a further torrent of abuse. Grinning she bent down again to soothe a quivering Angus before tugging at his leash and setting off again at a smart pace.

"There you go, Angus," she said, once they were around the bend and on the main path to the village. "I defended your honour."

He wagged his stumpy tail in response and resumed his sniffing of the grass verge.

* * *

"I honestly don't know why Mis…Skelly seems to think there's a dearth of faeries in the world," she said to Sophie as they sat over a mug of steaming tea. "I can't seem to walk for five minutes without having one of them haranguing me and tormenting poor Angus."

She looked down at where Angus was sitting attentively beside her chair. Sophie encouraged people to bring their dogs into the cafe, as long as they were well-behaved, and Angus was currently on probation in that department. He'd been bribed to quiet occupation with a small marrow bone that Frances had picked up at the butcher after stopping in at the post office. Hearing his name, however, Angus wanted to be sure there wasn't any crumbs coming his way.

"What do you think that whole compulsion thing was all about?" asked Sophie, sneaking a large piece of her scone under the table where Angus quietly accepted it. "Do you really think Moss was over-reacting? Maybe there's something to it. I mean, we've been here almost a year now - Uncle Phineas longer than that - and we've never known there was an old boy farming sheep nearby."

Frances pushed aside the gnawing suspicion that Moss was right and shook her head.

"Well, I can't say anything to that, other than he's an odd fellow who seems to prefer his own company. And you know Moss, he's got a flair for the dramatic. No, I just think he's lonely and likes a bit of company and a slice of lemon drizzle from time to time. Maybe he has a grandfatherly concern for me living in the studio."

Sophie frowned, unconvinced.

"I don't know, Fran. I think you'd best be on your guard. I don't like that you're out there on your own. I wish you'd come and stay with Stuart and me."

Frances smiled at her friend, reaching out to squeeze her hand.

"You've barely enough space for the both of you up there," she said, chuckling. "Besides, you know how Stuart feels about Angus."

Sophie wrinkled up her nose.

"True. Dog hair and excitability offend his delicate sensibilities. You know, I often wonder how we ended up together."

She grinned but Frances noticed that it didn't reach her eyes.

"Is everything okay, Soph?" she asked. "Here I am whinging

on about my problems and I never ask about you. God, I'm a terrible friend."

Sophie laughed.

"Don't be silly," she said. "Anyway, everything's fine. Now, can I interest you in our Share Your Work wall?"

She pointed over at the expanse of wall beside the cash register. It had been taken over by a large bulletin board which appeared to be festooned with various bits of paper.

"It was Melinda's idea," she said, beaming. "A way of encouraging people to sponsor the Creative Corner. The folk who use it leave pieces of art or writing, so that the patrons can know what their bottomless teapots are in aid of. Your wee friend has left a few of her drawings there."

"My wee friend?" began Frances, before she remembered. "Ah yes, Fiona! Isn't she a lovely little thing?"

Sophie smiled.

"She really is. I feel badly for the little tyke, though. Her mam works all the hours god sends and she's left on her own more than what's good for her, I'm sure."

Frances nodded, sipping her tea.

"But she's got this place, Soph. And that's a great blessing. I would've given my left kidney to have a place like this, and someone like you, when I was her age."

Frances looked around at the cafe and felt a sudden ache. She thought she'd had it all figured out - a thriving career as a gallery artist, a cozy flat in the heart of the arts district in the city, a circle of artsy friends to liven her days and evenings. When had life become so complicated? She shook her head, trying to rid herself of that very unhelpful thought. There was no sense dwelling on what clearly wasn't meant to be.

"Well, have you got something for the wall?" prodded

Sophie.

Frances blinked, bringing herself back to the present moment.

"Um, I'm not sure." She gestured vaguely at her sketchbook. "There might be something in there."

Sophie smiled and patted her arm.

"I can see you're heading into one of your fugue states," she joked. "I'll bring over a bottomless pot and let you get on with it, shall I?"

Frances gave her a weak smile as Sophie stood up and bustled off in search of a pot of tea. Her 'fugue states' had been notorious and a point of great humour when they were in art college. Not without irony, her other friends had referred to her faraway gazes and distracted manner as 'being away with the faeries' , mostly because they usually resulted in a flurry of productivity that gave birth to her signature pieces - her large canvases depicting the faery folk she'd seen, set in lush and detailed landscapes. She thought wistfully of those days. Those were the days when she felt like she was doing exactly what she was meant for - when she felt most rooted and certain.

She heaved a sigh and shook her head again. This was not helping matters at all, she told herself sternly. Now was the time for pragmatic pursuits. There were bills to pay.

Speaking of bills, she busied herself sorting out her post. There was an envelope from the same company for which she was currently designing. She slit it open with a convenient butter knife and there, as if by confirmation of her decision, was a sheaf of papers with specifications for another contract.

"See?" she said to Angus, who merely flicked an ear, devoted as he was to his bone. "This is how things ought to be. Me getting paid for my art instead of getting into debt over it."

She scanned the details, noting with only a mild twinge of disappointment that it required yet more geometric designs. People were greatly wanting sharp edges and distinct corners in their accent pillows it seemed.

Stifling another sigh, she pulled out the page that required her signature and rooted in her bag for a pen. Just then, Sophie came back with a large Brown Betty and a plate of currant rock buns.

"Here you go, pet," she said, placing it all on the table. Then she pulled a folded bit of paper out of her apron pocket and handed it to Frances.

"Here, I almost forgot. Uncle Phineas popped in yesterday on a flying visit. He's got the next section of his book finished and wants you to do the illustrations. I told him you would, I hope that was okay?"

Frances grinned and accepted the paper. It was a list of plants and animals that he wanted illustrated in the old-fashioned style of long-ago field guides.

"You know it is!" She rubbed her hands together with glee. "Finally, something that's not a concentric circle!"

Sophie laughed and bent down to ruffle Angus' ears. His bone had been thoroughly de-marrowed and the arrival of the plate of rock buns had not gone unnoticed. Sophie quietly scooped one off the plate and slid it to him.

"I saw that," remonstrated Frances, but without any real force. She was too delighted with the prospect of botanical illustrations to be cross. "When he's as big as a house I'll be bringing him to you to take for extra walks."

Sophie pouted her lips in mock irritation.

"And that would be just fine with me, you big spoily-fun.

You can't expect the poor wee dog to live on health food alone. Right, away with you to the enchanted places. I've work to do."

But Frances hardly noticed her leave. She was already turning the pages of her sketchbook, by-passing the robot daisies, as Moss had started calling them, her mind racing ahead to the possibilities of Uncle Phineas' project.

Uncle Phineas - or, rather, Great Uncle Phineas was a staunch supporter of the arts. It was he who had given Sophie the start-up money for Analogue Daze and was a source of great enthusiasm and encouragement to her and all of her friends during their college days. He was of the old school of country people - all tweed and argyle - and had made a lifetime project of documenting the flora and fauna of his vast estate. Unlike his contemporaries, however, he preferred shooting with a camera than with a rifle and was a great proponent of conservation. The illustrations which he hired Frances to do were for his many-volumed work on the denizens of the local countryside and Frances enjoyed it immensely. She suspected, too, that Uncle Phin could see the faery folk although they'd never discussed it. She'd tested her theory by hiding tiny drawings of pixies and elf-blossoms amid the illustrations she'd sent to him and he'd never once objected. She took that to be an affirmation.

* * *

Frances spent a happy couple of hours with the scrap of paper. Most of the plants she knew from sight but would need reference images to draw properly. The same went for the birds and animals. But nevertheless, she was able to do quick sketches from memory and her teapot emptied quickly.

It was the cold nudge of Angus' nose at her elbow that finally broke her flow. Startled, she looked up, blinking as if just stepping out into bright sunlight. She glanced at her watch and couldn't quite believe how much time had passed.

"I'm sorry, my boy," she said, tousling his ears. "You must be bursting for a pee by now. I know I am. That was a lot of tea."

She stretched and leaned back in her chair, feeling the quiet satisfaction of having done something she really enjoyed. It was exactly the sort of break she needed from her contract designs.

That's all I need to do, she thought, scrubbing a hand through her hair. I just need to balance the design work with something with a bit more soul. That'll stop me from getting sour. It's the perfect solution.

She was just about to pack up her pens and sketchbook when her eye caught on the Share Your Work board. She bit her lower lip and glanced at her sketchbook. Smiling, she tore out a page, tapped her pen against the tip of her nose for a moment and then bent over the paper.

There, she said to herself, a pleasing tingle of delight washing over her. That should keep everyone happy.

"Come on, Angus," she said out loud, picking up her satchel and slinging it over her shoulder. "A visit to the loo and then we're on our way."

Angus wriggled excitedly and trotted beside her to the front of the bookshop. She looped his leash over the hook, provided for just such that reason, and paid a quick visit to the facilities.

Collecting Angus on her way out, she paused to pin up the drawing she'd made. She stood staring at it for a moment - the face of the distressed faery from the other day looked back at her. But in the drawing, she'd removed the anguish and instead he smiled; rather than leaning on his friend, unable to stand for himself, he was lounging against the trunk of an oak tree, a piece of long grass clenched between his teeth. It was the first drawing of a faery she'd done since her gallery showing and it felt both thrilling and daunting at the same time. She stared a moment longer before a tug on the leash reminded her that Angus hadn't had his turn for the toilet.

There, she thought. It's not a painting but it's the next best thing. That will have to do.

* * *

The light was fading by the time they reached the lane leading to her studio. The hedge was darkening into shadow and Frances picked up her pace slightly. She'd forgotten to pack a torch, not expecting to be quite so late, and she didn't want to get caught in the dark. As safe as she felt in the relative isolation, she didn't want to step in a pothole and turn an ankle either.

Happily, Moss had turned on the lights in the studio and the scent of woodsmoke in the air promised he'd also switched on the electric fire. Moss wasn't usually inclined to use faery magic, but he made an exception when it came to ambience. She could find her way back by smell if she had to, she supposed, smiling happily to herself.

"Come on Angus," she said, waggling the leash merrily. "Let's get ourselves home. I bet Moss has got a pot of something lovely on the hob for dinner. Those rock buns were grand, but I could really use something substantial."

Angus wuffed in reply and trotted quickly beside her.

They were just about to turn from the lane onto the path to the studio when a blur of movement out of the corner of her eye drew her attention. She came to an abrupt halt, her mouth hanging open in disbelief.

Surely not, she breathed. She blinked and peered deeply into the closing gloom.

The faery perched on an outgrown branch of the beech hedge. He had an arm looped around a twig and he leaned out toward her, waving his other arm. A long blade of grass was clenched in his teeth.

Angus whined, tugging at his harness, straining towards the teasing creature, who just grinned and waggled a finger at the wriggling dog.

The anguish was gone from his features, just as she'd drawn it, and he was certainly in sturdy enough form, balancing as he was from the hedge.

"How?" asked Frances, faintly and to no-one in particular.

The faery merely winked and then stood straight up on the branch before sketching a courtly bow.

"Frances!" called Moss, from the open door of the studio. "Your dinner is getting cold!"

Frances glance toward the studio, opening her mouth to call back for Moss to come out and confirm what she was seeing, but when she turned back to the hedge, the faery was gone.

She blinked several times and rubbed her hand over her eyes.

"I didn't imagine that, did I?" she asked Angus, who was snuffling about on the ground, as if trying to pick up the scent of the faery.

"Frances!" called Moss again, impatience evident in his tone. "What on earth are you doing, standing out there like a gormless eejit?"

Frances sighed and went into the studio.

Chapter 10

Frances had decided to push all thoughts of the strange occurrence out of her mind. It seemed the only sensible option. She'd briefly considered talking to Moss about it but decided that would only end in frustration and a scathing lecture from him about meddling in faery business and how he wanted no part of it. After all, he'd made his decision and was happy to live with it so why couldn't Frances?

And that was ultimately what it came down to, reasoned Frances as she busied herself getting her materials sorted for another day of polygons and robot daisies. Whatever niggling doubts had made their way into her subconscious after the appearance of the previously-expired faery needed to be firmly dealt with. She had absolutely no reason to thwart the perfectly good situation in which she found herself.

Things were finally settling into place. She had a rhythm and routine to her days; she interspersed her design work with smatterings of botanical drawings for Uncle Phineas and she was beginning to feel like it was the best of all worlds. Not only that, she was expecting a sizeable payment from the design contract at any moment and just in time, too. She glanced surreptitiously at the calendar and then the clock. Her loan installment was due in a few days and she was certain that today's post would bring the cheque to more than cover it. She'd been assured, when she'd phoned to inquire, by their accounts department, that it had been sent to the higher-ups for approval and would be on its way imminently. Uncle Phineas had wired a generous amount to her as deposit for the illustrations, but Frances had hoped that she could hold onto that as savings.

The sun shone enticingly through the studio window. The sky was a startling shade of blue and the sound of the birds in the hedge was a merry chorus. Frances gazed, with a pang of longing, outside. What she really wanted was to pack herself a picnic lunch and take Angus for a great ramble across the fields. The beautiful weather wouldn't last much longer, after all. Autumn was a tenuous thing at best and she really ought to take advantage of it, perhaps get those blackberries picked. Moss would make a gorgeous jam and it'd do marvelously for Christmas presents.

She shook her head.

"No," she said, firmly.

Angus whined and looked up from where he lay, pressed against her legs. He was lobbying, in his own quiet way, for the picnic and ramble option, convinced that there were rabbits out there that wanted nothing more than a jolly romp with him.

"Work first, my boy," she said, more to herself than the dog. Her resolve was wavering. The lure of robot daisies was not strong.

"I have to be the grown-up here," she said, pouring herself a large mug of tea from the pot Moss had left. He had gone

144

out into the glorious day, bound for some foraging expedition or other, thought Frances, grumbling inwardly like a petulant toddler at the unfairness of it. "A couple of hours of work and then we'll have earned our outing. Maybe we'll stop by the bakery and pick up a lemon drizzle. We can go and visit Mr. Skelly. I'm sure he'd enjoy a visit."

Angus wuffed and took himself off to the sofa, resigned to the fact the rabbits would have to wait for his company.

Frances, feeling both virtuous for her restraint and buoyed by the idea of their proposed outing, settled down into her work.

A couple of hours and several cups of tea later, Frances shut off her computer with a sigh. Her eyes felt gritty and her back ached. Sitting for so long in front of a screen wasn't her idea of a good time but once her hand-drawings had been finished, she had no choice but to begin the digital work. That was, she explained to herself, the beauty of doing the work in the first place. She could do it from this funny little studio out in the middle of nowhere. Still, she thought, as she stood and stretched her arms above her head then rubbed her stiff neck, she should make it an absolute necessity that she only work for short bursts and then get out and move.

"See?" she said to Angus as she assembled herself a salad sandwich and sliced a wedge of cheese. "We can go and enjoy ourselves now, for the rest of the afternoon, without feeling guilty for not getting our work done."

Angus whined and trotted back and forth between the kitchen and the door. Clearly, he felt she was taking far too long with the provisions.

"Just a minute," she laughed, as the trot became a caper, "I have to wait for the kettle to boil. We can't assume Mr. Skelly will have his TARDIS flask of tea, can we?"

"You probably could," muttered Moss, appearing over the edge of the countertop as he climbed up the rope. "And it's not 'mister', remember?"

Frances clutched a hand to her chest and closed her eyes, trying to steady her breathing.

"Must you sneak up like that?" she said, through gritted teeth. "One of these days you'll give me a heart attack."

"I'm not sneaking," said Moss, indignant. "If you weren't talking to yourself like a nutter, you'd have heard me coming."

Frances scowled.

"I was talking to Angus," she said, primly, folding cloth wrappers around her sandwich and the lump of cheese.

Moss chuckled, diffusing the tension. He rummaged in the bag slung across his person and produced two large apples.

"Speaking of TARDIS vessels," said Frances, eyeing up the apples and then the bag. "What else have you got in there? A side of venison? I could use one of those bags for when I go to the laundromat. It'd save me carrying everything in bin bags."

Moss gave her a withering look.

"These are of faery-craft," he said, in a tone suggesting she was something of a simpleton. "Humans can't access the…um…dimensional attributes of them."

He stared at her with a pointed look, as if willing her to ask more questions but all she did was giggle and tuck the apples into her bag next to the sandwiches.

"Ah well, I supposed I'm destined to look like a college student forever," she said.

Moss heaved a dramatic sigh.

"Have you packed anything for Angus or is he meant to scavenge bits of dropped lettuce? You know he prefers it when you have paste in your sandwiches and giving him cheese isn't going to help his bulging waistline at all."

Angus wriggled excitedly at the door, less concerned with snacks than getting the day started.

Moss rummaged in the cupboards and pulled out a bag of dehydrated liver treats.

"Here, put a few of those in your bag. He thinks he doesn't care about the food now, but he will."

Frances took the treats and smiled at the little brownie. Moss had his arms folded in his default pose, a frown creasing his features.

"Thank you, Moss," said Frances, reaching over to squeeze his elbow. "I know I don't say it often enough, but Angus and I would be lost without you. I can't imagine a better companion for us, and I know it hasn't been easy for you, living out here…"

She waved a hand in a gesture encompassing the studio and the surrounding area.

"I know it's not what you signed on for and I'm grateful that you've stuck with us, with me,"

Her voice caught and she blinked hurriedly, looking down at her bag. She dug inside it for a tissue.

Moss cleared his throat.

"The kettle is boiling," he said, as the whistle shrieked. "Are you planning on letting it boil dry? Good grief, you're right to be glad of me. I think you'd end up setting yourself on fire or else starving your wee dog to death otherwise."

He pushed passed Frances, who was busy blowing her nose, and poured the hot water into the teapot.

"Go and get yourself together," he said, flapping a hand at her protest. "You didn't time this very well. Angus is having an apoplexy and this tea has to steep for another three minutes if you don't want to be drinking hamster piddle. Have you any crackers to go with that cheese? What about a bit of pickle? Honestly, how have you survived to this point? You can't expect to walk for miles on a rabbit-food sandwich. You need substance…"

Frances smiled, watching as Moss busied himself, scooping pickle into a little jar and tucking crackers into a square of cloth. She really would be lost without him, she thought, no matter his surly temper and impatience with her bumbling humanity.

"Get on with you!" he exclaimed, handing her the full flask of perfectly brewed tea. He blushed furiously as Frances leaned down to kiss him on the cheek. "I've no time for this emotional nonsense! I've things to do and you two are just under my feet."

"Are you alright?" said Frances, frowning. "Only you felt a bit clammy. Are you overdoing it? You've been going out rather a lot lately. Finally joining in with the local revels are you?"

Moss snorted.

"As if I'd lower myself. I'm fine. Go on, off you go. A bit of peace and quiet is what I need."

"As long as you can manage without us?"

Frances grinned at the level of wither he put into his glare and clipped on Angus' leash.

"We'll be back for supper," she called to him.

"I'm sure you will," he shouted back. "Aren't you always?"

He watched as the door closed behind them and they disappeared down the path towards the lane.

"Just make sure you are," he said, quietly, worry in his round green eyes. He pulled out a paisley patterned handkerchief and wiped it across the sheen of cold perspiration on his forehead.

* * *

"Right," said Frances, her face turned blissfully towards the sun. "First we have to go into the village,"

Angus trotted happily beside her, his stump of tail held high and his black nose held low. He was in a state of utter delight and couldn't have cared less what the route entailed, so long as he was outside and with his very best favourite person. Such were the needs of a little dog.

"We'll stop by the post office first, to pick up our cheque. It's been over a week since I spoke to that lady in the accounts department, ample time for the money to arrive. And then we'll go to the bakery for a loaf of lemon drizzle cake. I'm sure Sophie will forgive us for opting for that, but perhaps we should stop at the cafe before the post office and get half a dozen of those currant rock buns to take home for supper. Moss would like that; he loves anything to do with our Sophie. And it would feel good to do something nice for Moss for a change. He looks after us so well, attitude notwithstanding. And I really do think he's been working too hard. He's trying to uphold standards that the studio simply can't support."

Frances lapsed into a contented silence. The air was crisp with the sort of crispness that only comes with the perfect balance of warm sun and cool air. There wasn't so much as a breath of wind and the sky was a vast, cloudless blue. The scent of woodsmoke drifted on the air, combining in satisfying symphony with the sweet smell of windfall apples.

* * *

"Isn't it odd?" mused Frances, to the unsuspecting girl behind the counter at the bakery. "That the smell of rotting apples is actually a pleasant thing? And leaves, too, for that matter. The smell of damp leaves has to be one of the best smells of all. It's like a great finale, isn't it? Autumn is the great finale..."

Her voice trailed off at the expression on the girl's face as she handed over the wrapped loaf. Her heavily made-up eyes looked warily at Frances, as if she was deciding whether to call the police or just ignore her as a harmless nutter.

Frances smiled what she hoped was a harmless smile and thanked the girl, walking quickly over to the cashier. She paid for the loaf and retrieved Angus, stifling the laugh that was bubbling up inside her.

"I believe she thinks I'm quite mad," she said, untying the leash. "Although, I'm sure standing here talking to myself doesn't disavow her of that notion."

She looked through the window and met the raised eyebrows of several customers. Grinning, she gave them a wave and set off towards the post office.

* * *

"Is Sophie about?"

Frances handed over the money for the rock buns and took the paper bag from Melinda.

Melinda shook her head, smiling.

"No, she's off to the city today," she said, passing back Frances' change. "She had to go into the office to see to some accounting stuff."

Melinda leaned forward and lowered her voice.

"Stuart read her the riot act again and she couldn't really

150

put it off any longer."

Frances grimaced.

She knew how much Sophie hated dealing with the money aspects of her little business. And while she could certainly understand that, she knew Stuart was right in insisting she keep on top of things.

"Why doesn't she hire a bookkeeper?" asked Frances. "Wouldn't that take the pressure off?"

Melinda shrugged.

"That's what I said. But Stuart is insisting that she needs to take responsibility for it herself. That she has to at least learn how to do it before she hands it off. That way she has control of the situation. Or that's the theory anyway."

"Hmmm." said Frances, biting her lip, torn between defending her friend and not wanting to sound like she was disparaging her friend's fiance in anyway.

Melinda nodded.

"I know, I think the same. I don't believe people should be forced into things that are so very contrary to their nature. It might work for a time, but it ultimately cripples a person. And I think maybe Sophie is just one of those people who need to stay tuned into the magic, rather than being forced into muggle life, you know?"

Melinda was smiling but her joking tone belied a real seriousness.

Frances felt her stomach lurch slightly. Not only that, a tingle of recognition rippled up from somewhere deep in her chest.

She just nodded, schooling her features into gentle concern.

"I think you're right, Melinda. I really do. I know Stuart means well and he's right in a lot of ways, but he'll make her miserable if he keeps trying to turn her into something she's not. Our Sophie is definitely not a muggle!"

The two women shared a laugh and then Frances left to retrieve Angus, her thoughts churning wildly.

"Nothing today, love," said Mrs. Reeve. "Are you expecting something, like?"

Frances nodded, trying to wipe the concerned frown off her face. She was sure the cheque would have arrived by today. She wondered if it would seem too desperate if she phoned the accounting department again. A small knot of dread wound itself tightly in her stomach. She wanted to scream in frustration.

Instead, she smiled and shrugged.

"Well, I was hoping," she said, accepting the humbug that Mrs.Reeve passed to her. The elderly post office attendant seemed to have a never-ending supply of humbugs and barley sugars. "But that's alright, I might be being a bit optimistic I'll check again in a few days. We were just passing through on our way for a ramble and a picnic and thought I might as well stop in."

"Aye, lass. The old post isn't what it used to be, that's for certain."

Mrs.Reeve grinned a gap-toothed smile and reached under the counter, pulling out a paper bag. She rummaged inside and pulled out a large dog biscuit, then wrapped it in a square of grease-proof paper.

"Take that for your wee doggie," she said, with a wink. "My own recipe. Lots of good stuff, none of the rubbish they put in things nowadays."

Frances accepted the biscuit with genuine delight. The people in Thistlecrag were unfailingly kind and she remonstrated herself for feeling peevish over something so relatively small. When had she become so obsessed with the material things?

"Ah, that's lovely Mrs.Reeve, thank you!" she said, tucking it into her bag next to the provisions Moss had packed for Angus. He'd gone from getting leftover sandwich scraps to having a gourmet picnic all of his own. "I can say with absolute certainty that Angus will very much enjoy your present."

Mrs. Reeve beamed.

"'Tis my pleasure lass. My husband kept dogs for all our married life, and it was always me who did the cooking for 'em. They lived long and healthy lives and worked long into their teens, I can tell you that. Enjoy your ramble, then. You've a lovely day for it."

* * *

"Let's take the path out toward the sheep meadows, shall we?" she asked Angus, who was darting about at the very end of the lead, following some scent trail or other. "Maybe Mr....um, Skelly will be out tending his flock and we can catch him for a bit of tea and cake."

She didn't quite know why, but the events of the morning had stirred up some deep unease in her and she felt a strange pull to talk with the old sheep farmer again. For the first time since moving out to the village, she was beginning to seriously acknowledge the quiver of doubt that niggled at the back of her mind. Maybe she wasn't doing the right thing after all? But what other options were there? None that appealed, that was for certain.

"Ugh!" she said aloud, startling a flock of starlings which exploded into the air from the long grass. Angus yelped and skittered aside, and Frances giggled at the look of embarrassment on his whiskery face.

"That's what happens when you're so engrossed in your work," she said. "You forget the rest of the world exists."

She frowned, then whispered,

"At least, that's how I remember it."

Sighing heavily, she shifted the weight of her backpack and turned her face to the sun.

"Come on, my boy. Enough of these maudlin thoughts. Let's just immerse ourselves in this lovely day, shall we?"

Angus wriggled beside her, tilting his head to one side in the way that generally melted all resolve in his mistress's heart.

Frances narrowed her eyes.

"Do you promise to behave?" she asked, sternly. "No running off to chase rabbits or play with the sheep? We can't afford to get into trouble you know."

Angus whined, tilting his head to the other side and then back again.

Frances groaned and muttered, "Butter wouldn't melt…"

She bent down and unclipped his leash.

"We may both live to regret this," she said, laughing as Angus ran back and forth in excited dashes. "But it's so much more fun when you can have a proper run, isn't it? After all, what good is it to live in this beautiful area if you can't be off your leash? Much better for body and mind to have a bit of freedom."

Having convinced herself of that, she set off in the direction she hoped she might find Skelly. Although what she hoped to find in his company, she wasn't quite certain. Every exchange with him left her feeling more and more confused and unsure and yet, here she was, seeking him out. It made no sense. She silenced the unwelcome voice of reason and resolved to enjoy the walk.

* * *

She walked for about an hour, reveling in the glorious early autumn weather. The fields rolled in gentle undulating hills, still bordered by ancient hedges and tumbledown stone walls. The profusion of rocks and boulders in the meadows were likely why the land had escaped large scale cultivation, making it far more suitable for grazing. Whatever environmental perils that entailed, at least the old hedges were preserved. Frances smiled, imagining them to be filled with the busy goings-on of the birds and small creatures that used the hedges for travel and protection. And of the larger ones that used them for hunting. It was all a perfectly balanced system and she found that a great comfort. Indeed, giving herself over to those sorts of ponderings, she felt the tension and worry of earlier starting to dissipate. She could even look magnanimously upon the hedges as the thoroughfares of the faery people as well.

Her blissful musings were suddenly interrupted by the sound of an engine and the excited barking of a dog.

Oh no, Angus!

Frances looked wildly around, thoroughly furious of herself for losing track of him. Again! He would be perfectly fine if only she kept her eye on him.

"Angus!" she shouted, scanning the area. "Angus!"

There was no sign of him.

Frances started to jog slowly up the incline, hoping a slightly higher altitude would help her see. The sound of the barking seemed to be coming closer, so perhaps he'd heard her calling.

"Angus! Come on, my boy!"

Just then, a small motorcycle crested the top of the hill. It was the sort that people used to ride around muddy tracks and jump over old oil barrels. And just behind it, in hot pursuit, was a small, brown and white form, barking madly.

"Oh no!" groaned Frances, torn between terror and inappropriate hilarity. "What is he doing? And why doesn't that idiot just stop the stupid bike?"

She stopped running and stood still, waiting for the inevitable.

The loud, smelly machine pulled to a halt about ten feet from her. The stink of petrol and clouds of black exhaust prickled her eyes. The whole vision of it seemed the perfect insult to the peace of the day. Angus continued to run around the bike, darting in and out as if to try and bite it, barking and yapping. Frances tried fruitlessly to catch his attention. There was no point in shouting for him, he was too engrossed in his work and besides, the horrid machine was too loud.

The driver pulled off his helmet, revealing a red-faced, middle-aged man. His dark hair was greying at the temples and was cut in a short style that was unmarred by the confines of the helmet.

He looks like one of those people who are never untidy, thought Frances, even when they've every right to be.

She glanced quickly over his attire, taking in the expensive leather jacket and designer jeans. His hands were bare and the nails clean well-manicured.

So, not a farmer out checking on his sheep, thought Frances, with a hint of superior derision.

He appeared to be trying to talk to her.

She cupped a hand to her ear and looked pointedly at the motorbike.

With a scowl, he turned off the bike. The absence of racket made the quiet of the field almost magnify. Frances closed her eyes briefly and felt her muscles unclench, not realizing that she'd been holding such tension in the first place.

Angus gave one more bark, with a tone of triumph, dashed at the motorbike and attempted to bite the rear tire.

In one smooth movement, the driver swung his helmet at the little dog.

"Get out, you little bastard!" he shouted, in the cultured tones of somewhere not from around the village.

Frances let out a yell and lunged forward, knocking his arm. At the same time, Angus jumped back and escaped being hit. The momentum of Frances' lunge carried her forward, hitting the man and the bike with more force than she'd intended. She just managed to save herself from toppling into a heap along with the man and his bike.

"Oh, my goodness!" she said, frantically trying to pick up the heavy bike where it lay on top of the struggling man. "I'm ever so sorry!"

The man cursed and swore, managing to wriggle out from under his vehicle and stood up. His crisply ironed jeans were streaked with mud and the shine of his boots marred by a scuff, probably from some piece of his motorcycle.

"What in the bloody hell do you think you're doing?" he barked, glaring at Frances. "Do you have any idea how much this machine is worth?"

Frances was hit by a surge of rage.

"That machine?" she said, her voice rising with incredulity. "You were about to bludgeon my dog with your helmet, and you expect me to be worried about some smelly pile of bolts?"

In the interim, Angus had come to sit beside her, mouth open in a happy grin, panting. As far as he was concerned, he had saved the day. Frances crouched down to check him quickly over before snapping his lead onto his collar.

"You're lucky I don't inform the authorities," said the man, "Letting that animal run wild over the fields, endangering the lives of people and livestock."

Frances swallowed hard, a stab of worry piercing her indignation. He wasn't wrong about Angus running wild, although he was far from a danger to anything other than himself.

"And you're lucky I don't report you for abuse to animals," she retorted. "Not to mention the fact you're destroying the peace and tranquility of the countryside with that wretched machine."

The man smiled, a slow, hateful smile.

"For your information, young lady, this piece of the countryside *belongs* to me. And as such, I'm entitled to use it however I see fit."

Frances found herself momentarily speechless.

He *owned* this land?

"Well, that may be so," she said, struggling to think of something to say. "But it doesn't excuse your actions either."

"Shall we see what the police have to say about that?" he asked, glaring down at Angus. "What will they say when I tell them that I was chased by a loose dog, and then accosted by its owner, who was trespassing on private land? Do you imagine they'd care about the peace of the countryside then?"

His tone held such a vicious sneer that Frances felt herself flinching.

He actually means to report us, she thought, suddenly frantic. What if they try to take Angus away from me? What if they declare him a menace and want to put him down?

Her thoughts spiraled wildly out of control and she imagined every horrifying scenario that could happen, and many that wouldn't ever.

She swallowed and took a deep, steadying breath.

"You're absolutely right, sir," she said, infusing her tone with contrition and humility. "I'm so very sorry if either my dog or I have caused you any distress or lasting harm. I had no inclination we were trespassing; I've not lived in the area very long and I'm still getting to know it. We were just out for a walk on this lovely day and we clearly strayed where we shouldn't have."

Her stomach roiled and clenched, inner rebellion for having to eat such a large helping of crow.

Fixing a smile on her face, she added,

"I do hope you can forgive this misunderstanding."

The man regarded her for a moment, his dark eyes narrowing.

He looks like a snake, she thought, sizing up a mouse for his dinner.

"Where are you living?" he asked. "You're new to the area, you say?"

"Yes," said Frances, "I'm renting the old converted outbuilding on the outside of the village."

"Ah, yes. That old heap," he said. "I was surprised my agent found someone willing to use it."

"Oh, it's quite nice," she said, laying on the flattery. "I'm very much enjoying living…um, being there. I'm an artist," she said, cursing herself inwardly. "I work there." She added, hoping he wouldn't have noticed her slip.

"I see," he said, climbing back onto his motorcycle, having apparently lost interest. "Well then, see that you keep that bloody animal on a leash."

And with that, the machine roared into life. Angus took up his barking again, lunging to the end of his leash. The man and his bike sped away, back in the direction it had come. Frances sagged onto the ground, hugging Angus tightly to her.

"You absolute idiot," she said, tearfully. The adrenalin rush of the conflict had dissipated, leaving her wobbly and full of emotion. "You could've got yourself killed or seriously hurt. He would've done it, you know. I could see he meant to hit you."

She let herself cry, then. Great heaving sobs into the wiry ruff of her dog's neck.

* * *

After a short while, Frances sat back, still cradling Angus on her lap. She rubbed a hand across her face then rummaged in her coat pocket for a tissue.

"Right, I'm finished," she said to Angus, blowing her nose. "I suppose that's been building for a while, hasn't it? Nothing like a bit of terror to open up the floodgates."

Angus whined and reached up to lick her face.

"Get off, you silly sausage," she laughed, gently tipping him onto the grass so she could stand up. "You're an incorrigible menace and I don't know why I ever put up with you."

Angus wriggled and tilted his head.

"Oh no you don't," she said, bending to untangle his lead. "I think I may have finally learned my lesson for good. There'll be no more freedom romps for you anytime soon, young sir. Now, let's get ourselves back to the path and find our way off that horrible man's land. Not that I have any idea where that boundary might be, mind you."

The pair walked for another half an hour, hopefully, thought Frances, in a direction away from the motorcycle man's land. There were no clear boundaries, so she simply had to assume that she was on the main footpath.

The events had succeeded in dimming her joy in the day and she found herself wishing they were already on their way back to the studio. She worried for the possible consequences. Who was that man and why had she never seen him before? Surely someone in the village would have warned her so she could have avoided walking on his property. The knot of dread which seemed to have taken up more or less permanent residence in her stomach tightened when she remembered the look on his face as he raised his arm to Angus.

"I think he's quite evil," she said, aloud. "I really do. But in one of those menacing, sneaking ways. I bet he's some kind of high-powered businessperson. Maybe he owns a pesticide company or he's a builder, who tears down ancient forests to build pesticide factories. What do you think, Angus?"

Angus wuffed.

"Yes, I'm sure that's it. Then again, perhaps he's something to do with mining - tearing down rainforests and absconding with aboriginal land just to get to a deposit of oil or coal or something."

She cheered herself up with various scenarios of the man's extreme evil. It helped quell the very real worry of what might transpire.

Eventually, they made their way back to familiar territory.

Frances felt certain that the land closer to the village couldn't possibly belong to him as there were always ramblers and picnickers to be found on the footpaths there.

"Let's see if we can find somewhere for our picnic, shall we?" She asked, "I don't much feel like bothering to find Skelly now. I think I've had my fill of the human race for one day."

Angus wagged his bottom with great enthusiasm. Any mention of picnic was bound to get his vote.

"Here," said Frances. "I think if we cut through this gap in the hedge, it looks like there's a bit of a clearing on the other side. I even think I can hear a stream tinkling nearby. Perfect! Just what we need to rid ourselves of all that yuckiness."

They squeezed through the hedge and emerged into what turned out to be an utterly delightful little patch.

"Oh!" said Frances, her eyes wide. "Isn't this lovely? Look, Angus, there's even a convenient half-wall there for me to sit on."

She frowned briefly. It did seem rather perfect and arranged very conveniently. She looked around, scanning the area for signs of mischief.

Then she laughed, shaking her head.

"Look at me, I'm getting paranoid. Whyever can't there be a lovely little spot for picnic? I only wish we'd found it sooner. I'm letting my imagination get the best of me. Come on, I'm gasping for a cup of tea and this pack is digging into my shoulders."

Frances spread out their picnic blanket and then settled herself against the tumbledown stone wall. She firmly ignored the fact that it seemed entirely out of place in the small clearing. I'm sure it's a relic of times gone by, she told herself. A leftover from some other division of property or grazing land. The sun had warmed the stone and it felt good on her aching back and shoulders. How much of that was from carrying the pack and how much from sheer tension, she didn't know. Still, she could feel the discomfort seeping away.

"I'm sorry, my boy," she said to Angus as she wrapped the end of his lead around one of the fallen stones. "I can't take a chance. Besides, you've got lots of yummy things to eat, I can't imagine you want to be gadding about. Surely you've had enough of that for one day."

Angus wuffed, eyeing up the wrapped bundles she was pulling out of the backpack. His nose twitched in anticipation. Patience was its own reward as he was soon presented with a veritable feast. Besides the liver treats and the homemade biscuit from Mrs.Reeve, there was also a small marrow bone.

Frances frowned.

"I don't remember putting that in there," she said, placing it on the square of grease paper from the biscuit. "Moss must have tucked it in. You're a lucky dog, you know. I'm not certain you deserve all of this devotion."

She smiled as Angus gobbled the liver treats and biscuit and set to work on the bone.

"I'm sure Mrs. Reeve would have expected you to savour that a bit more instead of hoovering it down without hardly chewing. I'll have to tell her you enjoyed every bite."

Pouring herself a cup of tea from the flask, Frances un-wrapped her own sandwich and leaned back against the wall.

Pure bliss, she thought. I won't let that horrid man spoil this perfect day.

She finished her sandwich and drank her tea, tucking the loaf of lemon drizzle back into the bag, pulling out her sketchbook as she did so.

I'll let Angus have his bone and then we'll start back for home, she thought. I'm too tired to bother trying to find Skelly.

She flipped through her sketchbook, by-passing the pages of repeating designs which, she admitted, were lovely in their own way, and settled on a blank page. She ran her finger over the ridge of paper that stuck up from where she'd torn out the faery drawing for Sophie's bookshop. Such a strange thing, she mused. She cast her mind back, with a bit of discomfort, to what Skelly had told her. Part of her had to admit that the idea of pure-hearted creativity being the force that cultivated magic in the world appealed to her; that artists were tasked to remind humanity of that magic and that would be what held the faery people here. It was a truly lovely concept; one of give and take, of perpetual, mutual benefit.

She shook her head.

A coincidence, that's all. And let's face it, she thought wryly, faeries were masters of mischief and could very easily glamour themselves to look any way they fancied. They didn't need people; they had enough magic of their own.

That's it, she decided. It was simply a trick to get her back to painting.

With a contented sigh at having sorted it all out, she settled in to sketch in the glorious autumn sunshine, her darling dog gnawing happily away beside her.

Chapter 11

The sound of Angus whining jolted Frances from her work. She'd been sketching out some of the botanical drawings for Uncle Phineas, all the while pondering whether she ought to make up some little notecards for the Thistlecrag Christmas market. Her mind had wandered to the possibilities as her pencil scratched across the paper.

She felt a sudden chill, as if the sun had passed behind a cloud. She looked at her watch, which appeared to have stopped again.

"Oh for heaven's sake!" she exclaimed, tapping the glass face. "I really must have this looked at," she glanced at the sky. "We must have been here for ages, Angus. I suppose we should get moving, it's going to get dark soon. Sorry, my boy, I got a bit absorbed in my work."

Angus wriggled. He was used to it.

Frances gave him a steady look.

"Right, I'm going to trust you for five minutes. Can you behave?"

She unclipped his lead.

"Go and stretch your legs for five while I pack up the things. Do *not* go out of my sight, do you hear me? We've had enough trauma to last several lifetimes by now."

Angus trotted off to investigate the hedge border, ears flopping, and stump tail held high.

"Are you sure that's a good idea?" said a familiar voice behind her.

Frances started, dropping her sketchbook and whirled around to see Skelly's creased face smiling at her.

"Skelly!" she breathed, her heart pounding. "You gave me such a fright! Why didn't Angus bark at you? Oh no, did he…"

She glanced quickly over, making sure the little dog was still there. Sure enough, there was his brown and white bottom sticking out from under a bramble.

Sighing a wobbling sigh, she turned back to the old man.

"We've had a bit of bother," she explained. "I'm especially terrified that he'll run off and get into trouble. I only just let him off his lead to stretch his legs while I pack up our things. And I promise you, he hasn't bothered any sheep while we've been out."

Skelly chuckled, laying a hand on her arm. The strange electric tingle buzzed up her arm causing her to pull back slightly.

He tilted his head and smiled again.

"I couldn't convince you to pause a wee while longer, could I? I fancy there's something in yon bag for me?"

He patted his overcoat pocket, "And I've a nice full flask of tea."

Frances glanced over at Angus and then back to Skelly.

"Put the wee creature back on his lead, then," he said, settling himself onto the wall. "We'll only be a minute or two. You wouldn't want to walk all that way back without a bit of extra sustenance, now would you?"

Frances smiled back at him. He really was a lovely old thing and a few more minutes wouldn't make much difference. She glanced up at the sky.

"Never you worry yourself," he said, pulling the flask out of his capacious pocket. "The light will hold."

They sat munching in companionable silence once again, Angus sitting quietly at Frances' feet, gazing hopefully at Skelly. In his experience, the old farmer was prone to dropping large crumbs.

"So, what happened then?" asked Skelly, after a while. They had finished their cake and were sipping steaming mugs of his delicious brew.

Frances shrugged, not really wanting to go into it. Neither she nor Angus looked very good in the telling and Angus' wayward ways had been the reason Skelly had come looking for her in the first place. She didn't want a lecture about keeping her dog on a leash.

"Oh, apparently we were trespassing on some fellow's land earlier. He came roaring up on one of those off-road motorbike things and upset Angus. Then he tried to hit him with his helmet when Angus wouldn't stop barking."

Skelly raised a bushy eyebrow.

Frances blushed and looked down at her mug.

"I might have given him a shove and knocked him and his motorbike over."

Both of Skelly's eyebrows disappeared under his tweed cap.

"I didn't mean to," explained Frances, hurriedly. "I just got frightened when I thought Angus was going to get hurt and I sort of just…lunged at him, I suppose."

She allowed herself a small smile.

"It was a bit funny, actually. He was all dressed in these fancy clothes. They weren't so clean and fancy when he got up."

Skelly threw back his head and roared with laughter. The sound reverberated around the clearing, like waves booming in a cave, thought Frances. It had the soothing effect of making her feel as if everything would be alright.

"Well done, then lass," said Skelly, when his laughter had subsided. "I'm sure you made a grand impression. Nasty bit of work, that, wanting to hurt a wee dog. Likely some toff from down south that uses this land like it were his personal playground." The old fellow sighed. "Same as it ever was."

He looked down at Angus who was pouring all of his heart's desire into his brown eyes. Skelly still held a piece of cake in one hand. He grinned and passed it down to Angus who took it very gently then gobbled it up in one bite.

"He was horrid," agreed Frances. A frown crossed her face. "But I'm a bit worried that there'll be consequences. You know, he seemed the sort that would complain to the authorities or something. I imagine I'll be getting a fine or something for having a dog at large or some such."

"Well, if that's all that comes of it, I reckon it was worth it to see him lying in the muck, aye?"

Frances shrugged, her face still creased with worry.

"I suppose."

"Never mind all that for now. What have you been scribbling in yon book then? Given any more thought to what I've told you?"

He regarded her sharply, his flinty green eyes narrowed. Frances felt herself flinch under his gaze. She placed a hand, protectively over her sketchbook. She wondered if she should tell him about the faery that she'd drawn and what she'd seen afterwards.

No, she decided, that would only encourage him and his

mad notions for what she ought to be doing. And besides, she reminded herself, she'd decided that it had simply been some otherworldly prank on the part of the two little faeries.

"I'm actually very busy right now. I have a second graphic design contract and I'm also doing some botanical illustrations for a friend's uncle's book. Then there's the Christmas market coming up and I was just thinking that I'll do up some notecards and journals and such."

She held her head high, giving him back the same considered look that he was giving her.

His eyes flicked to her sketchbook and then back to hers.

She felt her eyes prickle, she wanted very much to look away.

"Is that so, then?" he asked, his voice soft and faintly menacing. "Can I see?"

Frances looked down at her sketchbook, breaking his stare, her brain working furiously. What was it about this old man that unsettled her so? He seemed to shift from doddering old farmer to potential serial killer and back again in a matter of seconds.

She looked up, the doddering old farmer was back, smiling benignly, his gnarled hand tousling Angus' ears.

Frances sighed. If Angus thought he was alright, then he must be. Aren't animals supposed to have a good judge of character? Then again, she thought grimly, the little dog belonged to anyone who would give him a scrap of food.

She passed the book over.

"I don't see why not," she said, with a sigh. "There's nothing of any great consequence in there. It's just where I sort out what I plan on eventually doing."

Skelly took the book from her and opened it. He turned the

pages slowly, an unreadable expression on his face.

"The first half is mostly my design work," she explained, suddenly feeling like she wanted to justify the subject matter. "It's not really my personal style but it's what pays the bills."

Skelly nodded, wordless, as he kept turning.

Suddenly, a wolfish sort of smile spread across his wizened face. He stabbed a finger at the page he'd just turned to.

"What about this, then?" he asked.

It was the last page she'd been working on that day. She craned her neck, trying to see what he was looking at.

"Those are the kind of drawings I'm doing for Uncle Phineas," she began, "He wants them done in an old-fashioned style and I was trying to mimic the font they used to use…"

"No, lass," said the old sheep farmer, turning the book around and handing it back to her.

"I meant this."

Frances stared, disbelieving. Swallowing, she took the book from Skelly's hands.

As she'd said, there was a series of drawings - foxglove and hellebore, a few sprigs of cow parsley, a study of a branch of hawthorn. The several attempts at recreating a swirling copperplate wound around the illustrations. But what had caught Skelly's eye were the pixies. Not just idle sketches, but complete renditions. They were situated amongst the flowers, hiding in the foliage, strange, pointed faces peeking out from under leaves. They looked to be a part of the illustrations, as essential to them as the petals of each flower.

Frances blushed. She didn't remember doing those! It must have been when her mind was wandering around the Christmas market and what she might try and sell there.

"I honestly don't remember drawing those," she admitted,

closing her sketchbook gently and pulling the elastic band over it. "I was daydreaming about the market and…"

"That's what comes natural to you, then," said Skelly, a hint of triumph in his voice. "It's what your hand does when it's able to wander without your brain interfering."

Frances shrugged.

"Perhaps," she said, standing up. "But it's not anything earth-shattering so don't go and get yourself excited about it. Just because I doodle a few faeries in my sketchbook doesn't mean I'm going to go back to painting - them or anything else. I really don't know why you have this ridiculous interest in what I'm doing anyway."

She stared defiantly down at the old man, who remained seated on the wall, his walking stick leaning beside him.

He narrowed his eyes at her, then shifted his gaze down to his boots, fingers drumming on his knees.

"Have you a mind to listen to a story, lass?" he asked, finally.

* * *

Frances sat, dumbfounded, as Skelly had spoken.

It was something out of a children's tale — one of the old-fashioned kind where the stories were touched with a hint of delicious menace.

A lord of the sea — who, if he were to be believed, Skelly had once been — battles with an ancient forest god over possession of the sea-lord's (again, Skelly's) only daughter. She had, apparently, married the forest god but then changed her mind about having to live on land. Somewhere in there, the north wind, as a magical entity, had wreaked havoc at the behest of a vindictive sea queen, and all manner of treachery and betrayal ensued.

"A thousand years ago, then? Did I hear that bit right?"

Skelly grinned.

"Give or take, aye. Time moves at a different pace for us, you see. I would only be guessing. Could be four hundred, could be two."

Frances sighed. She had the beginnings of a headache forming behind her eyes.

"Why should I believe any of this? What's to say you're not some mad old man with delusions or dementia or god-knows-what other mental instabilities or impairments?"

"Well, nothing, I suppose," replied Skelly, turning away to look out at the sea. At some point in the telling, they'd started walking, Skelly leading the way. As he'd said, the light had held, although Frances was sure it ought to be twilight. Their walk had led them back to the place they'd gone the last time, to the boulder-strewn meadow with the sea on the horizon.

His gnarled fingers went to his throat, fishing inside his collar to pull out a long, leather, thong. A green-blue stone wrapped in wire hung from the end of it.

"Do ye know what this is, lass?"

Frances leaned closer.

"Looks like a bit of sea-glass,"

"Aye, that's what it looks like, true," replied Skelly. "But back when I was, well, different than I am now…"

"When you were a lord of the sea, you mean?" interjected Frances, immediately despising herself when she saw the look of pain cross the old man's face.

"Aye, lass. 'Tis hard to grapple with, I know. But I wouldn't be telling you the tale if you weren't already halfway there to believing me."

172

Frances looked down at her hands. She was twisting Angus' leash around her fingers until it cut off the circulation. She nodded. He was right. She did believe him. She'd finally allowed herself to take in all of the strangeness that seemed to come with every exchange she had with the old farmer. Moss had tried to tell her there was something more to him, but her logical brain had interfered in places where she normally did not allow it to tread.

"I know," she whispered. "That's what frightens me the most - that I believe you."

Skelly reached across and squeezed her wrist. The rippling warmth seeped up her arm.

Skelly chuckled at her expression.

"It's all right, lass. It'll not harm you — just the touch of the fae, you see. It's how you'll have a knowing of who we are. As long as it's warm you're feeling, and not a biting chill, you're in safe hands."

Frances smiled a watery smile.

"Good lass," he said, patting her arm. "That's more like it."

Frances took a deep breath, her hand steadying herself on the top of Angus' head.

"So, is this what are you now?" she asked, gesturing at his tweed cap and battered overcoat. "You aren't very impressive, I have to say."

She smiled at him, trying to make light of the situation. The surreal nature of what she was being told was one-part delight at the sheer magic of it all and several parts terror at the fact she was sitting in a clearing, obviously not of her own reality, with a self-professed lord of Faery.

Skelly's eyes were gentle. He leaned back, stretched and stood up. In a shimmering instant, gone was the diminutive, elderly sheep-farmer who had rapped on her door and sat sipping tea in her studio. Instead, he stood straight and tall; he had an immense, quiet, strength and an almost regal bearing. The walking stick, which Frances had long since realized definitely was not a mobility aid, remained propped against the stone.

Frances grinned.

"You were telling me about the sea-glass," she prompted.

"Aye, I was," he said, turning toward the sea. He stood staring at the improbable view for some minutes.

"In our way of things," he said, turning back to look at Frances, "there aren't many rules, as you may already know."

Frances grimaced. That certainly wasn't a revelation.

"But the ones you have, seem to serve you well," she said, "'Just enough to ward off chaos', or so Moss tells me."

Skelly reached for the piece of sea glass and held it up to Frances.

"This," he said, "is the result of greed, arrogance and selfish pride. And my punishment for breaking a fundamental law of my people was being cast from my home, cut off from the life I had known for a hundred, hundred years, and more again. It's the very reason that I'm sat here, trying to convince a mortal lass to paint pictures of my kin so they don't vanish from the world before I can find my way back. If you knew, I've been waiting so long to find the likes of you…"

His voice broke, then, and his eyes filled with tears. He'd shrunk, become an old man again, frail-looking and tired.

Frances reached across and grasped his hands in her own, her heart breaking for him. She was instantly overcome with the urge to do anything in her power to help him.

"It's all right, Skelly. I believe you. I promise, whatever it is that I can do to help, I will."

* * *

They walked back to the main path in relative silence. Frances was lost in thought, mulling over all that she'd been told. She kept darting surreptitious glances over at Skelly, in the hope of catching him doing... what, she had no idea. Morphing into something else? Showing his true form? Because by now, she knew that what she was seeing in front of her was purely a glamour. What did a faery of the sea look like anyway? She couldn't remember much about water faeries, other than the usual sprites and naiads that frequented streams and ponds. She hadn't been to a larger body of water in what seemed like forever. Was it like fish, did saltwater produce different varieties? Were they like the ones she'd seen in her dreams? She thought she'd made them up. Her mind whirled.

"I'll leave you here, then lass," said Skelly, as they came over the last rise to reach the crossroads that led either to the village or back towards the studio. As he'd promised, the light had held, and it was no darker than it would have been if Frances had left her picnic spot at the time she'd intended. More faery magic, she mused. Moss was going to be livid.

"Thank you," she said, shifting her backpack on her shoulders. She glanced at him, somewhat shy, from behind the fringe of her hair. "For trusting me with your story. That's no small thing, I know."

Skelly nodded, a little stiffly. He'd been very reticent after his emotional outburst. A little embarrassed, thought Frances. He probably didn't mean to be quite so emotional. Her whole self had warmed to him then, sympathy and perhaps a little pity, for his state of exile.

"Aye, well," he replied. "Like I said, you were halfway to believing me all along. It seemed only right to give you the rest."

Just then, Angus barked and lunged at his leash towards the hedge. There was a rustle of leaves and snapping of twigs as something moved about.

Frances turned to look.

"Settle down, silly boy," she said. "It might just be a badger or something. Not every noise in the shrubbery needs to be a faery! Isn't that right, Skelly?"

She turned back to him, a smile on her face, only to see an empty laneway.

The laugh died on her lips and she felt her shoulders sag.

"Oh," she said, frowning. "'Bye then."

She gave Angus' leash a little tug, trying to quell the odd feeling of desolation that had suddenly crept up. It's been a long and upsetting day, she told herself. I have a lot to sort out.

Chapter 12

"That was absolutely delicious, Moss," said Frances, spooning in the last mouthful of blackberry crumble and custard. "Whenever did you find the time to go out and collect blackberries? I was meaning to go out in the next few days, I've seen some great places."

Frances kept up a steady stream of chatter, in direct opposition to Moss' sullen silence. She'd told him about her day and his expression got stonier and stonier from the confrontation with the motorcycle man right through to her conversation with Skelly when his face had turned an alarming shade of red and his lips pressed so tightly together, they'd vanished into his face.

"So, you were right," she'd said, imagining he'd be thrilled to gloat over it. "He *is* a faery and he most certainly must have some power if he can sustain that sort of glamour, not to mention whatever trickery he does with time and location. Do you know we ended up by the sea again? No wonder I got confused the first time. Of course, we're absolutely nowhere in view of the actual sea."

Moss had simply grunted and dished out the crumble and custard with unnecessary force. Frances ignored him. Moss' relationship with his people seemed to be a complicated affair and she never knew when he was just being a snob. Perhaps there was a thing about water faeries being lesser beings or some such prejudice.

"So, I said I'd help him," said Frances, turning on the taps to wash the dishes. The sound of the water running into the sink partially drowned out the shriek that finally erupted from Moss' tightly clenched lips. But it was loud enough to send Angus skittering out from under the table to dive onto the sofa and burrow under a cushion.

Frances let the sink fill and then turned off the taps, smoothing her face into a state of bland interest. The shriek had set her hair on end, but she wasn't going to let Moss know that.

"Something bothering you, Moss?" she inquired, raising an eyebrow.

"Bothering me?" he sputtered, his face scarlet. His clenched fists were set firmly on his hips and he leaned forward, staring into Frances face.

"Are you quite mad?" he asked. "What have I drilled into your thick skull since just about the day we met? What do we never, ever do in the company of faery folk? Especially, Pan forfend, one of the Old Ones?"

Frances frowned.

"You weren't listening, Moss," she said. "He's not actually old, that's just his glamour."

"Idiot!" exploded Moss, kicking a spoon across the counter. It clattered into the plates that were stacked beside the sink.

"That's Old with a capital O," he explained, as if to a simpleton. "Which doesn't always equate with actual chronology," he frowned down at the counter, then waved a hand. "Although it usually does, but that's beside the point."

"Well what *is* your point exactly?" said Frances, exasperated. "I haven't broken any of your rules."

"You agreed to help him!" shouted Moss. "That's as good as a promise, a bargain, a *deal!*"

Frances paled. Mild panic rushed up to her scalp in a wave of prickling adrenalin. Had she struck a bargain? Not really. There weren't any actual terms. Surely that didn't count?'

She said so to Moss who gave her one of his most withering stares. He folded his arms.

"Now, what else have I told you about dealing with faeries?"

Frances sagged against the counter, soapy water dripping from her fingers onto the flagstone floor.

"That they are masters of linguistic trickery and will bend your words to suit their needs," she repeated, having known this since ever she read her first proper faery story as a small child.

She clasped her wet hands against her head, groaning.

"Oh Moss, what have I done? It was all so innocent. He was just this sad old man who wanted help to find his way home."

Moss snorted.

"Good grief! You fell for that one? Honestly, I don't know. I thought you were an intelligent person, I really did. But that's the oldest and simplest ruse in faery lore. I really don't believe you could have been so..."

He paused for a moment, regarding Frances who still leaned against the counter, but was now staring blankly in the direction of the locked cupboard at the back of the studio. In an instant, his stance softened, and his face creased into a gentle smile as his eyes filled with tears. He cleared his throat and walked over to Frances, placing a hand on her arm.

"Never mind all that," he said, his voice soft and soothing.

"I'm sure it's nothing we can't sort out together, right?"

France smiled then, the bleak horror of what she might have done leaving her face. Because, just as Skelly had told her, a small frisson of warmth lay under her little friend's touch.

* * *

Frances slept fitfully, tossing uncomfortably on the narrow cot. She was troubled with strange dreams, visions of wild oceans and violent storms battering a small, rocky island. Fishing boats were tossed in the air and rain came down in drenching sheets. At some point, there were huge horses rising out of the waves, razor-sharp teeth bared in vicious, gaping mouths.

She awoke, trembling, from one of the more distressing dreams, one of a young woman being carried into the sea by one of the horrible horses as a group of people stood around and drank tea and ate lemon drizzle cake.

It was still dark when she got out of bed, padding to the kitchenette to put on the kettle. The sun was a faint orange streak just above the horizon, setting the hedge into dark silhouette as she stared out of the window. How was it that even the ordinary things suddenly weren't quite so ordinary anymore? It was as if time had splintered - to the time when none of this was real, and then the time after everything was changed. Ah, she remonstrated herself, I'm being far too dramatic. All he wants me to do is draw faeries. Surely that's not a bad thing.

The sound of the bread bin pulled her away from her internal argument. Moss emerged, his long, tasseled night cap askew. He wore a striped nightgown and felt slippers. Frances smiled, filled with affection for her friend.

"Sorry if I woke you," she said, her voice low. "I had a rotten night so figured I might as well just get up and get on with the day."

"Dreams?" asked Moss, blinking sleepily.

Frances nodded and he sighed.

"And so it begins," he said, ominously. He caught the look on her face and waved a hand, dismissive.

"Parlour tricks," he said, his tone light. "A sign of a lazy faery. Your best defense against that sort of low-brow enchantment is to simply do as you are now. Just get on with the day! Now, if you give me a quick minute, I'll get the porridge on."

After breakfast was tidied away and Angus had been taken for a quick walk up the lane and back, Frances decided that Moss' advice was ultimately the best. She was simply going to get on with her daily life and not worry herself over the strange turn of events. After all, it could all be more faery trickery meant to unsettle and alarm her more than anything else. Firming that up in her mind, she settled into a morning of solid productive work.

She was deeply engrossed in rearranging some trapezoids on her computer screen, contemplating adding a flourish of tiny triangles between the spaces when the shrilling of her phone jarred her concentration.

Swearing softly under her breath she crossed over to the back of the studio, rummaging under a stack of watercolour paper to retrieve and answer it.

"Morning, Frances!" came Sophie's voice down the crackling line. "Sorry to bother you so early but I'm on my way out and couldn't wait to tell you the exciting news!"

"Hi Soph," replied Frances, rubbing a hand over the back of her neck which had become stiff with sitting for so long. "No need to apologize, I've been up for ages and working. I need the break. What's up?"

"Melinda told me you were in yesterday, so you know I had to go into the city,"

Frances offered up a sympathetic grunt.

"I know, the stuff of nightmares," continued Sophie, her voice rising with enthusiasm, "but that's not the exciting bit. Do you remember Caitlin, that girl who used to run the art walks on Thursdays?"

Frances cast her mind back; she had a vague recollection of a pink and blue-haired girl who went around badgering people to set up mini-displays of their work on the last Thursday of every month. She was very persistent, and the walks were always well-attended and were great publicity for the students and the college itself.

"Sure, I remember."

"Well, I bumped into her in the coffee shop on campus - I was feeling like I needed an infusion of the old days after the most horrendous squabble I had with Stuart over my accounts, but never mind that…"

Frances frowned, whenever Sophie glossed over something to do with Stuart it usually meant she *should* be talking about it.

"…we got to catching up because she knows absolutely everyone and what they're doing, I imagine she should be writing a Where Are They Now? column for the alumni newsletter. Anyway! I digress! Wait 'til you hear this, you're going to be as thrilled as I am…"

Sophie was breathless with excitement and it was contagious. Frances felt the dull weight she hadn't realized was hanging over her beginning to lift.

"…had heard through some fellow I don't remember, that our very own Stephan not only applied for the National College of Art and Design Fellowship, but he got it! Can you imagine? Isn't that the most amazing thing? I literally squealed when she told me."

Frances felt a sharp twist in her stomach and a rush of something of which she was immediately ashamed. Envy, perhaps? Disappointment? Once upon a time it had been her plan to apply for that Fellowship. It was the logical next step in her career after her gallery opening. She'd had elaborate visions of spending a year in Ireland, soaking up all of the faery activity and rendering it on canvas. She still had the application packet stuffed into one of her boxes.

"Oh, Sophie," she said, pulling herself together with a sharp inner reprimand, "That's absolutely wonderful news. Stephan absolutely deserves it."

She meant it. It was wonderful news to know that one of her classmates, and a lovely, big-hearted, not to mention very talented, person at that, was achieving such great things. If only she didn't have that nagging, persistent and thoroughly embarrassing thought that it ought to have been her.

"He really does," said Sophie, "He's worked so hard at it, you know? Even when his advisor told him he should go in a different direction, he stuck with it. I bet he wants to march right up to that snooty cow and wave his Letter of Offer right in her pinchy face!"

Frances managed a small chuckle. She remembered that woman; she was an ancient creature, a contemporary of the old Masters, it was jokingly rumoured, who insisted the students conform to outdated practices. She would have had them all painting biblical scenes in oils had it been up to her.

183

It had been discussed at great lengths in the coffee shop and student lounges as to why she was actually still employed. General consensus had it that it was easier for the college to wait for her to either die or retire than try to fire her, so long had she been ensconced in the faculty.

"I think the old bird fancied him," said Frances, trying to claw her way back to good humour. "She seemed to always be wanting him to make appointments with her."

Sophie's bubbling laugh echoed down the phone, lifting Frances further out of her funk.

"Oh, Frances! That's awful!"

Frances laughed back at her.

"I know, isn't it? Anyway, that's brilliant. I'm really glad to hear it. It couldn't have happened to a truly more deserving person."

And Stephan *was* deserving, she thought to herself after hanging up the phone. He'd stuck to his artistic values and believed in his work.

"Not like some people I know," she muttered aloud, as she walked back to her workstation.

"Talking to yourself again?" asked Moss as he came through the door. He'd been off picking sloes after Frances had casually mentioned making some sloe gin for holiday gifts. He seems to prefer being outdoors more, these days, thought Frances. Not unsurprising, she added in her mind, with a brief, irritated look around at the studio.

Frances sighed and sat down heavily into her chair. She told Moss about her conversation with Sophie.

"I remember Stephan," said Moss dragging the sack of sloes across the floor. "Tall, skinny fellow with big glasses? Always wore those odd t-shirts with cartoon cats on them. He used to bring Russian vodka and foreign desserts to your parties."

"That's him," said Frances, smiling at the memory. She and Sophie had hosted lots of parties in their shared flat over the years, although they were more Sophie's doing than hers. Even back then she'd showed her talent for gathering people together and making them feel welcome.

She sighed.

"It seems like everyone is doing their best work," she said, a trace of bitterness in her voice.

Moss regarded her with a raised eyebrow as he leaned against the counter, a faint sheen of perspiration on his brow.

"Speaking of parties," he said, "the theme of today's is pity, is it?"

Frances scowled, refusing to meet his eye.

"Ha, ha," she said, sticking out her tongue.

When she got no response, she dared a look in his direction. What she saw made her forget her own silly troubles.

"Moss!" she cried, scraping back her chair and dashing over to him. Angus was already there, sniffing and nudging at the little brownie with his nose.

"Get that horrid beast away from me," mumbled Moss, from where he'd slid down onto the floor. His skin was a frightening shade of grey, dark shadows circling his eyes making them look sunken. His breathing was laboured and his hair lay in lank strands, plastered against his head with perspiration.

"What's wrong?" said Frances, reaching out to take his hand. It was cold and clammy. "You're ill. You never should've gone out to get those sloes! Why didn't you say something?"

She took the little sack of sloes and put them onto the counter, before kneeling back down beside him.

"I was perfectly fine when I went out," he grumbled, struggling to stand. The colour was coming back to his face and his breathing steadied, but he leaned wearily against the counter. "I've just been having these spells lately, nothing to worry about. It will pass. If you could be so kind as to help me up, I'll go and lie down for an hour."

Frances lifted him up, being careful to do so in a way that didn't make him feel, as he'd once remonstrated her, like a child's toy or a wayward puppy.

"Let me make you a cup of tea," she said, worriedly. "What about something to eat? It's been hours since breakfast."

Moss waved a feeble hand, shuffling towards the bread bin.

"Stop your fussing, I'm fine. I just need a rest. Slaving away trying to keep this hovel in livable fashion is rather a lot of work, you know."

Frances felt a stab of guilt at the same time as a jolt of relief. He was clearly feeling better already.

As Moss disappeared into the bread bin, Frances made a decision.

She glanced down at Angus who was still snuffling around the area where Moss had collapsed, whining softly.

"Fancy a walk into the village?" she asked him, already knowing the answer before he started capering around at her feet, Moss forgotten.

* * *

"This is what we're going to do," she explained as they set off down the lane. "First, we're going to the post office. I'm convinced that our money will be there today. Also, we'll need a stamp. Then to the bank to make our payment. Then a quick trip to Sophie's to buy one of those lovely cards that

Mrs. Robinson makes, the ones with the pressed wildflowers,"

She glanced down at Angus who was trotting along beside her, nose to the ground but with one ear cocked back to listen.

"Right, yes. We won't stay long, just long enough to write out the card and get Stephan's address. I'm sure Sophie must have it. She's organized like that."

Angus wuffed.

"Okay, it would be rude for me to not have a cup of tea and you really ought to have a biscuit…"

"You really are in the habit, then, of talking to yourself."

Frances let out a small shriek.

"Angus!" she said, crossly. "What sort of dog are you if you don't warn me when there's people lurking about in the bushes?"

Angus simply wagged his stump of tail and trotted over to greet Skelly.

The old man emerged from the other side of the hedge, squeezing between the brambles as if they weren't getting snagged on his cap and overcoat. Which, as Frances observed with a mix of wonder and irritation, they weren't.

"Hello," she said, stiff and unsure.

"And a good day to you, lass," said Skelly, nodding his head in what might be construed as a sort of bow.

Frances knotted her fingers in Angus' leash.

"Are you off rambling again?" he asked, gesturing to her backpack. "Don't you have work to do?"

Frances stiffened, scowling.

"I'm not off rambling, actually," she said, "We're going into the village to pick up a payment and to send a card of congratulations to a friend. And anyway, I've been up since before the crack of dawn working."

She glared at Skelly, inviting him to admit he'd been somehow responsible for her bad dreams.

He merely smiled, bright green eyes disappearing into the seams of his weathered skin.

"Ah," he said. "An early bird are you then?"

"Not usually," huffed Frances. "I didn't sleep very well."

Still nothing.

"Mebbe you need a cup of hot milk before bed," he said, helpfully. "Yon brownie of yours probably makes a lovely mug of that. He could add a pinch of something or other, to help it work. Nothing worse than a bad night, is there? Dreams bothering you, was it?"

Curbing a sharp retort, Frances gave Angus' leash a slight tug.

"Come on, my boy." she said to the little dog, who seemed reluctant to leave the company of someone who often had large crumbs of delicious things on hand.

"We haven't got time to stand around chatting today," she called over her shoulder. "Lots to do and I must get back to work, as you say."

She resisted the urge to look back, keeping her eyes firmly fixed on the lane. They were just about at the crossroads leading to the village. Angus trailed behind her and she tugged his lead again, willing him to walk faster.

"How is he, then?" called Skelly, his voice clear and loud, almost as if he was still standing next to her. "Your brownie. Is he alright?"

Frances felt cold fingers of dread clutch at her heart. Her scalp prickled and she felt a sudden rise of tears in her throat.

"No," she whispered, barely moving her lips. "This is absolutely not happening."

188

* * *

They were all of the way to the post office before Frances had shaken off the feeling of unquiet dread that had risen in the wake of Skelly's parting question. The ramifications were too horrible to entertain. Possibly even more horrid than the notion of Moss being in some sort of danger, was the hint of threat in Skelly's tone, as if he might be in some way responsible.

"But that can't possibly be," she'd said to Angus, her voice quavering slightly. "He wants to keep his people in the world, not help them out of it. I'm just letting this whole giant heap of nonsense get into my head."

They'd walked on, Frances resolving to let the peace of the countryside ease the tension of the exchange. It didn't have its usual effect, though, there were dark clouds threatening rain and she hurried more, her shoulders hunched and tense in the damp, chilled air.

* * *

"Got what you were hoping for then, lass?" asked Mrs. Reeve, smiling at the expression on Frances' face as she handed over the long white envelope.

Frances felt her entire body sag with relief. It was from the design company. and felt distinctly cheque-like through the envelope. Her face cracked into a wide, grin.

"Yes, finally! Thank you. This should keep the wolves from the door," she glanced down at Angus who was sitting tidily, an expectant look on his whiskery face directed towards Mrs. Reeve. "And biscuits in the dog bowl," added Frances, suddenly feeling magnanimous. The knowledge of being able to pay a large lump of her loan off filled her with ridiculous amounts of delight. I am getting boring, she thought.

"Oh, and a stamp, please," she said, passing over the money. "I have to send a card to a friend who's had some very good news."

"Well that's a nice change, isn't it? Better to send one when things are grand, instead of waiting until someone dies or some such tragedy," nodded Mrs. Reeve, sagely, tearing a stamp off the large roll.

* * *

Frances emerged from the bank with less joy than she'd gone in with.

Upon opening the envelope, she discovered that it was quite a bit less than she'd imagined it would be. Crestfallen, she made what turned out to be only slightly more than the minimum payment on her loan, keeping enough back for her and Moss and Angus to live on until the next payment was due.

"Never mind," she said, retrieving Angus from where he was tied to a lamp post. "At least I've got Uncle Phineas' deposit in case of emergency and they've signed me on for another contract. But I don't think I'll have enough money spare to buy the materials to make the cards for the Christmas market."

In low spirits, the two made their way to Sophie's cafe. The windows were steamed up, promising warmth and sanctuary. The rain had started, a light drizzle but enough to make things miserable and it was a welcome thing indeed to feel the rush of warm air carrying the smell of baked goods and hot tea as she opened the door.

"Hello, Melinda," said Frances, greeting the young woman as she got herself seated in a table by the window. She avoided the Creative Corner, knowing she really ought to get back to the studio and get on with her work. The sooner she got those new designs finished, the sooner she'd get paid again. She sighed, trying not to let herself spiral into money worries.

"Hi Frances," said Melinda, quietly cheerful. "And you too, Angus, lovely boy." She stooped to tousle the ecstatic Angus. In his experience, Melinda was another one of those people who often kept delicious morsels about their person.

"What will you have, this fine drippy day?"

"Just a quick cup of tea, please. And maybe a jam scone, if you've got any." Frances smiled at Melinda, determined not to add to the gloominess of the day. The weather had that covered.

Melinda nodded, smiling.

"Blackberry or apple?" she asked, her eyes twinkling. "We've got both. Or you could just eat it plain of course, no jam."

"Ha!" retorted Frances. "And that would be a crime against scones. Not to mention an affront to Sophie's jam-making skills."

The two women laughed, both knowing how proud Sophie was of her latest acquisitions. She had begged and pleaded with the local WI ladies to sell the cafe a selection of their jams and she'd finally worn them down.

"And for Sir Angus?" inquired Melinda, pulling herself up straight and adopting a stuffy butler manner.

Frances looked down at the little dog, who was vibrating with hope. He glanced, his heart in his eyes, between Melinda and his mistress.

"Oh, a nice sausage roll, would suffice I think,"

"Indeed," replied Melinda with a small bow and a wink and disappeared in the direction of the kitchen.

"You stay here," said Frances, wrapping Angus' lead around the table leg. "I'm just going over there to pick out a card."

Angus settled down with a contented sigh, visions of sausage rolls no doubt dancing in his head.

Frances and Melinda met back at the table, Frances with a card in hand, Melinda with a tray of tea and goodies.

"I know you said you only wanted a cup," said Melinda, lifting a classic Brown Betty and two mugs off the tray. "But Sophie's just come down and she saw that you were here."

Frances felt her mood lift again. Any chance to chat with Sophie always managed to put her perspective in order.

"Ooh! Lovely!"

She helped Melinda take the assorted tea-and-scone eating paraphernalia off the tray then watched as Melinda made a large fuss of presenting Angus with his sausage roll.

It was gone in an instant.

Melinda shook her head.

"If Gary had seen that, he'd have gone mad," she said, laughing. "I'm fairly sure he prefers his food to be savoured."

"Or at least chewed," added Frances, looking down at Angus who was snuffling on the floor in search of wayward crumbs.

"Right, here she comes," said Melinda, looking up. She untied her apron and folded it carefully. "I'll see you both later, I'm off to my class."

"Thanks, Melinda. Enjoying your studies, are you?"

Melinda had heard from the library sciences program and not only had she been offered a place, she'd been invited into a special class that was held before her official start.

Melinda's eyes sparkled.

"Oh, am I? It's like a bit of heaven, really. I can't quite believe that I'm actually going to uni. I never thought the day would come, I really didn't. It's all thanks to Sophie, oh, and Stuart of course. He's the one that sorted out the grant paperwork, after all. Anyway, I really must dash. I've got to get the twelve o'clock bus."

Frances smiled at her disappearing form, marveling at the change that had come over her. The shy, mousy young girl who could barely utter a sentence without stammering and blushing had transformed into a confident young woman, pursuing her dreams of being a librarian. Such was the influence of Sophie.

"Ah, I was just singing your praises," she said as Sophie approached. "In my head," she added, to Sophie's inquiring look.

"Well, better than calling me rude names out loud, I suppose," said Sophie, grinning. She leaned over to kiss Frances on the cheek. A cloud of patchouli wafted over Frances, immediately filling her with a sense of calm nostalgia.

"True enough. Shall I be mother?"

"Go on, then"

Sophie pulled out a chair as Frances poured the tea.

"Hallo, Angus," she cooed, leaning down to take his face in her hands. "I hear you had a sausage roll. Is that all your mean mistress gave you? Poor wee doggie must be starving."

Sophie made an exaggerated fuss of Angus, who absorbed it like the attention-starved creature that he most certainly wasn't.

Straightening up, she took up the large mug of tea and cradled it in her hands, closing her eyes briefly.

Frances studied her friend. While nothing was outwardly evident, other than perhaps a trace of shadow under her eyes, she could see that Sophie was troubled.

"Anything wrong?" she asked, watching her friend over the rim of her mug. "You look tired."

Sophie sighed a heavy sigh, then took a sip of her scalding tea.

"Ah, that's lovely, that. If I do say so myself."

Frances smiled, waiting.

Sophie continued to avoid her eyes and instead, spooned jam onto a scone and passed it over.

Still Frances waited.

Eventually, Sophie raised her eyes.

"Oh, alright!" she said, sounding as cross as she ever could, which wasn't very. "Stuart and I have been rowing again. It's becoming far too regular a thing and I don't like it. You know I don't like bad feeling."

Her lower lip trembled, and she took up one of the cloth napkins and began to wind and unwind it into a tight funnel shape.

Frances reached over and put a hand on Sophie's, giving it a squeeze.

"Soph," she said. "It's perfectly okay to have disagreements, you know. You don't have to agree on everything. Besides, you have to remember, you're very opposite in a lot of ways, that's what makes you such a great team. But it also means you're going to butt heads on certain things."

Sophie nodded, her eyes filling. She used the screwed-up napkin to dab at the tears that threatened to overflow.

"I know, of course you're right. I suppose it's just because he's so insistent on all the financial things being exactly so.

It's never been my strong suit, as you know."

Frances smiled, wryly then leaned over and whispered,

"Comes from being born into the idle rich, I suppose."

Sophie's features broke into a teary smile. The idle rich joke was one they'd shared since the very first day they'd met at college. Sophie had never been reticent about sharing the circumstances of her upbringing. Her family was one of very old money and title and she had always been forthcoming about that, which was not something that had always been well-received in an atmosphere of struggling artists and counter-cultural ideologies. But she'd more than overcome that by simply being herself - generous and big-hearted, enthusiastic and utterly unselfish.

"I know," she said, "it's my questionable heritage coming back to bite me in the backside."

"Exactly! And Stuart had the opposite experience growing up, plus he's an accountant so of course he's going to be panicked by your casual attitude to things like paying taxes and tracking expenses.

Sophie sighed again, taking another swig of tea.

"You're right, as always. How on earth did you get so wise?"

Frances grimaced, trying not to think of the myriad of questionable decisions she'd made, none of which could be blamed on her pedigree.

She shrugged.

"It comes naturally."

They chatted for a few minutes more, gobbling jammy scones and drinking tea. Sophie admired Frances' choice of card and, just as had been suspected, was able to procure Stephan's address.

"I'm really happy for him," Frances said, sealing the envelope and sticking the stamp in place. "I have to admit, I was a bit envious when I first heard…well, let's face it, I'm still a bit envious, but I realize I couldn't have asked for a nicer, more hard-working person to get the Fellowship."

Sophie nodded, sweeping crumbs off the table into her cupped hand and dropping them surreptitiously to the floor in front of Angus. Frances pretended not to see.

"I agree. He was the only one of us that never veered off track, wasn't he? He never once questioned what it was that he wanted to do. Even when that awful harpy of a supervisor gave him such a terrible time."

Frances felt a stab of regret, mixed with a touch of shame. Sophie certainly didn't intend it, but all Frances could think about was how far she'd veered from her own path. And not in a natural, artistic evolution sort of way.

"I really envy people who've always known what they wanted to do, like from being six years old," Sophie continued. "I think I wanted to be seventeen different things before breakfast every day of my life."

Frances gave a small smile, nodding. She tried to push down the memory of how it felt to see her ideal world crashing down around her in the wake of the gallery disaster. She'd never felt so unmoored in all her life. She *had* known, from being six years old, what she wanted to do with her life. And now, here she was, scrambling to salvage what was left of those dreams, trying to turn them into something else, rather than give up entirely. She turned Stephan's card around in her hands, musing over the events of her morning. The exchange with Skelly still lurked unsettlingly in the back of her mind.

"Soph?" she said, suddenly seized by an impulse. "Do you have some sort of connection whereby I can get a smallish amount of paper goods at wholesale prices?"

Sophie raised an eyebrow, her mouth in an 'oh' of surprise.

"Well, that's an odd and random sort of question!" She said, smiling. "What do you have in mind?"

Chapter 13

Frances and Angus made their dreary way home through the drizzle. The countryside was transformed; the grey chill of winter threatening to encroach upon on the fiery, abundant delights of autumn. When did that happen, thought Frances, miserably? I feel like I didn't get a chance to enjoy it enough.

"Ugh," she said aloud to Angus. "It's going to be winter before we know it."

Angus was unbothered by the weather. He trotted along with his usual enthusiasm, ears and nose attentive to possible activity in the bordering hedge. The faery folk had been quiet of late, noted France. Perhaps they, too, were retreating to warmer places, tucking themselves in beside their hearths, glasses of hot mulled cider clutched in their little hands.

She shook her head. Romanticizing the little menaces was never a wise idea.

Finally, the roof of the studio came into view above the hedge. Frances sighed, thoroughly fed-up but filled with a small tingle of delight at the thought of a hot mug of tea and a sit by the little electric log fire. It certainly wasn't the stuff of a Country Living spread but in comparison to the damp, grey day, it was pure heaven.

Just then, a low growl rumbled from Angus' throat.

Frances glanced at him, more surprise than alarm. It wasn't his usual 'there's a faery creature pulling my ears' sort of growl. This one he reserved for humans. His general good nature, however, meant he didn't use it often.

She looked up and around, suddenly anxious and very aware that she was in a rather isolated area with only a small dog for protection. She gripped his lead tightly and pushed back her shoulders.

"Hello?" she called, cringing at the wobble in her voice. "Is anybody there?"

There was no answer, but Angus maintained his warning grumble.

They turned up the lane and headed for the studio. The windows were dark, which were odd, she thought. On such a gloomy day, Moss would insist upon turning on all available lights to dispel the gloom. Perhaps he'd been aware of the intruder, thought Frances, and was trying to pretend there wasn't anyone home. Clever. That would also explain why she couldn't smell the faux woodsmoke.

Angus lunged at the end of his leash, startling her out of her thoughts. He barked, a high-pitched sound that Frances was convinced was meant to simply annoy any potential threats into giving up and going away in order to avoid having to listen to it.

"Hush," she said, glancing around.

Just then, a figure emerged from behind the studio. Further examination revealed it to be a woman, dressed in an oilskin. She carried a clipboard in one hand and a mobile phone in the other. On seeing Frances, her face formed itself into a scowl.

"There you are," she said, her tone clipped.

Frances wracked her brain, wondering if she'd had an appointment she'd forgotten about. That was certainly suggested by the woman's tone.

Frances pasted a smile on her face, admonished Angus to stop barking and walked forwards to greet her.

"Can I help you?" she asked, approaching the woman.

She was of medium height, her steel-grey hair matched her eyes and her expression was one of supreme irritation. The voluminous oilskin disguised her clothing and figure, but a pair of large green wellies poked out from under its length. She was certainly dressed for a rainy day in the country. Assuming she was on a grouse shoot.

"Are you the lessee here?" asked the woman, sharply. She consulted her clipboard. "Frances Mary Blackburn, is it?"

She looked up, piercing Frances with an inquisitor's look.

MI5?

The thought flashed briefly across Frances' mind, a hysterical giggle threatening on her lips. She imagined herself telling Sophie the story at a later date, both of them laughing into their wine glasses over the absolute ridiculousness of this entire exchange.

Frances got herself together and took a deep breath. She wouldn't be intimidated.

"And who, may I ask, is inquiring?"

The woman scowled, her eyes disappearing under her heavy brows. She passed her phone to her clipboard hand and rummaged in the depths of her oilskin, producing a plastic identification badge on the end of a black lanyard.

"Maureen Smith," she said, her tone grim. "I'm with the council. Housing by-laws."

She glared at Frances her expression one-part accusing, one

part questioning. As if she was trying to read Frances' reaction to her revelation.

Frances swallowed; a faint jolt of panic shot up from her belly. Deep breaths, she coached herself. Don't let her see that you're worried.

"Nice to meet you, Ms. Smith," she replied, smiling. "Not a very nice day to be out and about, is it?"

"It is what it is," said Maureen, her tone belying that of a longtime martyr. "I have a job to do and the weather conditions are of no consequence."

"So I see," said Frances, gesturing towards the vast oilskin. "You're certainly dressed for it."

"Could you please answer my question, Miss?"

"Question? Oh, yes. Yes, I am the lessee and my name is definitely Frances Blackburn. Is there some sort of problem? I paid four months in advance, so I'm fairly sure I'm up to date with my lease."

"Your financial arrangements are not my concern," said Maureen, an air of superior disdain on her face. "I'm here because we've had a complaint."

Frances felt her stomach flip. She glanced down at Angus who was quivering against her legs. His ears were back and his tail clamped tightly. A whining growl emerged in time with each shiver.

"Oh?" she said, her tone light but calm and polite. "I'm sorry to hear that. What was the nature of the complaint?"

Maureen Smith made a point of studying her paperwork. Her clipboard came with a handy plastic sheet covering the top of the paper. Even her clipboard had a raincoat, Frances imagined herself telling Sophie. She pinched her own arm in an effort to stop that train of hysteria. She concentrated on keeping her breathing steady, 'breathing the square' as she'd been taught by a friend who suffered from anxiety attacks.

Maureen looked up from her paperwork, narrowing her eyes.

"I'll need to see inside," she said, curtly. "There's a question that these premises are being used counter to the conditions of the lease."

When Frances stared in blank confusion, she sighed and added.

"This building is not zoned for habitation."

Frances fumbled with the latch; her cold hands being very uncooperative. The nervous tremble certainly didn't do anything to help but she maintained a tone of relaxed cheeriness.

"I'm a working artist," she explained to the dour-face woman, as they stood in the middle of the studio. There was no sign of Moss and for once, she was grateful that he hadn't left the studio bright and cozy. As it was, it looked and felt quite inhospitable - cold, dark and damp.

Maureen began wandering around, all the while taking notes on her clipboard.

"I spend most of my day here so naturally I thought to add some home comforts." She gestured towards the electric fire and the sofa. "I actually found the fire out in the rubbish heap at the back and the sofa was a gift from a friend. I sometimes have other artist friends over, and we have a bit of a meal and work on collaborations and things. You know, it's very much a thriving artist community in this area. It's been wonderful."

She was babbling, she knew, as she followed Maureen around, explaining the evidence of her habitation.

When they got to the back of the studio, Frances felt her

panic rising. Breathe, breathe.

"And this?" Maureen pointed at the little trundle bed.

Frances offered a silent thank you to Moss for his tidy ways. The bed had been made and the little alcove tidied. It looked entirely innocent, like the spare bed in a guest room - ready, but not in use.

"Oh, that!" Frances tittered. "Well, as I was saying, I often have friends over, and we sometimes get into the wine a bit. So, I have that there in case someone doesn't fancy crashing about along the lane in the dark. And," she added, as she saw the superior disbelief in the other woman's eyes. "I often work late into the night, so I might need a nap the next day. Or, if things aren't going well with my work, I'll have a little lie-down. It's an artist thing."

The barely suppressed sneer on Maureen's face told Frances that either she didn't believe her, or that she was laying on the Mysterious Ways of Creative People a bit too thick.

I bet she's never so much as glued sequins on a Christmas ornament, thought Frances, bitter at the idea she was being confronted by such an unappreciative person.

Maureen flipped the plastic cover of her clipboard over with a snap. Clicking her pen closed and putting it into her pocket she fixed Frances with a glare.

"I think I have all I need," she said, her tone giving nothing away.

"So, what now?" asked Frances, following her to the door. "What happens next?"

The woman sighed, clearly feeling an explanation was beyond her pay grade.

"Now I take my findings back to the council. They will review them before passing it back the landlord."

Frances thought of the pleasant, elderly woman who was, in fact, her landlord. Her family had owned the land around the studio for generations.

"Oh, Lady Wainwright," said Frances, somewhat relieved. Lady Wainwright was a great supporter of the arts, not to mention a contemporary of Uncle Phineas. That was how she'd found the studio in the first place.

"She's lovely," she added, feeling the need to assert that she was on great terms with her landlady.

A look of what may have been pity crossed over Maureen Smith's sour features, to be quickly replaced by grim superiority once again.

"Lady Wainwright is no longer managing her estate. Her eldest son is now in charge and has seen fit to do a thorough audit of all holdings, including this one."

Frances' tongue cleaved to the roof of her mouth.

"I see," she said, her voice barely above a whisper. "Well, I'm sure that nothing will be found to be amiss. I'm a responsible tenant and have only improved the conditions here. I see no cause for concern."

She closed the door behind Maureen and leaned her forehead against the old wood.

"This can't be happening," she groaned.

Angus whined, pushing his nose against her leg.

"I know, I know. It's dinner time. Let's get you something."

As she wandered into the kitchen a thought struck her.

"Oh no!"

She looked back at the little brown and white dog who was spinning himself in an excited circle of anticipation.

"You do realize who Lady Wainwright's son is, don't you?"

Angus stopped his spin, head tilted. He glanced at the dish

in Frances' hand and then back at her face, his concern being only for how soon she was going to fill it and give it to him.

She measured out his kibble, added a dollop of canned food and placed it on the floor. She watched him gobble it up, her heart full of love for the little dog.

"It's that awful man on the motorbike. It has to be."

Frances glanced around the dismal studio. Despite Moss' best efforts, it really wasn't a homey sort of place. It was greatly improved, but definitely not a *home.*

Thinking of Moss, Frances stood up.

"Moss! You can come out now, she's gone!"

The silence was broken only by the sound of Angus pushing his bowl around the floor, licking every last morsel of his dinner.

"Moss?"

Frances took a deep breath, trying to quell a surge of worry. She walked back to the kitchen and knocked on the bread bin. It sounded metallic and hollow, just as a bread bin would expect to sound.

"Moss? Are you in there? Please answer. I hope you haven't gone out in such awful weather."

Angus whined and followed her into the kitchen, sniffing the floor for crumbs.

"I'm opening the door," said Frances, her voice suddenly full of tears. "Sorry to intrude!"

Frances opened the bread bin and found only a loaf of bread.

Chapter 14

"Any sign yet?"

Frances shook her head, unable to meet Sophie's eyes.

"I'm sure everything's fine," said Sophie, "Perhaps he just went off on one of his rambles and lost track of time."

"For over a week? And he always lets me know if he's going to be gone for any length of time and he very rarely does that. Usually only for the Blue Moon Market."

Frances shook her head again.

"This is something different. Worse. I'm worried that…what if…"

Her voice cracked and she left the sentence unfinished.

Sophie handed her a tissue.

"I'm fine," Frances assured her friend after she'd wiped her eyes. "Thank you for the tea and commiseration."

She opened up her sketchbook, still avoiding her friend's gaze.

"Oh! I have the preliminary sketches for Uncle Phineas," she said, her tone, falsely bright as she reached down into her backpack to pull out a manila folder.

"Wow, that was fast," said Sophie, taking the offered folder. "He'll be delighted."

"Yeah, I've been working pretty hard the last few days. It fills the time between…"

"Are you going out every day?" asked Sophie, gently. "Still?"

Frances nodded.

"Absolutely. I'm not giving up on him, Soph."

She gave her friend a challenging stare, as if daring her to point out the futility of finding a house brownie in the vast expanse of field and lane around the studio. Not to mention the faery realms into which he may have wandered off.

Sophie nodded, pressing her lips firmly together. She reached out and squeezed Frances' arm.

"I wouldn't suspect that for a minute," she said, standing up. "Now, let me leave you to your work. I can come and help with the search later this afternoon if you like. Once Melinda comes in, I'm free."

Frances smiled, tears threatening again.

"That'd be great, Angus and I would love the company."

* * *

It had been over a week since Moss had disappeared, seemingly without a trace. The bread bin was even empty of his Collection. It was as if he'd never been there. Frances had walked the fields and lanes every day, sometimes two or three times, searching for her friend, to no avail.

"He wouldn't just leave us, would he?" she'd asked Angus one evening as they sat huddled on the tartan sofa. "Surely, he'd tell me?"

Angus had whined and burrowed himself further under the blanket. Even he seemed to be missing the temperamental brownie. There was certainly a shortage of delicious morsels to be added to his dinners.

Sighing, Frances turned her attention to her work. She'd almost completed the second contract and was trying to get it ready to send off so she could focus on doing up some cards and notebooks for the Christmas market.

"I have to have something other than robot daisies," she'd explained to Sophie when the order of blank cards and notebooks had arrived. True to her word, Sophie had managed to convince a small company that used only tree-free paper to send her a sample selection. It was a small enough order to be manageable and still at a wholesale cost. As it was, Frances had to dip into her emergency savings to pay for it.

"I'm very proud of you," Sophie had told her. "I think you'll be glad you took the risk. It's an important first step, don't you think?"

Frances had just stuck out her tongue and laughed

"Sure, if you say so, Miss Therapist. An important first step in my creative recovery, is that it?"

Sophie had giggled and shoved the box of paper at her friend.

"Smarty pants! Just go and do something beautiful, will you?"

Focus, focus, Frances thought, tapping her pencil against her lower lip. She stared at the page of triangles of varying sizes, interspersed with tiny circles. Groaning inwardly, she got back to work.

"Hi there, Frances!" piped a small voice.

Frances looked up, smiling.

"Fiona! How lovely to see you," she replied, genuinely pleased to see the little girl. "Ah, I see you have your sketchbook. Are you here for a bit? Would you like to sit together?"

Fiona was bent over, patting Angus who was wriggling in delight. She had her sketchbook tucked under her arm.

"I wish I could," said Fiona, straightening up, a small frown on her face. "My mum just came in to buy some buns or something. We have to go and visit my auntie today. Which I'm not thrilled about, I can tell you, because my cousins will be there and they're both boys and very loud and not at all interested in anything at all interesting."

She rolled her eyes.

"I'm sure you know people like that."

Frances suppressed a grin. The little girls' earnest nature spoke directly to some long-ago part of herself.

She nodded, her face serious.

"That's true. I've known my share of those sorts of people. The good thing about getting older, though, is that you're free to find people who are interested in interesting things. So, hang in there, it'll be alright in the end."

Fiona considered this for a moment, then nodded.

"I suppose you're right. I know when I'm bigger I'm going to live in a little cottage out in the woods and have a big flower patch and a black cat named Soot. My mum says we can't have a pet because they cost too much."

She glanced down at Angus.

"I might have a dog as well but it would have to be a big one, to scare off unwanted visitors."

"Ah," agreed Frances. "That would be handy. To discourage uninteresting people, then?"

"Precisely. I'm thinking perhaps a big black wolfhound-ish sort or something. What do you think?"

"I think that sounds the perfect choice," replied Frances. She smiled down at Angus and winked, lowering her voice to a

209

conspiratorial whisper, "Small dogs are lovely, of course, but uninteresting people might not take them seriously."

Fiona nodded, her ponytails bobbing furiously. They were wrapped in a star-patterned ribbon that twinkled as the little red head moved.

"That's true. I'm sure Angus is very ferocious but he's ever so small and an intruder might not see him until it was too late. I think it's best to discourage people before they get to your front door. The constant knocking would disturb me while I was trying to draw or make my potions."

Fiona paused in her chatter to lean over and get a look at Frances' sketchbook.

"What are you drawing? Oh."

Her face creased into a frown and she looked up at Frances

"What are those?"

Frances grimaced.

"It's a design I'm doing for a company that prints material for cushions and furniture and things."

Fiona stared, clearly trying to sort out the concept in her mind.

"Is that your job, then?" she asked. "Only, I thought you said you were an artist?"

Frances winced.

Fiona looked at her, her eyes questioning.

Out of the mouths of babes, thought Frances.

"I *am* an artist," she explained. "There are lots of different ways to be one, you see. And graphic design - which is what this is," she gestured to the page of triangles. "Is simply a different branch of art. I draw the designs here, you see, then I transfer them onto a computer and fiddle with them and..."

"Well, I *know* there are lots of ways of doing art," interrupted the little girl. "My teacher makes us do sculpting and weaving and things and they're mostly fun and okay. But don't you like drawing and painting better?" she asked, clearly unconvinced of the merits of graphic design. "Isn't that what you said when we were chatting the last time?"

Frances felt she was getting into tricky territory again. She glanced around, trying to catch sight of Fiona's mother. She seemed to be engrossed in a discussion of the bun selection with Sophie.

"Yes," she said, cautiously. "It's true, I do enjoy drawing and painting."

"So why isn't that your job? Aren't you supposed to be doing the thing you like best? Isn't that what you said?"

Frances felt a twinge of something just then. Alarm? Guilt? Trust a small child to pinpoint exactly the evidence of do-as-I-say-not-as-I-do. Which is precisely what had just happened.

"Well," began Frances, about to embark on an explanation of how sometimes we need to make money doing things we might not like as much just so we can continue to do the things we do like. But even as the words were forming in her mind, she could hear the inconsistency between what she believed and what was actually real. And she was fairly certain the little girl would see it too. Because while she did believe that it was often necessary to support one's art in other ways, that wasn't really why *she* was doing the graphic design work.

"Fiona! Are you bothering this poor lady again?"

Fiona's mother came to the rescue, a large brown bag full of the perfect choice of buns, no doubt. Frances noted that despite it obviously being a day off, she still looked harried. She smiled warmly.

"She's no bother at all," Frances assured her. "I enjoy our

chats."

She looked at Fiona who was clearly trying to make herself as inconsequential as possible.

"She's a very wise young lady. And a talented artist, at that."

Fiona grinned, her whole face lighting up.

Her mother smiled faintly and nodded.

"Yes, she does some lovely pictures, that's true. Still, that won't pay the bills now, will it? A nice hobby. Keeps her out of mischief, I'll say that. Come on, pet. Auntie Lois will be hopping if we're not there on time and the bus will be here in a few minutes."

Frances muttered a goodbye, reeling slightly from the way Fiona's mother had so casually dismissed her child's passion. Her heart broke into a million pieces. She'd heard those very words a hundred times growing up in her very sensible, very conventional household where people got regular jobs that paid well and produced a generous pension. It had been an extreme act of defiance to go to art college and she was still regarded with vague suspicion whenever she spent time with family.

Fiona's mother set off for the door, her daughter trailing behind. As she passed by Frances table, Fiona bumped Frances' elbow. She gave Frances a cheeky grin then turned to stick her tongue out at her mother's back.

Frances's eyed widened in delicious shock, looking around quickly to see if anyone else had noticed.

"A wolfhound," whispered Fiona, leaning in. "Definitely a wolfhound."

* * *

Frances walked back to the studio in deep thought. Her conversation with young Fiona had stirred up some feelings that she'd been happy to keep locked up in that special compartment in her brain.

It was Fiona's innocent and idealistic view of art that both delighted and distressed Frances. She tried to remember back to when she'd shared the same convictions. She had been so single-minded in her pursuit of her dreams and had never once stopped to consider that she wouldn't succeed. The failure of her gallery showing had been a crippling blow to her confidence and had left her rootless and unsure.

"I wish Moss were here," she said to Angus, as they made their way down the path. "He always manages to put things in perspective. Even if he's rude and impatient with me, I know he has our best interests at heart."

Angus wuffed softly and resumed his explorations of the hedge. Frances watched him, eager to see some reaction that would mean he'd scouted out a faery. Even if it wasn't Moss, she could at least enquire as to his possible whereabouts. She wasn't above catching a pixie and grilling it for information. She kept a small jar of milk in her backpack for just that reason. The neighbourhood pixies, she'd discovered, were rather fond of milk. But there was no excited bark or tug at the end of the lead, so they turned up the lane towards the studio, Frances' mood sinking as they went. It wasn't the same going back there knowing that Moss wasn't waiting for them

As they approached, Frances noticed something white fluttering on the door. Frowning, she reached up and unpinned the paper that was folded and attached to the peeling wood.

With a clawing dread and hands that trembled, she unfolded

the sheet of paper. The words swam in front of her eyes and it took her several attempts to read and understand. Her brain kept moving her eyes back to the large black type at the top of the page that read, 'Order of Eviction'.

* * *

"Oh, Frances! This is too awful! Can they really do that?"

Frances sniffled.

"I suppose they can, can't they? It says I've violated the conditions of the lease, so I have to be out in thirty days."

"Thirty days! That's ridiculous. How is that even reasonable?"

"It was that horrid man," said Frances, with a heavy sigh. She took a sip of tea, trying to collect herself further. Her first instinct, after making a mug of tea, was to phone Sophie.

"What man? Oh, Roger Wainwright. Ugh. Hateful, hateful beast. We're in for a miserable time if he's back in the area. Todger, we always called him." Sophie giggled then paused, "I can have a word with Uncle Phineas. He and Lady Wainwright are very chummy, I'm sure he could convince her to let you stay. He'd be utterly enraged to think this was happening. So would Lady W for that matter. Whatever was she thinking leaving her son in charge?"

"I don't suppose it would hurt," said Frances, "but I don't imagine it'll make a difference. This letter came from the authorities. I think they only consulted your man Todger out of professional courtesy. The building isn't zoned for living in and so it's a very tidy excuse to get me out. It's my own fault. There's no-one to blame but myself."

Frances was entering a phase of calm acceptance. It was as

if the eviction letter was the last in a too-long string of events meant to wear her down. She glanced over at Angus who was curled up on the tartan sofa.

There was silence on the other end of the telephone.

"Sophie? Are you still there?"

"Of course," came the hurried reply. "I was just thinking, that's all. Listen, Fran, I'm going to say something, and I don't want you to think that I'm doubting you in any way or that I'm encouraging any sort of change of direction. I just want to be a good friend and to make sure you're alright."

"Okay, but this sounds ominous."

Sophie chuckled.

"It's not meant to be, but you might think it so. I just wanted to repeat my offer of staying with Stuart and me. And there's also the option of a few hours in the cafe if you want them, for a bit of extra money. Melinda is finding it tricky sometimes to juggle her class and her work schedule so I'm sure she'd be glad to give up a couple of shifts to make it easier on herself. It's only going to get trickier once she'd properly enrolled. I know she wants to ask me about it, but you know Melinda, always trying to do it all."

"You're babbling, Soph," said Frances, smiling down the phone. "Don't worry, I'm not going to bite your head off for wanting to take care of me. Of us. Because you know I come with a menace of a little dog, right? What about Stuart? You know how he feels about Angus."

There was a small pause before Sophie answered, "Does this mean you're actually considering it? Oh, my goodness! And don't worry about Stuart, it won't kill him to bend his stiff neck for a change. He's getting far too set in his ways for a young person. He's turning into his father, for heaven's sake."

"As much as I appreciate this, Soph, with all my heart," said Frances, struggling to pick herself up from the floor where she'd been sitting, leaning against the cupboards in the kitchenette. "I haven't made up my mind just yet. It just feels like maybe the universe has been bludgeoning me over the head with the idea that I'm on the wrong track altogether, you know? Like maybe it's time I admitted defeat and started to act like a responsible grown-up."

After she hung up the phone, Frances made herself another mug of tea.

Moss would've just made a whole pot when he saw me walk through the door, she thought, an ache echoing around in her chest. He would've known exactly what to do to make me feel better when he saw my face.

"And no doubt given me a lecture along the theme of 'I told you so'," she said to Angus, nudging him along the sofa. "Shove over and give me some room."

Angus obliged, moving just far enough to make room, but not so far as to be out of reach. He settled back in, leaning comfortingly against her thigh. She placed an idle hand on his back, letting her fingers sink into the wiry fur.

"What'll we do, my boy?" she murmured.

The sound of someone knocking softly on the door jolted her from her musings.

Her heart leapt and she jumped up off the sofa, spilling tea and Angus.

"Moss?" she said, wrenching open the door.

"Oh, it's you."

"That's not a very pleasant way to greet an old man, parched for a cuppa as he is."

Skelly stood, smiling beatifically in the doorway. His much-patched corduroy trousers and vast overcoat combined with the tweed cap and bushy white eyebrows made him look like an extra from Last of The Summer Wine. *If only he was actually just an eccentric sheep farmer*, thought Frances, looking at the spectacle before her, *I would probably become very fond of him.*

"Well, will you invite me in for a drop of something?" he asked, tilting his head.

Frances opened her mouth then paused, narrowing her eyes.

"Is this like the whole vampire thing? That I have to invite you or else you can't come in?"

Skelly gave her a withering look.

"Vampires!" he snorted. "Bloody Stoker! But aye, a bit like that," he conceded. "It's a matter of threshold. Although yours is a bit of a weak one at that. I can get across it without any bother but it's mostly a matter of good manners, aye?"

Frances blushed, pulling back the door.

"Come in, please. I'm sorry to be so rude, I've had some upsetting news."

She went back into the kitchenette to fill the kettle.

"I'm sorry but I haven't got any cake," she said. She looked in the biscuit tin and saw that it, too, was empty. Moss used to keep it filled, she remembered with a pang. Rummaging in a cupboard, she found a packet of HobNobs which she opened then spread a half dozen on one of the little enamel tea plates. Moss again. She sighed, audibly.

"That's a heavy old sigh for such a young soul," remarked Skelly, who'd sat himself down on the sofa next to Angus.

"Yes, well. I've enough troubles for a soul twice my age," replied Frances, carrying the tea tray over to the table.

"Is that so?"

Skelly raised a shaggy eyebrow, accepting the mug of tea that Frances offered.

"Yes, it is so, actually. I've just had an eviction notice for the studio, if you must know," Frances stirred her tea, not making eye contact. The whole thing felt very shaming for some reason.

"Aye well, then."

Frances looked up, surprised.

"What does *that* mean?"

Skelly shrugged, reaching for his second HobNob.

"It doesn't mean anything," he said, munching happily. He broke off a small piece of his biscuit and handed it to Angus, who was waiting patiently, his head on Skelly's knee. Traitor, thought Frances, glaring at her dog.

"Of course, it means something," said Frances, feeling her temper rising. "It means I'm not going to have anywhere to live in a month. And on top of that, Moss has vanished."

She looked closely at Skelly, trying to see if he reacted to the last bit of news. His face remained impassive as he chewed his biscuit with apparently deep reverence and concentration.

Eventually, after swallowing the HobNob and taking a large swig of tea, he spoke.

"I told you, didn't I?" he asked, his voice soft. He was looking intently at the plate of chocolate biscuits, perhaps contemplating having another. Frances reached down and picked up the plate, moving it along the table, just out of reach. She wanted to find out everything he knew about Moss' disappearance.

"Told me what, exactly?" demanded Frances. "Did you have something to do with it? Have you done something to him? Because if I find out you have, I swear to you I'll find the biggest lump of iron, wrap it in hawthorn and club you with it!"

Skelly's eyes twinkled with amusement then shifted to brief longing as he looked at the distant plate of biscuits.

Frances pushed the plate further away.

"Answer me," she said, through gritted teeth, a hint of uncharacteristic menace creeping into her voice. She clenched and unclenched her fists. "Did you make my friend disappear?"

Skelly turned his eyes to her. The green of them startled her. The colour flickered between emerald and a darker shade, like that of cloud-shadowed moorland.

"No, lass," he said, softly again. "It had naught to do with me."

"Who then?" demanded Frances, "If you're some sort of faery lord, exile notwithstanding, surely you know something."

Skelly licked his lips. It was a strange and disturbing gesture and Frances felt a brief chill flicker up her spine.

"It had naught to do with me," he repeated, staring intently into her face. "And everything to do with you."

Chapter 15

"Tell me about the paintings in the cupboard."

Frances sat, reeling. Her mind raced, trying desperately to sort out what Skelly was telling her. It couldn't be, surely.

According to Skelly, the reason Moss and, apparently, many of the other faery folk in the area, had disappeared, was solely down to Frances and her refusal to draw and paint. It wasn't just because she wasn't drawing the faery folk, he'd explained, it was more to do with the fact that she wasn't truly putting her heart into her work.

"Of course, I am," she'd spluttered, deeply offended. "I always do my best. I have an obligation to the people who hire me, and I never submit anything that isn't my best work."

"Aye, that's as may be," he'd replied. "But is it the work of your heart?"

He'd reached over and pointed a gnarled finger, just hovering over left side of her chest.

"That's what matters, you see? That it's your heart's work. Everything else just skims the surface."

"But Moss was fine. Well, mostly fine. We've been here for a good while. I've been doing the design work since ever we got here."

She paused, not wanting to think about the times he'd looked unwell in the weeks before he vanished.

Skelly shrugged.

"He's an odd one, that brownie," he said. "It mebbe that because he was more bonded to you that he managed to hang on…"

"The botanical illustrations," murmured Frances. "I've been doing those for the last few weeks. He had a bit of a worse turn a while ago, then he seemed more or less okay. Could it be because I was doing those? I've always loved…"

She'd broken off then, waving a hand in a quick, dismissive gesture.

"Forget it! I don't believe this. This is just some sort of faery trick to make me do what you want."

She'd lapsed into a confused silence then, trying frantically to rationalize her way through the situation.

"The cupboard?" repeated Skelly, "Tell me."

Frances emerged from her haze of thought, blinking. She shook her head, wanting very much to disbelieve what she'd been told but having gone over the events of the past few months in her head, she could see the dots joining up. But that didn't mean she wanted to dig into the cupboard and all that *that* entailed.

"I need to know more about this," she said, firmly. "I have questions."

Skelly smiled, acknowledging her stalling.

"Fine then," he said, winking. "I've got time."

Frances winced at that. She wasn't really up for the humour of a thousand year exile.

"Why can *I* see them?" she asked, surprising herself. She hadn't ever really consciously questioned it. She'd seen faeries

221

since she was a very young child and it was simply a part of who she was. "If what you told me on the hill that day is true, then shouldn't every artist, every creative person, be able to see faeries? And what about people that aren't explicitly creative? Can any of them see?"

Skelly shrugged.

"I don't know, really. Some of you can, most of you can't. The children always can, until the world gets at them, and sometimes the old folk start seeing again. It's mainly your creative ones." He shrugged again and added, "Not all of you, mind."

Frances scowled.

"That wasn't very helpful," she said.

"Does it matter?" he asked. "It's like asking why some folk like walking in the woods and some folk would rather sit in front of yon telly boxes. It's just the way of things. My people have always been drawn to the creative ones; they're always going to gather where there's music and art and dance and grand inventions. More than that, though, it's cleverness and an open heart that attracts them."

"So why are they disappearing then?" asked Frances, becoming increasingly frustrated. He was talking in circles and not saying very much. "There are heaps of people doing all that, every day. *I* am doing that every day. Just because I'm not creating masterpieces in oils doesn't mean I'm not creative."

Skelly shook his head.

"You're not getting it through your thick skull, are you?"

"Well maybe if you explained it better I would!"

"Pass me a bloody biscuit and I'll try again. Thick as two short planks, you lot,"

Frances sighed and pushed the plate of HobNobs towards him. He took two more.

"What?" he said, seeing her raised eyebrows. "You might take the plate away again."

Frances sat, impatient, as the old man munched his way through a biscuit and slurped several mouthfuls of tea.

"Right," he said, finally, dusting the crumbs from his beard. "Try and pay attention because the truth of it is, there's no easy way to explain it. All I know is what I see in front of me, what I've seen happening and what needs to be done to, hopefully, turn it around."

Frances bit back a retort and nodded, placing her hands on her knees and sitting up straight, like an attentive student.

Skelly held up his hands and started ticking off his fingers.

"Point one, faery people are drawn to creativity and the arts. Are you with me on that one?"

Frances nodded, fighting the urge to roll her eyes.

"Point two, the attraction is not so much to the product of the creativity," he paused, tilting his head and giving Frances a meaningful look.

She scowled and nodded.

"Got it, thank you."

"But to the...och, what's the best way to say it...to the life of it, mebbe? To the force of it?"

"The energy," said Frances, leaning forward. "Is that what you mean? The creative energy?"

Skelly smiled, touching a finger to the side of his nose.

"Aye, the energy. That's the one. Sorry lass, there's some things that a body *knows* but doesn't always have the word for, aye?"

More nodding.

223

"Right. So, point three," continued Skelly. "This energy, if you like, is strongest when a person is doing the work of their heart. You know what I mean by that?"

Frances nodded again. She was starting to feel like a bobblehead doll but at least it was all beginning to make sense.

"Now, we have to step sideways for a minute to explain the next bit. In the old days, folk believed in the faery people as a matter of course. There wasn't any particular effort required on the part of the wee folk to be in the human world, see?"

Frances frowned.

"Wait a second, so what you're saying is that faeries actually *need* humans to believe in them to exist? That seems a bit stupid."

Skelly shook his head.

"No lass, not quite. We only need mortals to believe if we want to walk in *this* world. To be here," he gestured around the studio. "We're well enough, in a way, to stay in the enchanted places and the in-between."

Frances pursed her lips.

"But what's the big deal about here?" she asked. "Everything I've heard of Faery is that it's a far superior place to be. Why wouldn't faery folk want to live in their own world anyway? Given a choice."

Skelly frowned, his shoulders sagging.

"That's one of the things I can't rightly explain," he said, his voice rasping.

Frances blushed, suddenly remembering the reason behind his exile and the dissolution of his people. She reached out a conciliatory hand.

"I'm sorry, Skelly," she said. "I didn't mean…"

Skelly patted her hand.

"No matter, lass. It is what it is."

He took a slurp of tea.

"So, you're understanding so far, then?"

"Yes, thank you." She held up a hand, a thought occurring to her. "Does this mean that Moss is okay then? That he's just gone back to Faery? This is great news!"

Skelly avoided her eyes.

"What?" she said, alarm bells ringing in her mind. "What's wrong?"

The old man cleared his throat.

"You're not wrong" he said, slowly. "Only that once a faery has spent any length of time in the mortal world, it's not so easy for them to be in the otherworld."

"Meaning?"

"Meaning, there are creatures of the otherworld, of Deep Faery as we call it, that don't hold with the mingling of faeries and mortals. They don't look kindly on the ones who, they believe, have betrayed their kind."

Frances winced, remembering again what he'd told her about the nature of his exile. Her brain whirred, trying to make sense of the situation and what it might mean for Moss.

Her gaze flicked to the locked cupboard and back again. She straightened her shoulders and put her hands back on her knees.

"Point four?" she prompted.

Skelly nodded his head in a manner of a bow.

"Point four," he said, "is that the mortal world benefits from the faery folk walking abroad. There's a sort of magic that we bring with us, a belief in…"

"Impossible and wonderful things," interrupted Frances. "You don't need to explain that one, I understand. Although," she added, "I would argue that it's not all benefits. There are rather a lot of rotten apples in your midst."

Skelly chuckled.

"Aye, right you are. On to point five then?"

Frances nodded.

"Point five, the final point, is that the only way I know of, to keep the faery folk in this world, is for humans to be doing the work of their heart. The way I see it, it benefits all of us. That's the energy that's strongest so that keeps us here and the bonus of it is that you humans get to do your best work."

Frances mulled that over for a few minutes. She drummed her fingers on her knees.

Finally, she sighed and shook her head.

"I don't know," she said, frowning. "It all seems a bit simplistic to me and, well," she waved a hand dismissively, "something out of a faery tale or something."

She paused, smiling at what she'd just said. Skelly merely regarded her, his lined face without expression.

"It's just that nothing I've ever read about faeries suggests that they're in any way philanthropic towards humans. They're mostly just out to serve themselves."

Skelly scowled.

Frances looked at him, tilting her head.

"And why do *you* even care?" she asked. "I mean, obviously you're strong enough to be here without my input. What does it matter to you what the rest of your lot are doing? I would've thought that the way you'd been treated would be enough to make you want nothing at all to do with them."

Skelly made a slow gesture of placing his mug onto the little table. He paused, staring down at nothing, his gaze directed at the floor then took a deep breath. He seemed to grow in stature, the slight old man straightened and a hint of the regal bearing he once had returned. Frances felt herself involuntarily leaning back.

"I can't explain much of what you ask," he said, after a time. "Things have changed a lot since the days when we walked the earth without conditions. As for me, though, it's not without effort that I'm here," he gestured to the studio with his crooked fingers splayed, "it drains me fierce, but I have a place to go when I'm finished here, a place that's easier. And I do better out of doors. Which is why I have my sheep."

Frances nodded, it was starting to make some sense, but she still had so many questions. She was extremely reluctant to believe that anything she could offer would be of any help. She may have abandoned her heart's work, according to Skelly anyway, but she doubted very much that she'd be able to go back. There was just too much baggage attached to it.

Skelly watched her turning it over in her mind. He smiled, a crooked mischievous smile.

"It'd be easier for me, aye, if there was some of that creation energy, but I manage, more or less."

Frances narrowed her eyes, very aware of what he was trying to do.

"And it *is* a matter of belief," he continued, looking sideways at Frances, who was lost in thought. "Of believing in something that you can't rightly explain, that maybe doesn't hold up to hard logic, but you know, somewhere deep in your own self, is true."

Frances felt her eyes fill with tears. She blinked them away, clearing her throat.

"That wasn't really an answer. Why are you doing this?"

Skelly shrugged again, deflating to his familiar form. His

skin was touched with a greyish hue and tiredness was written all over his face.

"Penance, mebbe?" he said, his voice low. "To make up for what I did."

"But you didn't really do anything wrong," argued Frances. "Your people made their own choices. You couldn't exactly force them to stay in the sea if they wanted to leave."

Skelly nodded.

"Aye, true. But it were me that allowed them the possibility, you see? And besides, I am, *was*, responsible for what they did. It was right and proper that I was punished."

Frances snorted.

"Well, I didn't have you pegged as a martyr," she said, but then seeing the expression of deep sorrow on Skelly's face, softened her tone. "Thank you for explaining it to me properly," she said. "It makes a bit more sense now."

Skelly nodded, sighing wearily.

"So," he said. "Can we get back to the paintings in the cupboard?"

And so Frances told him, everything, this time.

* * *

A fresh pot of tea had been made and the rest of the HobNobs piled onto the plate.

Frances felt utterly wrung out. Dredging up the events of the past few months had sapped the last of her energy.

"That fellow was a right piece of work, wasn't he?"

Skelly shook his head in disbelief.

"I could probably arrange for a plague of boils, or some such. A pox upon his house; something from the good old days, if that would make you feel better?"

When he got no reaction, he continued.

"Be that as it may, mind you, I still can't understand why the opinion of one person could make it so that you don't ever want to paint your pictures again. It seems to me it'd be a grand thing to do to get back at the little shite by carrying on anyway."

Frances nodded, not really paying attention. Her mind was toying over the idea of perhaps doing some illustration work. If she absolutely had to go back to drawing her faery folk subjects maybe she could incorporate some of the them into that sort of work. It would have to do. Besides, Sophie had said there was always a good trade in cards and notebooks through the shop and at the various fairs and fetes in the area. She could set up a stall or something. She mentally shook her head and went back to what Skelly was saying.

He was giving her a strange look. She raised an eyebrow in question.

"It won't be enough, lass," he said, his voice low.

Frances blushed, then scowled.

"Don't do that," she said. "It's intrusive and inappropriate."

Skelly put up his hands in a placating gesture.

"I didn't do anything," he protested. "I don't need to read your mind to know what you're thinking."

"And what exactly is it that I'm thinking?"

"You're bargaining with yourself. You're thinking that you can just shove a few drawings of faeries into something else. Add them in, like."

"And what's wrong with that?" she demanded. "If drawing faeries is my heart's work, then won't that be enough to bring..."

Her voice broke slightly.

"To bring your friend back?" finished Skelly, something like pity in his eyes. He shook his head. "I can't promise he'll be back, lass," he said. "And even if he did get back, there's no guarantee he'd be the same wee fellow that you knew."

"What do you mean by that?"

Skelly shrugged and avoided her eyes.

"I told you. They don't always take kindly to the ones that have chosen to live amongst you lot. And he's a bit of a special case; his family line has spent generations choosing to actually live *with* mortals, to serve them. Look at what they did to my folk. The Unseelie court…" his voice trailed off and his eyes got a faraway look.

Frances clapped a hand to her mouth, feeling a shudder of terror go through her. Her imagination ran wild at the extent the horror to which Moss could possibly be exposed. The faeries of the Unseelie court were the worst of the worst. Her breathing became ragged and she felt dangerously close to hysteria. Which, she briefly mused, would help no-one, much less Moss. She tried to get a grip of herself, closing her eyes and imagining a square in her mind.

"Now, now," said Skelly, reaching over to pat her arm. The tingle of his touch coursed warmth and comfort through her. She felt her breathing slow. "There's no point in working yourself up."

"What else am I supposed to do?" she snapped, pulling her arm away from under his hand. "My friend is trapped in some godforsaken faery realm, enduring heaven knows what sort of horrors, and now you're telling me I won't be able to bring him back?"

"I never did say that, lass," he replied, his voice barely above a whisper. "I said that what you're thinking will help him, won't."

"And why not? You're talking in circles again! One minute you're saying that drawing faeries is my heart's work, the next minute you're saying it's not enough. Which is it?"

Her voice rose to a high pitch then broke. The tears she'd held in since Moss had vanished rushed up in a flood from where they'd been trapped, lodged in her throat.

"I just want to help my friend," she sobbed into her hands. "I just want him to be okay. Can you please help me?"

A slow smile spread across Skelly's features. If Frances had been looking up at him rather than down into her hands, she might have been alarmed at what she saw there. The air shimmered slightly and as it coalesced, his features blurred and shifted. The windburned, lined face of the elderly sheep farmer was replaced, ever so briefly, by smooth blue-green skin and high angular cheekbones. The eyes were the same colour, a bright, emerald green, but were vaguely almond-shaped and tilted slightly upwards.

Frances sniffled and blew her nose noisily. Looking up from her hands, she blinked, her vision blurred with tears. Frowning, she blinked again, unsure of what she'd seen. The air seemed to quiver slightly and then all she saw was Skelly's wizened face, looking on with great concern. He reached his hand out again to squeeze her arm. This time she let it stay there, feeling the soothing warmth flood into her weary soul.

"I think, lass," he said, "That you'll find that we can help each other in this."

She nodded, smiling weakly.

"Okay," she said. "Tell me what I need to do. Whatever it is, I'll do it. I just want Moss to come home."

231

"That's a good girl," he said, patting her arm before leaning back. He picked up his mug of tea and took a big gulp.

"Right, if you'll not show me yon paintings, we'll just have to go a different way." He cocked his head at her, but she remained impassive. He waved a hand. "It doesn't really matter, anyway. I was just being nosey."

Frances' eyes widened and her mouth hung open. Skelly winked, mischief dancing in his eyes.

"Do you mean to tell me we've sat here arguing for," she glanced at her watch and winced, "three hours and you don't even actually need to see the paintings? What sort of lunatic are you, anyway?"

Skelly ignored the question.

Frances sighed.

"Just tell me what I need to do."

"Paint," he said, his voice firm. "Paint whatever it is that's in yourself." He tapped his chest. "Don't be thinking on whether it's good or proper or will help you pay the rent."

Frances winced, thinking of her plan to sell faery cards at the Christmas market.

Skelly nodded.

"There's time for that, lass," he said. "You'll be needing to get your things out in the world eventually, of course. But it needs to start here," he tapped his chest again. "That will be the only thing that could bring your wee man back."

Frances frowned, struggling with the idea.

"But how's that going to help?" she wailed. "It's no different when I draw in my sketchbook. It feels exactly the same to me. What about the faery that I drew that came back? Why won't it work to just sketch a bit? Why do I have to go back to painting?"

Skelly sighed, frustration creeping into his tone.

"We've been over this, lass. It's not the same. If it was the same, then why did your wee man vanish, eh?"

"But I don't understand, *why* isn't it the same?"

"Why does it matter?" he asked, his voice rising slightly. Angus stirred under the blanket, emerging to place his chin on Frances' knee. He regarded Skelly from under his eyebrows.

"Because I don't know if I can," said Frances in a small voice. "I don't know if I can do it anymore."

Chapter 16

"I know, I know," said Frances. Angus was in a fit of excitement. "We've been sat for ages and you need a bit of fresh air. *I* need a bit of fresh air!"

She bundled herself into her coat and wrapped a scarf around her neck. The weather had taken a turn for the wild, the wind whipping fallen leaves into a frenzy as they whirled past the windows. Like festive shoppers rushing along the high street to their next destination, mused Frances, her mind turning briefly to the Christmas market before bidding the thought a sad adieu.

She bent down to clip on Angus' leash, which was no small feat considering his wriggling and capering.

"I don't think you'll be quite so excited when you see what it's like out there," she warned him, laughing. "I feel like this will be our shortest walk yet."

But it wasn't. They did their usual route - down the path to the lane and then along to the crossroads that led to the village. The wildness of the wind helped blow away some of the murk that was hanging over them, the detritus of old hurts and congested emotion.

At the crossroads, Frances briefly considered walking into the village. She desperately wanted to get Sophie's thoughts on

234

everything that Skelly had told her. No, she thought eventually, after weighing it all up. I need to sort this out for myself. I don't want Sophie to offer me any more easy ways out, bless her heart.

"Come on, my boy," she said, turning down the other fork in the road. "We'll go as far as the sheep grid then turn around. This coat is supposed to be waterproof, but it seems to be letting the wind in."

Angus, ever agreeable, changed direction and trotted off along the other branch of the road. His stumpy tail stood aloft, wagging back and forth. They rarely went down this way so there were lots of smells to catch up on.

They walked on, Frances taking great gulping lung-fulls of the fresh, cold air. She felt as if she'd been locked in the studio for days, arguing with that wretched old man. Faery, she corrected herself. I need to remember he's actually a faery. And arguing with a faery was an exercise in abject futility.

She'd refused to unlock the cupboard, despite Skelly's elaborate arguments trying to convince her otherwise.

"No," she'd said, arms folded, as they stood beside the cupboard. "And that's absolutely final. I don't need to dig them out. They've no bearing whatsoever on what decision I make next. And," she'd wagged a finger at him as if he were a misbehaving child, "*You* said you didn't even need to see them and *I* haven't decided yet, what I'm going to do."

"But you're going to at least start with the drawings again?" he'd asked, finally admitting defeat. He was very drained. The energy required to hold him there for so long indoors had just about gone.

Frances nodded, more to herself than to him.

"Yes, I'll start with proper drawings first. I feel like that's the sensible approach before I try to tackle actually paintings."

He'd taken his leave then, limping wearily to the door and out into the wild wind and rain. Just before he disappeared into the storm, he turned back, his face ashen and the lines staring in stark relief.

"I want you to think on this one thing, if you get to fretting that you haven't got it in you. And that's this: you saw the sea with me, lass," he said, his voice hoarse with emotion.

"A thousand years, lassie. I've been away from my home for almost a thousand years. Never has anyone else ever seen my sea."

Frances felt a ripple of something as he left, and the light in the studio seemed to dim ever so slightly. The air seemed stale and stuffy and suddenly she felt she couldn't bear to stay there a moment longer. Which is when she'd decided she'd rather go walking in the foul weather than continue to sit, stewing in her own juices.

The girl and her dog reached the sheep grid and, as planned, went to turn around. Just then, a flicker of moment caught her eye. Angus went on high alert, his ears pricked and his body rigid.

"What is it, Angus?" asked Frances, tightening her grip on the leash, staring intently into the hedge bordering the path. She surprised herself, this time *hoping* for a glimpse of one of the faery folk.

Suddenly, a starling burst out of the hedge and soared into the air. Angus barked and Frances felt her shoulders sag.

She stood watching the bird for a moment, as it battled its way into the headwind; it would flap furiously for a moment or two, before stopping and allowing itself to be carried on the air currents. With short bursts of energy, it tacked into the oncoming blasts and made slow but steady progress in the direction it wanted.

Point taken, murmured Frances.

She looked around her, noting the bareness of the hedge. The wind had taken the last of the leaves; the only colour left being the coppery gold of beech, and even they were having a hard time hanging on in the force of the wind. The field stretched into a green expanse on the other side of the sheep grid, dotted here and there by clumps of shrubs and piles of stone. Something twinkled in the far distance and Frances squinted her eyes, disbelieving. She lifted a hand to shield her gaze from the wind and spattering rain.

"It can't be," she breathed, incredulous. "It absolutely can't be."

It appeared as if the glint on the horizon belonged to the sea. Frances remembered traveling to the seaside as a small child. They would take the train out of the city to the coast and there was a certain bend in the track that would give the first sight of the ocean, a strip of twinkling light on the horizon where the sun bounced off the rippling waves. It had never failed to both take her breath away and fill her with enormous excitement at the same time. More than that, down by the sea, she suddenly remembered, was where she'd seen her first faery. Some kind of water sprite splashing in the tide pools where a young Frances liked to play.

Frances scowled and urged Angus to turn away with her.

"Not bloody possible," she muttered aloud. "The sea is miles away and there's no bloody sunshine to make it dazzle. I don't know how he does it, Angus, but he's a tricky bastard."

Angus tilted his head, cocking an ear at his mistress.

"I know," she said, laughing. "Language, language." She

mimicked Uncle Phineas' plummy tones. The elderly fellow had very old-fashioned views on what real ladies said and did.

"Come on, my boy," she said, her mood lightening, despite the hideous weather and faery trickery. "Let's get back. I think a hot cup of soup is in order. Then we have to sort out how we're going to get our Moss back, right?"

Angus wuffed and set off at a smart trot, Frances scurrying behind him.

* * *

Frances heated up a can of tomato soup. She ladled it into a large mug, adding a splash to Angus' own bowl along with his kibble.

"Let it cool for a minute," she told him, putting a slice of bread into the toaster. "By the time my toast is finished, you can have it."

Angus sat, trembling with anticipation as she spread butter on her toast and cut it into long strips.

"Moss taught me this trick," she explained, "Soldiers aren't just for boiled eggs, you know. I can dip them in my mug, you see. And soup from a mug is even cozier than soup from a bowl. That's just a known fact."

Angus remained entirely focused on his bowl, which was still on the counter and not on the floor in front of him where he felt it ought to be. He had very little interest in toast beyond if there was going to be a piece for him. After what seemed an unbearable eternity, Frances placed his bowl on the floor and took herself off to the tartan sofa with her mug and strips of toast.

A few moments of sipping and thinking passed, before her

eyes traveled to the locked cupboard at the back of the studio. She sat, chewing her lip for a few moments, tapping her fingers against her soup mug. Her gaze shifted from the cupboard and began to scan around the studio. She noted the flaking paint and crooked windows. The curtains that Moss had hung in an attempt to keep out the draught moved slightly as the wind found its way into the cracks around the seals. Still, he'd turned the damp, musty space into something resembling a cozy space. The electric fire, despite its vintage was warm and cast a merry glow in the gloom of the afternoon and Sophie's tartan sofa added the final touch of homeliness in a space that was most definitely, she had to agree with the planning council, not really meant for habitation. She let her eyes wander back to the kitchen area, resting them firmly on the bread bin which, since Moss had gone, was something she'd avoided looking at.

"Right, Angus," she said, putting her mug down the table and standing up. She took a deep, somewhat shaky breath and walked over to the cupboard. "Let's bring him home."

Chapter 17

Frances sat staring at the half-finished canvas. Several paintbrushes had dried, criminally, on the palette where she'd left them earlier in the afternoon. Sighing, she scrubbed a hand across her face and placed the dried brushes in a jar of warm water, hoping to soften the stiffened bristles.

All else aside, it was true what Skelly had said; it was unforgivable to not be enjoying the art she made. And the undeniable truth was that she absolutely did not enjoy the graphic design work, no matter how much she tried to convince herself otherwise. Generic abstracts reproduced over and over again were simply not the stuff of divine inspiration for her. She hadn't *truly* enjoyed her work, other than the botanical illustrations, since she'd come to the studio. It had become a way to make money until….

But that was it. What was the "until"? What did she think she would do after her loan had been paid? Would she continue with the design work? Would she become a regular of the craft fair circuit? She really hadn't given it any thought. Considering it now, she couldn't find any part of her that was excited by any of those prospects.

Vibrant seascapes where the ocean seemed to heave and

churn; strange, mist-shrouded forests with monolithic trees in a hundred shades of green and brown and gold; and the creatures that lived there - fauns, satyrs, slant-eyed pixies and baleful faeries. Those were the things that set her heart pounding and her hand reaching for the paintbrush.

She flicked a gaze at the cupboard.

Those were the things she'd poured her soul into only to have them ridiculed and declared infantile and outdated. The world, apparently, didn't need that sort of thing anymore.

Frances shivered, remembering the conversation with Skelly.

How could it be? It was impossible. It was far too risky. She was only setting herself up for more failure and humiliation. It was entirely without logic, insisted her logical mind.

But her logical mind was losing the argument.

She stretched her arms above her head and reached for a clean paintbrush.

The shrilling of the telephone jolted her from deep concentration. She started violently, dropping a brush onto the floor, or, rather, onto Angus' back where he lay on the cushion at her feet. He yelped in surprise and stood up, a streak of cadmium yellow marring the blob of black hair on his coat.

"Sorry, love," said Frances, picking up the brush. "It suits you though."

"Hey, you," said Sophie, down the crackling line. "I thought I'd check to make sure you're alright over there in your ramshackle shed. Have you lost your electrics?"

"No, why? Have you?"

"Yes, the whole village is out. I'm actually surprised the phone is still working to be honest. It's this rotten wind. Apparently, there's a really nasty storm further north and we're getting the edges of it. If this is just the edges, I hate to think what those poor souls are dealing with."

"Oh, yes, it must be awful."

Frances was having trouble focusing on the conversation. She felt a bit disembodied, as if the rest of her was still sitting at her easel. She glanced over at the painting. She was almost finished.

"Are you working?" asked Sophie, with a chuckle, picking up on the familiar symptoms of Frances art-fugue state. "I can tell, you sound a million miles away. Are you doing those cards you were talking about? Only I was speaking with Mrs. Carpenter, she's the woman in charge of the stalls at the Christmas market and she says that the tables are all spoken for but if you want to add onto the end of our stall, nobody will kick up a fuss. After all, the stuff you're selling fits our inventory. Fran? Are you still there?"

"Hmm? What? Sorry, Soph. You're right, I'm a million miles away. And no, I'm not working on the cards just yet. I have…well…another project on the go."

"Oh?"

Frances pretended not to hear the implied question, choosing to assume it was an expression of disappointment that she wasn't doing the cards.

"Don't worry," she said. "I can get the cards done in plenty of time. And Soph?"

"Yeah?"

"I wanted to thank you for offering me a place at yours, the bookshop and your flat, but I don't think I'm going to take you up on it."

"Really?" said Sophie, her voice full of surprise. "Have you sorted out the studio thing?"

"No," replied Frances. "I think that ship has sailed for shores unknown."

"What are you going to do then? Where will you go?"

"I'm not sure yet," said Frances, smiling over at the painting. "I'll think of something."

She looked down at the paint splattered on her jeans and towards the bread bin, where the faint sounds of someone moving about ought to have been heard. The joy of immersion in her art dulled and cold fingers of dread squeezed her heart.

"I have to," she whispered, barely audible.

* * *

Frances leaned against the sink, examining her fingernails studiously for signs of ground-in paint. It was taking every ounce of will-power she had to not look at Skelly who was standing in front of the row of paintings she had leaned up against the studio wall.

It had been a week since the two of them had stood, arguing, beside the locked cupboard. It was a week of Frances sitting down at her easel, only after her design work was finished, to listen to what her heart wanted. She'd painted every afternoon, well into the evening, and after every session she'd strained her ears, hoping for the sound of Moss moving around in the bread bin or clattering plates in the kitchen. Still, there was no sign of the little brownie. She and Angus had walked miles, scouring the hedges and fields, exploring the banks of streams and the scattered copses of hazel and oak, and while there had been a few more sightings of faery folk, none of them were Moss and none of them were inclined to share any information on his whereabouts.

243

Eventually, unable to bear it any longer, Frances peered up from under a curtain of hair.

Skelly had pulled the three-legged stool up in front of the paintings and was sitting, straight-backed, gnarled finger clasping his corduroy-clad knees.

"Well?' he said, breaking the silence.

Frances started.

"Well? Well what?" she asked, gripping tightly to the edge of the apron she wore when she was painting. "What would you like me to say? Those are them. You stood here long enough badgering me to see them and now you have."

She glared at him, her tone was defensive, but her eyes darted between the paintings and his face, trying to gauge his reaction.

Skelly chuckled. He rose from the stool and stood facing Frances. The early sunlight slanted through the open studio door and cast the old man in a halo of yellow-gold light. He shuffled his feet and a million dust motes spiraled into the air around him like a cloud of dandelion wishes.

"I thank you, lass," he said, lowering his head in a gesture of deference. "I thank you for entrusting me with your paintings."

Frances felt the hunch of her shoulders subside slightly. Still though, he hadn't said what he thought of them.

"I've been painting all week," she said, waving her hand at the two canvases at the end of the row. One was finished, the other still a sketched outline.

Skelly turned back to the row of images. He walked along to the newest ones. The completed one depicted a tide pool strewn with shells and seaweed. A small, blue-skinned faery sat at the edge, washing something in the water. He squinted and leaned in for a closer look.

"Is that…"

"Yes," interrupted Frances. "It's sea glass. I took the memory of the very first faery I saw, down at the seaside when I was only little and then added in the sea glass. Sort of a juxtaposition of past and present. I wanted to…"

Skelly held up a hand, smiling and shaking his head.

"There's no need for the fancy explanations," he said. "You've no need to justify it to me. Or to anyone, for that matter."

Frances blushed, looking down at her hands which were twisting her apron into tight folds.

"Sorry," she said, "Habit."

"It's grand," he said, coming back to stand beside her. "It's a grand thing altogether."

"But Moss isn't back," blurted Frances, unable to hold it in any longer. "You said if I painted these," she pointed at the new canvases. "Then he'd come back. That it would be the right sort of magic."

Her face crumpled; disappointment etched in her features as she tried very hard not to burst into tears. She reached into her apron pocket and pulled out a paint-splattered handkerchief.

"I don't know what else to do," she said, her voice muffled by the square of linen.

"It's not the paintings, lass," said Skelly, his voice low. "You have the magic in them by the cart load."

"Well, what is it then? You're so full of riddles and I'm sick to bloody death of it. Just help me get my friend back, please! I'll do whatever you want!"

"That's three then," muttered the old man, the wolfish smile spreading over his face.

Angus, who had been dozing on his cushion underneath the easel, woke up and trotted over to Frances, bumping his nose against her leg. When she didn't acknowledge him, he stood up, front paws tapping on her thigh.

"What is it, my boy," she said, absently tousling his ears. She was staring at her paintings, but her attention was miles away. "We'll go out shortly. Just sit quietly."

Angus whined, glancing at Skelly before sitting himself, back straight and ears pricked, between them.

"Och, wee doggie," murmured Skelly, moving his hand in a sweeping gesture. "Let's not be like that, aye?"

Angus wuffed and sank to the ground, tucking his nose onto his outstretched forelegs. He whined softly and wagged the stump of his tail.

"That's better," said Skelly, his smile fading.

Reaching up to his neck, he pulled out the leather thong with the piece of sea glass threaded through it.

"D'ye speak any of the Old Language, lass?"

Frances started out of her reverie in surprise and shook her head.

Skelly sighed heavily.

"They not teaching it in those schools anymore?" he asked.

"Not really," replied Frances. "Not for a long time, I don't think."

The rest of the tension had gone out of her shoulders - tension she hadn't realized was still there until it had gone.

At least he doesn't hate them, she thought, her gaze returning to the paintings. Surely, he would've just come out and said it if he did.

"I think they still teach it on the north islands," she offered, by way of apology for the mainland's lack of cultural preservation. "Things are a bit more, you know, oldy-worldy, up there."

246

"Aye, lass. That they are."

Skelly turned his head to look at the paintings again.

Turning back, he smiled again, still wolfish. Frances' eyes widened briefly, before sliding away from his face and back to the artwork.

"You've done well, lassie. I couldn't have asked for better."

His voice lilted in a soothing sing-song rhythm.

It was Frances turn to smile widely. A wave of warm relief washed over her. Finally, she thought, absently, approval.

Skelly laughed again, shaking his head. The soft chuckle had gone, the timbre, changed. It was bitter and sharp-edged.

Frances frowned. Wait, she thought to herself, attempting to shake off the fuzzy glow that had descended. Where on earth did that come from? Approval? She put her fingers to the bridge of her nose, feeling the twinge of a headache forming. She fought the urge to stare at her paintings and turned to face Skelly.

In the cast of the sunlight, the old man's face seemed altered. The deep, furrowing lines had smoothed and his features became more angled.

Angus, stirring from where he lay at her feet, whined softly.

Frances felt something sink in her stomach, her scalp prickled, and her tongue cleaved to the roof of her, suddenly very dry, mouth.

Skelly shook his head gently. He was taller by now, the air shimmering around him in undulating waves. The dust motes, Frances noticed absently, were flickering and darting like live things in the wake of his glamour.

Glamour, she mused, feeling herself slipping back into a state of giddy calm. Of course, it's a glamour.

"Aye, lass," he repeated, his voice rolling gently like waves

247

across sand. "They'll do the trick just fine."

He tilted his head to one side, the same, bird-like mannerism that she'd noticed when they first met. Back then, he'd reminded her of a curious sparrow or robin. Now, however, given his sudden, alarming-yet-not-alarming, alteration in appearance - the broad shoulders and long, silvery-blue hair woven through with strands of kelp and clacking seashells, the expression had a slightly more predatory air.

"I've no argument with you, lass. You needn't worry that there'll be harm to you. In fact, you might say I'm doing you a great service, taking you in to my charge, as it were. We have plenty to offer each other. This will be of mutual benefit. And you're coming to it willingly, aye? Three times now, you've asked and promised. Besides, you want your wee man to come back, don't you?"

"You're what?" choked Frances, fear trilling up her spine, dispersing the feeling of benign fatigue. She willed Angus to stay where he was, sensing the little dog's distress and confusion. What was happening? "What do you mean, taking me in your charge?"

Skelly waved his hand dismissively. The fingers were long and straight and beautiful.

He's beautiful, thought Frances, immediately repulsed by the thought. In her mind, he was and probably ever would be an elderly sheep farmer.

He grinned, showing sharp, white, teeth.

"'Twas a convincing approach, aye? It suits me just fine and besides, it seems to me you young ones are far more likely to trust the old man with the sheep."

Frances swallowed hard. Her stomach churned. She smiled weakly. Maybe she could talk her way out of this. Faerie had a fondness for banter and riddling. Maybe she could lure him into an argument, distract him from whatever it was he already had in mind.

"So, what is it that you want from me then? More paintings?"

She had a sudden vision of herself being spirited off through a faery hill to spend an eternity painting portraits of Skelly's relatives. It was like some sort of punishment for her artistic vanity, or other moral-of-the-story fate usually reserved for the vain or greedy.

Skelly laughed again. This time it wasn't unpleasant - the sound of the wind through the trees, thought Frances, her mind growing misty and her attention wavering again She swallowed hard and fought to keep her wits.

"Nothing that we hadn't already talked about, lass," whispered Skelly, suddenly standing next to her. "It's for the best. For both of us. For all of us." He towered over her, leaning in to speak softly in her ear.

He smells like the beach in summer, she thought, feeling her knees give way.

Skelly caught her as she fell and lay her gently on the floor.

"I'm sorry lass," he said, pushing a strand of hair back from her face. "I truly am. This wouldn't be my choice but it's all I've been left with."

Angus whined again. He padded back and forth, nosing the prone form of his mistress, unsure of the current situation.

"Come on, wee dog," sang the lord of the sea. "It's alright. Nobody is going to harm you."

Angus wagged his stumpy tail and slithered across the floor on his belly until he was lying next to Frances. He burrowed in as close as he could get, ears flicking worriedly toward Skelly.

Skelly reached out and tousled the little dog's ears, murmuring something under his breath as he did so. Within moments, Angus was snoring alongside his mistress.

"Right then," said Skelly, straightening up to his full height.

Holding the piece of sea glass in one hand, he began to hum. It was a low, droning, sound at first but then slid into a higher pitched, more melodic harmony.

Frances stirred on the floor, her hands twitching where they lay across her stomach.

"Aye, lass - that's the way. Know that, whatever happens, I'm glad to have met you and grateful for the help. We all are. I just can't take the chance of you giving up. You're a feckless lot, you are."

The air around them began to shimmer - shapes ghosted in and out of view and colours swirled in a kaleidoscope. There came the sound of the ocean - waves crashing against determined rock and the keening wail of the wind through crevices and cracks in cliff edges,

Ceangailidh mi thu ri m'adhbhar
   Ceangailidh mi thu ri mo bheatha
   Is e mo bhròn do bhròn
   Is e mo bhròn do stri

 I bind thee to my purpose,
  I bind thee to my life,
  My sadness is your sadness,
  My sorrow is your strife.

Chapter 18

When Frances woke up, she was alone but for Angus lying beside her, snoring gently. Sitting up, she fought a wave of dizziness, and put a hand to her buzzing head.

"What in the hell was *that*?" she asked aloud, speaking to no-one in particular. There was no sign that Skelly had been there, bar the empty tea mug on the table.

"Wake up, you useless beast," Frances nudged Angus in the belly, "Aren't animals supposed to be able to sense these things? What good are you if you can't warn me of faery treachery?"

Angus stirred in his sleep, opened one eye and yawned, well aware that the accusation was groundless. As far as he was concerned, he'd done his duty. It wasn't his fault if he'd been ignored.

"Just as I thought," sighed Frances, "Utterly, bloody, useless." She leaned over and buried her face in his wiry fur, breathing in the warm doggy scent of him. "I'm sorry, my boy," she said, her voice wobbling slightly. "I'm glad you're okay."

Rising gingerly to her feet, she tested the weight of her head before mincing over to a chair.

"Now what?" she said aloud to the empty studio. The row of paintings were still there and she fought the urge to look at

251

them. The room felt very much as if it were larger than it had been and smelt faintly of ozone.

"People will wonder if you keep on talking to yourself."

"Jesus!" swore Frances, starting violently and immediately regretting the sudden movement.

Skelly raised a bushy, white, eyebrow.

"No, not quite," he said, grinning. "Although I have been told I bear an uncanny resemblance to your one, Moses."

"What did you do to me? I feel like I've been drunk for a week." she waved a hand up and down, indicating his appearance. "And where did the dashing, silver-haired lord of the sea get to? I think we're past pretending, don't you?" she snapped.

"Och, sorry about your big head," said Skelly, spreading his hands in a gesture of helpless apology. "'Tis always a bit hard the first time. You'll get used to it." He walked across the studio to retrieve the tea mugs, patting her on the arm as he passed.

Frances flinched at the jolt of electricity that sparked under his touch.

"What the…"

His touch was no longer just a pleasantly warm tingle but more of a prickling jab.

"Oh, aye - there's that an' all," said Skelly. "You'll be a bit of a lightning rod for the next wee while."

Frances stared, disbelieving. Skelly, in his original guise as elderly farmer, stood washing mugs at the sink as if nothing untoward had happened.

Mustering up the combined force of her anger, fear and confusion she took a deep breath and opened her mouth.

"Keep your hair on, lass," interrupted Skelly, before she could even form the words. He returned to the table with the clean mugs and his flask of tea. "There's time for the explanations yet."

"No! I'm not listening to any more of your lies and circular arguments. Not to mention the giant gaps in information."

Skelly held up a hand. "I never lied to you," he said, softly.

"Really?" retorted Frances. "And what do you suppose *that* is,"

She gestured toward the patched, brown, overcoat and wellies.

He shrugged, his mouth quirking up into a small smile.

"I suppose it's what you might call a truth-telling loophole." His eyes twinkled and Frances felt her indignation seeping away into resignation.

She sighed heavily, reaching across to unscrew the lid of the flask. She bent down to the opening and sniffed.

"I thought we might need something a bit stronger than tea," explained the old farmer. "It's faery brew, the last of the summer wine."

Frances glanced at him sharply, but his face was impassive.

"Right then, get on with it," she said, pouring generous slugs of the amber coloured liquid into the tea mugs. "What've you done to me?"

* * *

Frances bit back the torrent of fury that was rising from her chest. It burned, but she swallowed hard and tried to focus on steadying her breath. What Skelly was saying was one-part horrifying and one-part pure wonder.

She took another of several deep breaths.

253

"So, what you're saying then," she said, slowly enunciating each word. "Is that you've put some sort of binding spell on me whereby you have access to my thoughts and can influence my action. Mind control, in other words. And," she held up a hand as Skelly opened his mouth to respond. He closed it and sat, knobbled fingers clutching his mug of wine. "And, you did this without my consent."

Skelly remained silent, his gaze flickering between France's red face and the row of paintings behind her.

"You do realize that describes a rather heinous form of assault, don't you?"

The old man nodded.

"Aye lass, I suppose by your reckoning it is. Although I would argue that it wasn't without your consent."

Frances raised an incredulous eyebrow.

"Three times," explained Skelly. "Three times you asked for my help and so that was the invitation."

"Invitation?" Frances finally exploded, sloshing summer wine over the rim of her mug. It was quite delicious and was going down rather easily. "You're suggesting I *invited* you to invade my mind?"

Skelly shrugged, taking a large slurp of wine.

"That's the way of it," he replied, his eyes challenging. "And it's not as if it's a secret. Mortals have been making bargains with faeries since the mists parted. I honoured the thrice-asked rule, which isn't so much a rule as a courtesy and not one I'm compelled to honour, let me hasten to add."

"Oh, well then," said Frances, her voice dripping with sarcasm. "Let me take a moment and feel some gratitude for your chivalry."

"Ignorance of the law is no excuse," he continued, warming

to the topic. "It's what trips you lot up all the time when it comes to our dealings."

"Ah, so I suppose it's *our* fault that we get trapped in Faery for hundreds of years or end up with our hair tied to bedposts and cattle whose milk runs dry."

"Et cetera, et cetera," finished Skelly, grinning over his mug.

Frances sighed, feeling the anger deflating out of her. There was no point in arguing it, that much she knew. She was exhausted and she already knew that the old man could argue until the cows came home. Likely without milk in their udders, she thought grimly.

"Okay, let's set aside your gross violation for a moment and revisit the point of it."

Skelly nodded, leaning back on the sofa, resting his mug on his belly. He was on his third mug of summer wine and it was obviously taking an effect.

"If I'm to understand correctly, there are three reasons you felt this criminal act was necessary,

Skelly rolled his eyes heavenward and nodded.

Setting her mug down on the table, Frances ticked the items off on her fingers.

"One, to help me stay true to my heart's work so that I can bring Moss home. Two, to ensure that other humans have access to my work so that the magic spreads and other faery folk are saved."

She glanced at Skelly after that last one, her eyebrows raised in question.

"Did I get that one right? Only it seems a bit lofty and far-reaching, don't you? Thistlecrag isn't exactly the hub of culture and influence and it's already been made clear that my work isn't welcome in the wider sphere of the art world."

Skelly suppressed a groan.

"You're missing the point on that one," he said, waving a lazy hand over to the paintings. "There are more ways to bring the magic to the world than in some toff gallery. How many real people actually go to them places anyway?"

He didn't wait for her indignant reply.

"Not many, I don't reckon. Anyway, that'll all come clear in its own time. Go on to the third point so I can finish my brew and get away. I'm fair sick of the nattering by now."

Frances swallowed down another angry retort but fixed him with a steely glare. He flinched. Or at least, she felt him flinch rather than saw it. He put a hand to his head and gave her a sly wink.

"Aye, lass. The bond works both ways. You don't need to tell me you're in a rage, I can bloody well feel it."

"Three," she said, her voice clipped. "I am apparently one part of some magical threesome which you've been charged with assembling to perform some great service to your people. The second part of this trio I am yet to meet, and the third part is currently unknown. Also unknown is the exact service we shall perform and how we shall perform it."

She tilted her head at the old man and asked, in a sweetly sarcastic voice, "Did I get that quite right? Only it sounds a bit like the plot of every superhero movie ever made. Have you been partaking of comic books and film during your stay with us?"

Skelly scowled and heaved himself forward, banging his mug down on the table.

"Right, lass. I understand you're a wee bit cross with me. But I won't have you making a mockery of what's happened to me or my people. And I won't sit here and try to justify what

I have to do to protect them."

Frances blushed, suddenly feeling like a truly horrible person. Her fear and panic over what had happened manifested as rage and indignation and she told him as much.

"I don't like feeling out of control," she admitted. "And this feels very much beyond my control. Asking me to throw myself back into my painting is pushing all of my giant fear buttons and I suppose I'm not managing it well at all. I'm sorry for belittling your plight and that of your people. That was wrong of me."

She pushed back a strand of hair and placed her own mug on the table, gently.

"But I'm not sorry for being angry with you. You can talk all you like about the thrice-ask rule or whatever it is, but I didn't know about it and that's a fact."

"And would you have chosen to help your wee man, or my people if I'd just told you that the only way to do it was to paint your pictures and put them into the world?"

Frances glanced quickly at the paintings and then down at her hands.

"I don't know," she whispered. "I mean, I want to. I want to help you and I want Moss to come home. But,"

She paused, rubbing her hands across the knees of her paint-splattered jeans.

"But?" prompted Skelly.

"But, you're right, I don't know if I could be brave enough on my own."

She looked at the old sheep farmer, raw vulnerability on her face.

Skelly looked quickly away. He may have walked among mortals for hundreds of years, but his ancient faery instincts were still there. And they were not always kind. What the young woman sitting before him didn't know, was that there were other ways to the same end, far more efficient ways, but he'd made his own choice on that long ago. Because he knew something of what it was to have that power taken away.

He slapped his hands on his own knees and stood up, far more smoothly and quickly than what might be expected for an elderly man who'd worked the land his whole life.

"Not that you'd believe me, lass, but I think you're quite brave enough on your own. But you don't trust that, and that's the truth of it and I'll not convince you with my words," he paused, clearing his throat. "So, we're agreed then? To disagree on the nature of the How but to agree on the necessity due to the nature of the Why?"

Frances nodded.

"A year and a day," she said, her voice softly. "I don't suppose that's very long at all, really."

"It'll fly by," said Skelly, in a no-nonsense voice as he pulled open the door. "Now get back to work, I'll start making the arrangements."

"Wait!"called Frances, as the door slammed behind him "What arrangements?"

* * *

"You're leaving?"

Sophie's voice wobbled. She cleared her throat, putting a hand to her chest.

"Where are you going? Why? What's happened? Melinda!" She called back to the young woman who was unboxing books

"Be a love and bring us a pot of tea, will you?"

Melinda smiled, dusting her hands down her apron.

"A plate of something as well?" she asked, setting off for the kitchen.

"Lovely," replied Sophie with a warm smile, turning her attention back to Frances "I rue the day she leaves us," she added. "I'll never find anyone as truly wonderful."

Frances nodded.

"She's a gem alright," she said. "But, give yourself some credit. She was a meek little mouse of thing when she wandered through your doors. It was you believing in her that gave her the courage to do all the marvelous things she's done."

Sophie waved a hand, dismissive.

"Not at all. All of my belief in her wouldn't have done a thing if she didn't believe in herself first. All I did was give her the space to find it. But anyway, enough of our Melinda, what are *you* up to now? Obviously, you're off on adventures anew? And here's me thinking Thistlecrag had got you in its charming clutches."

Sophie had clearly managed to get control of her initial emotion and, for that, Frances was grateful. She couldn't bear it for her best friend to get all teary-eyed at her leaving. Mostly because she, Frances, was feeling very teary-eyed at the thought of leaving Thistlecrag. In the short time she'd been there, she'd become very fond of the little village. It had welcomed her at a time when she felt very much on the outside of everything.

"Well, do you want the whole unbelievable story, or just the pertinent facts? Dates, times, destinations…"

Sophie giggled, just as Melinda arrived with a tray laden with teapot, mugs and a plate piled high with chocolate-covered biscuits.

"Why do you think I sent Melinda to gather supplies?" she said, "Don't leave anything out."

* * *

A pot of tea, a plate of biscuits and two cheese and onion rolls later, and Frances had told her tale.

Sophie rubbed a hand across her face, bangles jingling and sat back in her chair, a rueful smile on her face as she shook her head slowly.

"You know, when you first told me you could see faeries, I thought you were utterly mad. I assumed you'd been into the absinthe or something,"

Frances giggled.

"I'm not surprised. It's not exactly something I went around telling people. At least, not after about aged ten anyway."

"But then I saw your paintings and I knew it was true. I don't think anyone could paint like that who didn't have firsthand knowledge of their subject."

Frances shifted uncomfortably in her seat.

Sophie saw her discomfort and leaned over to squeeze her friend's hand.

"You're going to have to learn to take a bit of praise and adoration, lovey. You're a brilliant artist and it really does shine through when you're working from…what was it that horrid man said? Your heart. Your heart's work. Now that's a grand way to put it. I could almost forgive him all other transgressions for that."

"Don't hold a grudge, Soph," said Frances. "Now that I've got my head around it, I can see how it all came about. He's a

260

trickster and I fell for it; it's just that simple. It's a year and a day, pretty light sentence as far as faery bargains go, and it's not like I'm being held captive in a barrow or something."

"I suppose," said Sophie, frowning. "I suppose you're right. You could've been whisked off to the land of Faery only to emerge when the rest of us were reduced to dust."

Frances shuddered, holding up a hand in protest.

"Please, don't say things like that. It's the stuff of nightmares."

"Sorry, I know. I shouldn't joke."

"And besides," continued Frances, "this whole thing does solve one of my more immediate problems. That of my impending homelessness."

"True, true. Where is this place you're going then? Somewhere up in the back of beyond?"

"Glencarragh," said Frances. "It's a small island, just off the northern mainland."

"Never heard of it."

"Yes, you have. They had that terrible storm there a bit ago. You know, when we had all that wind and rain? Apparently, they had it about a hundred times worse."

"Ah, right. Well, it certainly sounds like the weather isn't one of its attractive features," said Sophie, wrinkling up her nose. "Better get yourself some decent waterproofs."

"Ha, ha," said Frances, sticking out her tongue.

Sophie grinned and returned the gesture. The two women sat, sipping the last of the tea, each lost in their own thoughts.

After a moment, Sophie put down her mug.

"Are you sure, Fran? I mean, is this really what you want? It's a lot to ask and you don't really know what you're going to find there. What if it's some awful primitive place where

261

the people there shun strangers and keep to themselves and are all strange-eyed and secretive?"

Frances barked a laugh.

"Sophie, you've been spending too much time sampling your own merchandise," she said, gesturing towards the section of the book wall book devoted to fantasy novels. "I'm sure it's a perfectly normal place. Besides, they have a pretty thriving tourist trade, I looked it up. Boat tours and the like. Apparently, there's rumours that the seals in one of the coves are actually selkies."

Sophie grimaced.

"Fine, then. I just worry about you, Fran. All alone up there with just Angus for company."

Frances felt a stab of grief. It really was just the two of them now. Moss was the subject left unsaid. But one of the reasons she hadn't fought Skelly too hard, was knowing that going to Glencarragh was her best chance at bringing Moss home.

At the sound of his name, the little dog had wuffed softly and sat to attention. There had been no tasty morsels thus far, something to do with chocolate being bad for dogs, or so he'd been told.

Frances smiled down at him and reached to stroke his wiry head.

"Still no biscuits, my boy," she said. "No matter how high you turn up the charm."

"I'll get him a sausage roll," said Sophie, rising abruptly. "I'm sure you need to get on. Lots of packing to do, I suppose?"

Frances frowned up at her friend, who stood looking down at Angus, her eyes filling with tears.

"You can visit, Soph," she said. "I'm allowed visitors, you know. I'm not in exile or anything."

Sophie blinked, wiping a hand over her eyes as she nodded. "I know, I know," she said, her voice hoarse. "Don't mind me, I'm being silly. It just hit me all of a sudden. It's just that I've so enjoyed having you nearby. It was nice to know I had somewhere to go when," she waved a hand, vaguely. "Well, when I needed room to breathe."

"Are you alright, Soph? Is there something else bothering you?"

"No, no. It's all fine. I'm just feeling sorry for myself. And anyway, I'll be taking you up on your offer for a visit. Maybe I'll want to expand the business to another location. The tourist trade sounds promising!"

She laughed, her usual burbling chuckle and reached over to plant a kiss on Frances' cheek.

"Yes, I'm going," she said to Angus who was wriggling with anticipation. "One sausage roll coming up."

Frances watched her friend bustle towards the kitchen. Whatever Sophie may have said, she knew there was something bothering her. But, never one to lower a mood, and selfless to a fault, she was unlikely to be forthcoming when Frances' own world was turning itself upside down. Again.

Chapter 19

"I think Moss would approve, don't you?"

Angus wagged his stump of tail, thrilled with life, as usual.

"Not a sign of damp, good windows and a proper bedroom. Not to mention a real woodburner."

Frances looked around the room where she and Angus were nestled on the old tartan sofa. The woodburner was pumping out delicious warmth and the various bits of furniture that had been left behind by the last tenant were sheer perfection. A couple of sturdy lamps and a lovely Welsh dresser, along with a large, scrubbed pine table, fit perfectly into the warm rustic charm of the small cottage. The minute she'd got out of her car and saw the little building, white-washed stone nestled in the lee of a hill, Frances knew it was where she wanted to be.

"I don't rightly think either of those will even fit through the door," the landlord had said, gesturing at the solid, wooden forms of the dresser and table.

Frances had answered an advertisement for 'shepherds croft for rent' that was tacked onto the notice board in the Glencarragh post office, making an appointment the same day to come and see the place. It was love at first sight.

"I can't imagine how they got them in. Must've built around it, aye?"

The landlord was a tall, broad-shouldered man in his early fifties, named Duncan MacFinlay. Black hair peppered through with grey and smiling blue eyes in a weather-beaten face. Frances had taken to him instantly.

"My family has had sheep on these moors since as far back as anyone can remember and this croft has been here just as long," he'd said, slapping a large hand against the grey stone. "Solidly built, like. They don't make things like this anymore, I warrant."

Frances nodded, not usually one for questioning construction standards. And then he'd said the thing that made her absolutely sure it was the place for her.

"You know," he'd said, with a conspiratorial wink. "Legend has it that the place is haunted."

Frances raised a questioning eyebrow.

"Not the ghosties mind," he'd assured her, a serious expression on his face. "No, it's the wee folk."

"Wee folk?" choked Frances, her eyes darting to the corners of the cleanly swept corners. "You mean faeries?"

"Aye," said Mr. MacFinlay, "Not that anyone's ever seen them with their own eyes, you ken? Just that they're supposed to frequent the place."

He shrugged and splayed his large hands.

"'Tis naught but stories, like. Not likely to be any truth in it at all. I just thought you being an artist type would appreciate the atmosphere."

Did you know about that? she'd asked Skelly later, after she'd signed the lease and given Mr. MacFinlay her deposit. She made her way back to the bed and breakfast where she

265

and Angus were staying to pack up their belongings. The croft was available for immediate occupation and as much as she enjoyed the home cooking of The Primrose Inn, Bed & Breakfast, the landlady's clear disapproval of Angus was wearing their welcome thin.

A low chuckle echoed through her mind.

She'd soon discovered after leaving Thistlecrag that the main term of her 'agreement' with Skelly was that he was somehow in her head.

Just a way for us to keep in touch, he'd assured, after the first time his voice had echoed somewhere deep in her mind. She'd shrieked aloud, startling the young woman who sat beside her on the ferry. The woman had quietly taken the hand of her small child and moved to a different seat.

Aye well, I might have had a notion, came the response. *Yon croft has been around a long while now, as have I.*

"Well that was utterly vague and noncommittal," muttered Frances, aloud. "Typical."

"Hello?"

"Yes?" replied Frances, opening the door.

Mrs. Taggart peered around her, trying to get a look into the room.

"Oh, only I thought you might have a visitor," she said, mild disapproval on her face. Although, thought Frances, I think that's her default expression. "I was going to see if you'd like tea served. Only we don't allow visitors in the rooms, you see. We must insist you entertain guests in the sitting room."

Frances bit back a retort. The "we" was strictly of the royal variety. Mr. Taggart seemed to be either fictional or absentee.

"Sorry, Mrs. Taggart. I must apologize. I have this silly habit of talking aloud to Angus. There's no-one here but us."

Mrs. Taggart pursed her lips, looking down at the wriggling terrier who, having used all of his charm, couldn't understand why the woman who smelled so deliciously of sausages didn't like him.

"I see. And are you leaving us then?" She peered around Frances again, catching sight of the suitcase on the bed.

"Yes, thank you. I've just signed a lease for the croft I was telling you about. It's just lovely."

The disapproving look melted slightly.

"Good lass," she said, her tone slightly less clipped. "The MacFinlay's are good people. Very well respected around these parts, for several generations. And I hear that croft has been very well maintained over the years."

She frowned at Frances.

"It's a wee bit remote, though. Are you sure you'll be alright up on that hill all on your own? It's not on the phone, you know?"

Frances smiled, her animosity fading. She really is a kind old girl, she thought. Her main, and unforgivable, flaw being she doesn't like dogs.

"Yes, Mrs. Taggart. We'll be fine. I actually prefer to be a bit away from things. It helps me concentrate on my work."

Mrs. Taggart nodded sagely, as if thoroughly intimate with the inner workings of the artistic mind.

"Right you are then," she said briskly, her mask of disapproval sliding back into place. She turned to go back down the steep staircase but then turned again.

"I'll pack you a bit of something to take with you, shall I? I don't imagine you'll fancy starting proper supper after trekking all the way up that hill at this time. I think if you ask at Henderson's they have a lad who'll bring your shopping up

267

for a small fee. It'll be worth it, I warrant. And if you get stuck into your painting, you might forget to pick it up yourself."

"Thank you, Mrs. Taggart," said Frances, grateful. "That would be very kind. And thank you for the tip about the shopping, you're quite right."

Mrs. Taggart nodded primly, accepting her due, and disappeared down the stairs.

Frances leaned against the closed door, silent laughter shaking her shoulders.

It's good to hear you laugh, lass, said Skelly. *Only you might want to practice chatting with me on the quiet, like. You've a terrible habit of talking to yourself.*

* * *

Frances leaned her head against the back of the sofa, her arm draped around Angus who snored happily at her side.

"Well," she said aloud. "This isn't getting the work done, is it? I can't be resting on my laurels."

Angus grunted and rearranged himself on the sofa, stretching out to receive the full benefit of the warmth of the fire.

Frances walked over to the other side of the room where she'd set up her studio space. The croft was basically one large room with a small bedroom and bathroom leading off the kitchen. It had surprisingly large windows which Frances assumed, like the separate bedroom and bathroom, had been added in after the original construction. She was grateful for them and had no qualms about how they affected the authenticity of the place.

Her easel stood to catch the best of the natural light and her latest canvas was propped there. Beside it was a new drafting table, a gift from the staff at Sophie's cafe. It, along with the tartan sofa, had been shipped across on the ferry, paid for by Sophie and Stuart as their going away present.

On Skelly's advice, she'd started with smaller pieces, ones that could be easily stocked in the gift shop in the village and so she sat down at the table to work on one of those.

It was a drawing of Moss, dusting the shelves of an imaginary apothecary. She was doing a series of him, in a hopeful effort to boost the magic in his specific direction.

It can't hurt, Skelly had told her when she suggested it. *Mind, you have to give them up. You have to take them into the shop.*

He'd known exactly what she was thinking. Seeing the drawings come to life, she'd wanted to keep them. As if keeping them in the croft would draw Moss directly to her.

So, behind her, stacked with several others, including some prints of her gallery paintings that she'd had done before she left the mainland, were the drawings in the series so far. She had an appointment with the owner of the gift shop the next day and having already told the woman the number of pieces she had to offer, couldn't possibly back down.

Can I keep my sketches? she'd asked, a bit tearfully. Seeing Moss, if only on paper, had stirred up her grief and pangs of loss rolled over her in waves, as if giving up the drawings was losing him all over again. *They're only pencil sketches, very rough. Nobody would buy them. It's the watercolour copies that people might want.*

Aye lass, you can that. And don't worry. Sending them out into the world only makes the magic stronger. You'll have the wonder of all the folk who see them and touch them and hang them in their homes to add to your own.

Frances sighed, smiling fondly at the image of the little man with his feather duster and surly expression.

Alright, my friend. Let's get you home.

She picked up a paintbrush and got to work.

Chapter 20

Dorothy McShane may have been a rude, pinch-faced, ogre, but she knew a beautiful piece when she saw it. She decided right then to only ever stock the gift shop with a few of Frances' pieces at a time.

"It creates a need for them," she told Frances, feeling she ought to explain away the look of crushing disappointment that flashed over the young woman's face. A bit sensitive, this one, she thought, watching Frances wrestling with her facial expression.

She sighed. It wasn't her way to pander to the flighty whims of artists and craftspeople. She had more than enough folk wanting to bring in their bits and pieces. But this one, she eyed up the prints and watercolours, this one was worth hanging onto. Pasting a smile onto her heavily made-up face, she reached across the counter to pat Frances' hand.

"Dinna worry, pet," she said. "I'm going to buy more than I display. It's a matter of just trickling them out, aye?"

Frances nodded, feeling a wave of relief washing over her in a hot tide. As it was, she'd had to sit in the car for fifteen minutes, working herself up to it, before she'd come in, clutching her wrapped bundle of art with white-knuckled hands.

Dorothy continued to flip through the paintings.

The small seascapes - like the ones with the seals sunning themselves on the rocky crags in the bay, and the curious images of what looked like horses cresting the whitecaps - would fly off the shelves, she was sure of it. Glencarragh used its remote and somewhat mysterious landscape to its advantage. It was no use pretending it wasn't often gloomy and grey with inhospitable weather, the advisory fellow from the Tourist Board had told them, you just have to use it to your advantage to attract the visitors. It was simply a matter of good marketing. And so, they had. Somehow, word had leaked out and now people came from all over, especially to watch the fat, lazy seals and browse the quaint high street. Dorothy's shop was featured in the brochure and many of the visitors came just to buy the handcrafts and artwork.

"You've got a lovely sense of light in these," Dorothy admitted, somewhat grudgingly, holding a print at arm's length.

"Thank you," replied Frances. "I was trying out a new…"

Dorothy flapped a hand impatiently. She favoured filing her fingernails to sharp points and painting them garish colours.

"Do not tell me your secrets," insisted Dorothy. "If I know your secrets then the magic is lost and I cannae sell the magic to the customers. I must have the air of mystery to be genuine and the punters cannae get enough of the mystery and magic."

Frances blinked, not quite sure what to say next.

Dorothy continued to unwrap the paintings, muttering quietly to herself all the while.

No doubt she's imagining how much magic she'll sell them for, thought Frances wearily. This whole expedition had been so draining.

"Yes, those will do very nicely. Now, terms of payment?"

Dorothy peered over the top of her purple-framed cat's-eyeglasses (which were entirely unnecessary, herself having 20/20 vision).

Frances swallowed hard. Sophie and Stuart had sat her down before she left and coached her on what to ask for when she sold her work. Stuart, particularly, had been very explicit in his explanations of cost ratios and time spent and the inherent value of an artist's reputation.

She took a deep breath and named her fee.

Dorothy frowned.

"That might be alright for the mainland," she said, taking off her glasses and folding them neatly. "But that's a bit steep for out here in such a remote area."

Frances felt her resolve waver. It did seem like rather a lot. But she'd done her own research and assured herself it was fair.

"I suppose that's true," she conceded.

Dorothy face widened into a toothy, crocodilian smile. She knew she'd judged correctly. The girl lacked confidence. Enormous talent, but she clearly didn't believe it herself.

"If it were local people to whom you were marketing your wares," continued Frances. "But it's my understanding that most of your custom comes from visitors? Mainlanders, who, obviously, not only expect to pay mainland prices, but also accept that being tourists, they're inevitably going to pay more."

She returned Dorothy's smile, scenting victory and realizing she very much enjoyed it.

"If those fees aren't to your liking," she added, "I'm happy to consider selling privately." She reached over to start packing up the prints. "Who knows, maybe I'll set up a little shop myself. I hear studio shops are becoming quite popular."

She grinned, enjoying the torment of indecision on the shopkeeper's face.

A set of garishly clawed hands reached out to stop her own

"Those terms are fine, lass," said Dorothy, "You're a rare talent and I'd be honoured to display your work in my shop."

Frances nodded, understanding what it had taken for the other woman to say that.

"Lovely, thank you," she said, beaming at Dorothy.

* * *

"She wants the mainlanders to think she's a person of great eccentricity," Frances mused to Angus on their way back to the croft. "I bet that's why she wraps those ridiculous chiffon scarves around her head and plays New Age music in the shop."

Angus wagged his stump in agreement, gnawing on the knuckle bone that Frances had got at the butcher in celebration of their successful mission.

Frances inhaled a deep breath of air. Despite the chill, she'd rolled down the window of her little car, letting in the salt breeze and the distant hum of the waves. She slowed down and stopped, pulling over to the side of the single-lane road that let up to her croft. She leaned out of the window, turning her face to the wind so as to get the full effect.

Arriving on Glencarragh, although fraught with the stress of moving to an unknown place, with no-one there to greet her, Frances had felt an immediate sense of everything falling into place. Tension that she didn't even know she was holding melted softly away, leaving her feeling quietly determined to make the best of her strange situation. Despite her years of immersion in otherworldly culture, being bonded to an exiled lord of Faery was something far beyond her scope of experience but, so far, it hadn't proved too terrible. Sometimes, when the last of the light had faded and she was standing at her easel in the firelit croft, she could hear the slow murmur of the tide pulsing with her own heartbeat. That and a dull ache, somewhere deep in her chest, if she went too many days without walking down to the beach. Skelly's sorrow, she'd learned, but a vastly diluted one. He tried hard to hold back the immensity of it, knowing it would be more than she could bear. All he really wanted of her was that she commit to her painting and he'd sworn to do whatever he must to protect her from the worst of the binding.

Why here? she'd asked him, as she stood overlooking the sea from the cliff path that led from Glencarragh village.

Here is where it all began, answered Skelly, his voice as clear as if he'd been standing beside her. *And as long as you're here, then so can I be.*

How?

You'll be a beacon, lass. That's as best as I can explain it. I'll find my way by you.

And the others? The ones who are going to help?

In time, lass. Soon enough.

Frances hadn't known what to say to that and so had stood, eyes closed, letting the boom and hiss of the waves crashing below lull her into a peaceful state. Whatever the reason Skelly wanted her there, on Glencarragh, she was glad of it.

Frances took another deep breath of the sea air and turned to look at Angus, who was very much occupied with his bone. She reached out a hand and smoothed it over his wiry head. He

275

paused briefly to lick her hand then went back to his chewing

"You know what, my boy? I think we're going to be just fine here, I really do. I have a great feeling about this. But this isn't getting the work done. Pinchy McShane wants another ten pieces by the end of the month. And then there's the Christmas market to consider. I'd better get painting, eh?"

Angus picked up his head, bone clenched firmly in his teeth and wuffed enthusiastically.

Throwing her head back in a laugh, Frances put the car in gear and headed home.

The End.

About the Author

Melanie Leavey was born and raised in the north-east of England before emigrating to Canada with her family at the age of nine. An aspiring hermit and passionate gardener, she likes nothing better than drinking tea and thumbing through the pages of the latest David Austin rose catalogue. A country mouse turned town mouse, she lives with her husband, two children, a badly-behaved Jack Russell and a cat named George in Fort Erie, Ontario.

Learn more and stay up to date with new releases by visiting her website and/or signing up for her newsletter.

You can connect with me on:

🌐 http://www.threeravens.ca

🖇 https://www.instagram.com/inkblotmoon

Subscribe to my newsletter:

✉ https://tinyurl.com/ufgrrqh

Printed in Great Britain
by Amazon